PHONY FACES

Rex Lilly

DISCLAIMER:

This is a work of fiction and creativity. The story, all names, characters, and incidents portrayed are fictitious. No identification with any actual personal living or deceased, places, buildings, locations, or products is intended or should be inferred.

Phony Faces © 2024 Rex Lilly

All rights reserved. No portion of this book may be reproduced, stored in a retrieval system, or transmitted in any form or by any means—electronic, mechanical, photocopy, recording, scanning, or other—except for brief quotations in critical reviews or articles, without the prior written permission of the author.

ISBN: 9798343470093

Imprint: Independently Published/WindRose Press

WindRose Press is dedicated to publishing the past and the present to master our modern mission. With so many wonderful books and stories from the past being quickly forgotten and left behind, WindRose Press seeks to identify and curate the best of the past while also equipping new authors with the knowledge and tools to achieve their writing and publishing dreams.

Prologue

Hello, my name is Marshall Cayman, I am a Private Investigator located in central North Carolina; I cover all of North Carolina and South Carolina, specializing in auto insurance fraud and major crime defense. Like most private investigators, I'm a former law enforcement officer that needed a break from the bull shit surrounding the hidden issues with the so-called profession. Some of the biggest criminals I met wore a badge and somehow managed to make it in the positions of power.

It took years to develop my business, and I rarely work cases near my home. I could never explain why my cases end up in the same areas back-to-back. It is very common for me to be at the beach or mountains and for some reason get several assignments close together. Another strange occurrence is the caseload. Any time I run out of cases; I suddenly receive a couple of weeks of work.

As a small business owner, you always worry about cash flow and having enough work to keep going. I have been doing this for years, and for some unexplained reason, this strange flow seems to occur over and over. My only answer seems to be the Universe has a bigger plan for me, and I need to accept and be thankful for everything that comes my way.

I have learned that I do not have all the answers, and often my thinking is challenged. I know I am a very different person today than I was twenty years ago and wonder what changes are ahead. This story is about one of those life-changing challenges.

Whenever I introduce myself to people, I often get the response of "How interesting" or "How exciting". Of course…the topic is followed by asking about domestic cases. Fortunately,, my business has grown to escape the need to work on those cases except for very few special incidents.

I really enjoy what I do, and I'm sure most people find it fascinating and glamorous. I am reluctant to talk about myself or tell my stories. I don't want to sound like I'm bragging and quite frankly I'd swear I was lying half the time if I hadn't experienced some of the things I've seen and done firsthand.

I've decided this story had to be told because It is the one that changed my life. I'll never be the same again, and hopefully, it will have a positive effect on you as well.

1

I was headed back home from a weekend case at Carolina Beach when I got a text on my phone. The text said, "Come Quick, I need your help!" The address provided was only about twenty miles away from my home, which also serves as my office.

I decided to go check it out before going home. I hate to text, so I tried to call the number. All I got was a recording that said the customer was unavailable in the network. The number was from outside my area code, and I guessed it might be a pre-paid phone. I tried a couple more times and got the same recording.

I arrived at the address on Academy Road, which turned out to be a church with a private school. There was a Sheriff's car in front and no one in sight. I ended up walking around the buildings for several minutes before I located an unlocked door. I was a little uncomfortable just walking in, but I did it anyway.

I called out several times hoping to locate someone. I did not get a reply, and I turned to walk out.

I almost ran over a girl that was standing right behind me. She seemed to be about twelve years old with long blonde curly hair and striking bright blue eyes that were staring right at me. Her expression was blank and showed no emotion whatsoever that I could read.

Startled by the sudden encounter for a moment, I stuttered a bit trying to explain why I was there. I finally got the words out that someone had sent me a message to come here. She said, "they're in the house," and pointed toward the back of the building.

I was hoping for an escort, but it became apparent that I wasn't going to get one, I said, "thank you," and headed in the direction where she had pointed. When I reached the door, I turned to look back, and the young lady was still standing in the same spot watching me. I smiled and waved and said, "thank you." She turned and walked down the hallway and entered what appeared to be a classroom.

The encounter with the young girl left me a bit shaken. Not from being startled by her. She scared me for some vague reason. Something about her was wrong. I paused for a moment looking back through the glass in the door hoping I would get a feel for what I had just experienced.

At that moment, a group of girls about the same age all appeared in front of the building. The odd thing was that the girls were all dressed in the same long denim skirts and blue polo shirts, same as the first girl I'd encountered in the hallway. At least these girls were talking, and a few giggled as they passed by as if sharing some inside secret joke.

I walked to the house and rang the bell. A woman came to the door dressed just like the young girls in the same long denim skirt and a blue polo shirt. Her hair was long, and curly blonde like the young girl from the hallway, except hers appeared to have lost its luster. She seemed just as drab as the young girl. For a moment I thought I recognized her from a previous meeting or something. I couldn't place her, but I'm sure I'd figure that out later.

The woman invited me in and led me to the den without saying another word. Normally I'd introduce myself upon entering a room, but there was a heated debate going on between a uniformed deputy sheriff and a man I presumed to be the preacher of the church or school administrator.

I heard the deputy tell the man that there was nothing he could do at this point. The man later identified as the preacher was holding his Bible in the air, spouting verses and demanding action from the law enforcement community to take him seriously. He made his last plea and yelled, "drag her back here!"

The deputy finally said, "sorry, please feel free to call the sheriff himself and file your complaint." The deputy then turned and walked toward the door; I heard a muffled "good luck" as he passed by.

I finally got a chance to introduce myself to the preacher, and said I'd received a text to come there. Someone said they needed my help. The preacher seemed confused and said no one had called from there needing a private investigator; he was a taxpayer and didn't need my kind. He'd make the sheriff do his duty one way or another. He said cell phones and computers were not allowed in his home or church. I pulled out my phone and showed him the text and confirmed the address. He said that was his address, but no one there had a cell phone. I told the preacher that I was sorry to bother him and started to leave. I was just about to the door when he asked how much you charge to kidnap someone and drag them back home.

When I turned around the woman quickly got up and walked between the preacher and me. She asked, "do you believe in the Lord?" She took my hand and placed it on an open Bible. There inside I saw a note and a stack of one-hundred-dollar bills. She quickly closed the Bible, pushed it toward me and said, "please accept this as a gift from the church."

The preacher took the woman by the arm and told her to sit down; he would handle this. The preacher then said that his wife doesn't know her place sometimes. I thought to myself, *that's okay*, I know where her place is. She's my new client. I made sure we made eye contact and gave her a nod as I tucked the Bible under my arm. I told her I'd make good use of the gift and asked if I could call if I had any questions. She said that I was welcome to come to their service, that they didn't have a phone.

I wanted to hear what the preacher had to say and asked him about the deputy. The preacher started yelling about teen whores running off with devil worshipers. It took a while between the ranting and sermon, but I finally got the idea that his daughter had run away from home.

The preacher said he would pay me if I could find her, drag her back home and not let anyone talk to her but him. I told the preacher that I work on retainer, and that I get paid for my time up front. I heard something about my duty to do the right thing and such. The truth was, I'd already heard all I needed. I looked to the woman and thanked her for the gift and said, "maybe I'll see you on Sunday."

I was curious about the Bible, and what I'd seen inside. I got to my van and placed the Bible on the passenger seat. I opened it to be sure that what I'd seen was real. Sure enough, there was money and a note inside. I got out of there; I didn't want to take a chance that the preacher would walk up on me reading the note.

I drove down the road about a mile and found a place to pull off. I opened the note, and all it said was "PLEASE HELP ME. I'll explain everything later."

I picked up the money and counted five hundred dollars. I was a bit disappointed since that would cover about one day of local work. I tossed the Bible back into the passenger seat and saw another one-hundred-dollar bill sticking out from another page. I opened the Bible up and discovered that it wasn't a Bible at all. This was an American history book that had a black leather cover on it to make it look like a Bible. I noticed the outer pages had been painted gold and were stuck together. I opened the book to about the middle and found that it had been hollowed out and there was a stack of one-hundred-dollar bills inside.

That made me look around to be sure no one was watching me. I figured I'd better get home and see what else I might find in here.

I've been doing this for a long time and rarely get excited about a case. I was fired up that maybe I had a real mystery on my hands for a change. I watched my mirrors the whole way home to be sure no one was following me. I don't know why, I've never been paranoid about that kind of thing before unless there was a reason. All my senses were on edge, like a rookie on his first assignment. I tried to do a little self-talk and make myself settle down. After all, I didn't even know what this was about. I was still pretty stoked up until I had the thought that this might turn out to be a bull shit nut case, and I'd have to return the money. That killed the mood.

When I pulled into my driveway, I barely had the van in the park before I grabbed the book and pulled the money out. There were an additional ten thousand dollars in the hollowed-out area. I looked for another note but didn't find one.

I called the number again but got the same recording. There was nothing else to do but unpack and think about this situation.

Over the next few days, I called the number and sent text, but never got a reply. I rode by the church several times hoping to catch a glimpse of the woman and have an opportunity to talk with her. I never saw her and didn't want to burn dead time trying to figure out what I was supposed to be doing on this case. I decided that I would attend the service on Sunday and see if I could get an answer then.

The church service—Sunday

I arrived at the church and parked in the visitors' space right up front near the door. As soon as I did, I thought that maybe I should park elsewhere and not draw attention to myself. I didn't want to talk to anyone else but my client.

Before I could move my car, I saw my client enter the church. She turned and made obvious eye contact before walking in. I got out and hurried in hoping to get a chance to speak with her. Unfortunately, she was near the pulpit area, talking with another woman. I noticed the church was divided in two sections with the men on one side and the women on the other.

Normally, I go with the flow and not do anything to stand out, but in this case my defiant side won out, and I took a seat in the last row of the women's side. I saw my client smile and almost laugh. She quickly sat down in the first row with a group of teenage girls.

The first three rows on each side appear to be reserved for the students, again boys on one side and girls on the other. I got strange and unapproved looks from some of the men, but the women just kept their eyes focused towards the front. I stood up and a few of the women nearby glance over their shoulder to see if I was changing sides. I moved closer to the wall away from the isle so I wouldn't be bothered by anyone trying to correct my behavior. Before I sat down, I wondered if it was a mistake and should consider my clients' needs first. I looked up and saw that she was standing near a door at the front of the church. Her smile and slight nod of her head told me that she approved and found humor in my defiance.

When the service started my client came back in and gave me a quick glance to see if I was still there. I noticed a slight grin as she sat down at the piano and started playing. The congregation sang two hymns, and then the preacher took his place at the pulpit.

Right away, he asked the students to stand and face the congregation. What I saw was the faces of terror. The preacher did a lot of yelling and preached about the ways of the world and the outside influences of the world on our young people. Only the church and God's people can save these kids. He was there to relay the words of God and keep them on the correct path. The preacher talked about the fact that only twenty percent of kids attend church after they leave high school. The rest are lost to the sins of the world and never attend church again.

The preacher invited the congregation to give testimony on the bad influences they have witnessed upon their children. The people seemed to enjoy gouging the kids telling how bad the world is and there is no hope for our future. I heard about the public schools, alcohol, homosexuals, drugs, sex, TV and the evil internet that is robbing them of their children. The kids looked beaten. The preacher told them to sit down and listen to the word of God.

The preacher looked straight at me; I think this was the first time he he noticed my presences.

He said, "I see we have a visitor here today, stand and introduce yourself."

I stood and gave my name and started to sit down again.

The preacher then said, "tell everyone who you are and what you do for a living."

I told them I was a Private Investigator, and I was invited there by his wife.

The preacher then asked, "Is there a special reason my wife invited you here on this special day?"

I replied, "I don't know. I haven't had the opportunity to have a conversation with her. Maybe we can talk after the service?"

The preacher held up his bible and asked, "Do you believe in God?"

I said, "I assume this is a Christian church, am I correct"?

The congregation laughed, and the preacher was outraged.

He yelled, "What else would we be?"

I responded, "I'm no biblical scholar, but I assumed that the Christian church is to follow the teaching of Jesus. Somewhere in there I remember hearing something about love, compassion, understanding and forgiveness. I sort of think that he would be more interested in hearing the problems of his followers and offering a loving solution rather than telling them to just go to Hell. God works in mysterious ways. Wouldn't you agree?"

I scanned the first three rows as all eyes were on me. I saw a glimmer of hope. I looked straight into the preacher's eyes and smiled. I thought to myself, *game on, I'm going to kick your ass!*

I sat down and the service continued. I noticed a few people as they took quick glances in my direction. I was not here to hurt these people and felt a little sorry for them. I remember a lot of bad experience at the hands of people like the preacher. I was lucky. I was one of the eighty present that fled the church as soon as possible. I returned many times over the years looking for something only to find more lies and hateful judgmental people. I just don't understand how people can think this kind of religion is a good thing.

As soon as the service was over, the preacher and his wife walked to the front door of the church to speak to the people as they left. I wanted to be the last person they saw today. I moved closer to the aisle and waited. A few of the adults nodded or murmured some sort of greeting as they passed by, but it was obvious that my presence made them very uncomfortable.

Most of the youth departed from the side doors. A few walked past and said hello as they passed.

I approached the preacher and his wife, and I finally asked their names.

My client said, "Christy McFerrin."

The preacher took her strongly by the arm as a signal to shut up. Then he said, "I'm the Reverend McFerrin, and I run this church and school."

He said, "I don't like outsiders trying to undermine me and God in my own church."

I couldn't help but notice he said "me" first. I let it go. There was no point in having a conversation with this idiot. I thanked Mrs. McFerrin for the invitation and walked toward the parking lot. I was thinking that I really hadn't gained any information about the case. The thought struck me as I was getting in my car. Maybe God thought getting me pissed off was his way of motivating me on this case. At this point I'm pretty motivated, I just didn't know what my next move would be.

I went back to my office and finished my reports and videos for the week. I wanted to get the short cases out of the way so I could spend some time on the McFerrin ordeal. The deadlines for my insurance and criminal cases were all several weeks away; I updated the handwritten notes, expenses, and sent out a few invoices.

After finishing up with the office work, I opened my safe and got out the book and money I received from Mrs. McFerrin. I opened the book and scanned every page that wasn't glued together looking for an additional note or maybe something underlined that would give a clue to what this was about. I even looked at each bill to see if there was something I had missed. I couldn't find anything, so I put it back in the safe feeling a bit defeated.

A little time away

I wasn't about to sit around and allow that feeling to consume the day, so I grabbed a cooler and made some sandwiches headed for the lake. It had been a few weeks since I'd been sailing and couldn't think of any reason I shouldn't be there today.

I arrived at the lake later in the day. It was your typical Sunday where the sailors arrived as the motor boaters, jet skiers and those jerk wake boaters are leaving. I can't understand why they have to run up next to you with their blaring crappy music, while you're cruising along on a light breeze relaxing in peaceful nature, then the next thing you know you're dipping the bow under their waves.

I unloaded the van and headed down to the dock passing several of my dock mates along the way. I paused just long enough to say hello as I passed by. I didn't want to hang around long since I'd be losing daylight soon. It was obvious from the overflowing trash cans and grills set up in the area that I had missed out on an eventful weekend. I'm kind of envious of the groups around the lake and often wonder if I'm missing out on too many fun things in life. There is nothing I can do about that now.

It was good to see the old boat again. I spend a lot of time alone working, but it is a different kind of alone when I'm sailing. Although there is plenty of room on a 26' boat for others to join me, I've come to enjoy sailing her singlehanded. I don't claim to be a highly skilled sailor, so being alone I don't have to explain my mistakes to anyone. I just chalk it up as practice and move on.

When I'm sailing, I have no place to go and no certain time to get there. The cell phone reception is poor over most of the lake. That is a special kind of freedom. I feel a little guilty about being out of contact with my clients if they need me, but I justify it by telling myself that I get to take breaks too. I just hope I never have an emergency and need to call for help.

I spent the first half hour moving things around, opening hatches and checking for leaks. This boat was rescued from a horse pasture and then restored. It took a while, but it looks like my repairs are holding up. After that I just sat back on the couch, closed my eyes and tried to unwind. It had been a busy and successful week. My energy is renewed when I'm able to nail an insurance fraud and stay within my budget. I was feeling incredibly pleased about that, but the thought of my new assignment was totally outside my comfort zone.

I live each day with uncertainty. I rarely have a game plan on how a case is going to be worked. I guess I've done this for so long I recognize the patterns of behaviors and things seem to fall into place. I've often questioned if it were possible that I could be somewhat psychic because so many times I'm in the right place at the right time. I would never tell anyone that. I just say I'm very lucky. No one looks at me funny when I say it that way.

This case was different. I somehow knew it was going to be incredibly involved, even though I had no idea what I was supposed to do. I mean it's not every day I get a $10,500 retainer and no instructions whatsoever. I sat there for a while longer and remembered. Nothing in my life is routine, I've been in this situation many times before. There was no point in trying to figure it out now, I'll work it out later.

I jumped up and climbed into the cockpit then prepared to cast off from the dock. I fired up the outboard, untied the boat, then motored out of the cove slowly checking out the other boats and looking to be sure there were no swimmers out in front.

Most of the slips are occupied by boats, and I rarely see them on the lake. I often see the same few people at the lake sitting on their dock, cooking out, mostly just hanging out while the kid's swim. We always wave as I'm passing by. I've only met a few of them. I'm the last slip in the marina and rarely anyone ventures that far since you have to cross a bridge and walk a short distance through the woods to get there.

I've walked the other docks a few times meeting the others. Unfortunately, I have a short memory for names and only know a few of my dock mates. Seems like all the ones I know come at different times than me.

The wind is up today, so there was no time to socialize. As soon as I passed the main marina area, I headed out to an open span of water to put up sails. It's not too often that I get to sail out of the marina, but today the winds were in my favor, and I wasn't going to miss the opportunity to get in a little more sail time.

This was indeed a rare occasion where I was able to sail directly out of the marina on a single tack with the boat at a comfortable degree of heel all the way out to the main section of the lake. Normally, I don't attempt this since all the motor boaters coming in the narrow section are headed in for the day. The wake boats are the worst if you're in light winds it causes you to lose your heading or sail shape. This wasn't a problem today, and I was able to plow through the large wakes and only had to tolerate their blaring poor taste in music for a short span of time. I've never understood why some people go out into nature and feel the need to pollute the air with the loudest speakers possible. You can hear the wake boats coming a mile away. Then they're yelling at whoever is riding the wake. You'd think they'd get a clue to turn the music down, and then they wouldn't have to yell at each other.

Maybe I'm getting old; I sure like it better when they all head in for the evening, and I have the main part of the lake to myself. Especially this evening, the winds were strong and steady.

The main channel of the lake was much less crowded for the moment, so I came about and headed further down toward the open waters. Soon the area just beyond the marina would be crowded with boaters sitting to watch the sunset behind the distant mountains. It really is an impressive sight and I've been known to drift and watch it myself. The steady wind was too much of a blessing to pass up, so I sailed on.

To non-sailors I'm sure we seem slow and boring, but I've scared more than a few people when we catch big wind and lay the boat over on its side plowing through the waters. This was one of those days; I've become pretty good at single handing the boat in all kinds of conditions. The tacks can be a little harder since the 150 Genoa sail takes a little more work to bring it across and actually land on my intended course.

On days like this it takes concentration to sail at top performance, which leaves little time to think about other things. I needed this time to unwind. Many times, I've thought it was too much trouble, but once I'm here and have a day like this I realize it is well worth all the effort. I pulled the sheets in and laid her over as far as I dare. I often wonder how much further I could go without taking on water in the cockpit. Sometimes I scare myself and must do some quick self-talk and say out loud "hang on and ride it out." After a few minutes of this, the boat seemed to settle into a workable position, and I held myself in my seat by putting my feet on the opposite bench for support. The boat creaks and pops from the stress of the wind on the aging sails and rigging. I'm feeling a bit adventurous, so I tug just a bit on the tiller, and she leans a bit further. All my gear down below was crashing about, and stuff falling out of the storage compartments.

My freshly opened beer was missing in action, but I really didn't care at this point. I made a few adjustments, and she came up around forty degrees and picked up speed. I tacked back and forth across the lake a few times repeating the process. Before I knew it two hours had passed, and I figured I'd better head back in.

As the sun began to set, I turned and started back toward the marina. It had been a short but satisfying time on the lake. I love to night sail, but I'm a little tired and this seems like a good night to do a little dock time by myself. I turned on the running lights and headed back. The winds had laid down quite a bit which allowed for a much slower pace on my return trip. I had a downwind run and just enough wind to run a wing, and wing without too much adjustment to maintain to keep the sails full and stay on a course toward the marina.

As I came closer to the marina, I noticed several people taking pictures of my boat with the mountains and sunset behind the full sails. The wing and wing makes for a beautiful sight. Only a full spinnaker can compete with such a majestic scene. All I could think of at the moment is all these jackasses admiring my boat while they're running around on pontoon and wake boats. Screwing around with my serenity. Actually, I'd like to have a copy of the photos, but I have no idea who these people are.

I sailed up the leg going into the marina. The winds were exceptionally light at this point which seemed like a good time to drop sails and motor in.

It takes a little practice to be able to walk up on deck and secure the lines and sails in the dark while maintaining your balance. It's a small feeling of accomplishment when you return to the cockpit proud that you were able to perform the task without falling overboard. This is one of the hazards of single handing a cruiser. I have real respect for people that can do this in the ocean.

I motored on past the boats sitting near the dam watching the sunset. My little outboard is kind of slow, and I wanted to get back before it was dark. Since I'm the last slip, it's not well lit on my end of the dock. Most of the time it's pretty quiet down there. Occasionally, I get late night visitors skinny dipping just across the cove. I guess I must expect that sort of thing sometimes. I did it myself not too far from here when I was sixteen.

I was glad the wind had eased off before I tried to dock. It can be a real pain trying to bring her in with the wind at your broadside. You get it lined up and the next thing you know you're five feet away, and I have to back up and try again.

Not tonight. I got in on the first try. I secured the lines and sails, then went below to see what damage I caused while tossing everything out of storage. It wasn't as bad as I thought. I opened the door to the head and thankfully I hadn't caused it to spill out. It has never actually been dumped out, but I always check to be sure.

It was pretty dark by this time, so I went topside to look around. I could hear voices off in the distance, but no one was in sight. I grabbed my cooler and jumped onto the dock. I opened my dock box and pulled out a fold out chair. This was the perfect night just to be here with a cooler full of beer and a sky full of stars.

I'm not sure how much time had passed when I heard voices again. I looked over to see one of my dock mates had arrived to go out for a late-night sail.

He said, "sorry, didn't mean to wake you."

I didn't realize I had drifted off to sleep. I said, "No problem."

He seemed a little uneasy about my presence. Most of the folks know I'm a private investigator, and I'd be willing to bet the pretty young thing standing on the dock is not his daughter or niece.

I picked up what was left of my beer, chugged it down, and then climbed back on to the boat. I was tired, so I just crawled into my bunk and went back to sleep listening to the chimes of the halyards pinging as they slap against the mast.

Text messages—Monday

I woke up to the sound of my phone receiving a text message. It was my client from the church. Mrs. McFerrin's text indicated that she only had a moment to text while she was out walking on the track; her husband was selling drugs, and the school was a cover for prostitution too. Then said, "I've got to go."

I sent a text back, but I never received a reply.

I checked the time 7:35 AM. One of the bad things about sleeping on the boat is the amount of light shining in. Actually, this is late for me; normally I'm up with the sun. I keep saying I'm going to get one of those dark masks so I can sleep later. What's The Point in taking time off and waking up at the crack of dawn?

Either way, I'm up, and my mind is racing now. The lack of information and purpose is driving me nuts. I crawled out of my bunk and sat on the bench seat for a while trying to figure out what I was going to do today. On one hand I had a retainer to work the case, but I had no idea of where to start. I hate burning dead time on a case just to eat up a retainer. At the moment nothing came to mind that sounded reasonable.

This is pretty normal in this business; not having a clear game plan in the beginning. Whenever this happens, I tend to fall back on an old saying of: "To thine on self be true."

I'm not sure if I'm applying the phrase correctly, but in my case, I use it to justify doing what suits me at the moment. Heck, I think it was just yesterday when I thought the same thing and ended up at the lake. I think I'll be true to myself and walk over to the marina for breakfast.

It was already getting warm out, and I was surprised to see so many people at the lake for a Monday. When I entered the marina restaurant it was crowded. I was able to find an empty table in the corner. I didn't recognize anyone I knew there this morning. These were mostly retirees and people that had houses on the lake.

My waitress was very busy and apologized for the wait since I had been there for quite some time before she came to my table. One of my weaknesses is food. I couldn't resist the biggest breakfast platter on the menu. I drank a couple cups of coffee waiting for my food to arrive. Looking out on the lake, my mind wandered through all the things I need to do at the office, what to do with my new case and wondering if this should be a screw-it day and go back out on the lake.

I was embarrassed by the size of the breakfast platter, but I made short work of it and was pretty stuffed by the end of it. I can't seem to get past my law enforcement days of wolfing down food between calls. Back in those days you shoveled it in and got ready for the next call, otherwise you may not eat at all the entire shift.

The walk back was kind of painful in my present stuffed condition. When I arrived back at the dock, I sat down in my fold out chair trying to make a decision about the rest of my day. I took out my phone and looked at the text for a long time. It was short and to The Point, but I kept looking at it like it was suddenly going to reveal some secret message.

I was still too full to do any serious sailing, so I secured all the sailing gear, and made sure everything was locked up before leaving. It's a little more than an hour back to the office and that would give me time to think. Just shortly before arriving at the office I changed my mind and decided to drive the other twenty minutes to the school and just have a look around.

It was getting close to noon when I arrived at the school. I saw an unmarked patrol car near the residence in the back of the school. A white passenger van arrived, and six girls got out.

I could only guess that these were new to the school because they were wearing street clothes and not the long denim skirts and blue polo shirts. The Reverend was driving the van, and he escorted them all into the residence.

I saw Mrs. McFerrin leaving the residence and heading out toward the athletic field. I really wanted to go out and talk with her, but something told me to just watch and see what happens.

Mrs. McFerrin was walking at a rapid pace, almost jogging around the track. Then she disappeared around the back of some bleachers. A moment later I got a text saying "Something's going on, there are new girls at the school, a detective is here. Robin is in Haven near Black Mountain…Go there and I'll fill you in later."

I was about to reply to the text when I saw Mrs. McFerrin walk back out onto the walking path around the field. She walked fast back to the residence. I was concentrating on her and didn't notice a marked patrol car until it was behind me with his blue lights on. The deputy asked for my license and registration then wanted to know why I was there. I still had my phone in my hand and said that I pulled over to send a text, and then I held up my pee bottle and said it was a good thing you didn't arrive a minute later, or I'd have been in an embarrassing position.

The deputy didn't seem to buy the story and spent a lot of time looking in my van windows. Luckily, this van is more like a camper than a surveillance van, and I had a bunch of my gear still in the front seat. My gun was locked in the back since I hadn't planned on doing anything more than a ride by and hadn't bothered to get it out. Since it was locked up, I didn't have to inform him about the gun, and I didn't identify myself as an investigator.

The deputy lied and said that someone called in my vehicle as suspicious. I didn't bother to argue the fact that I had only been there a few minutes and just went along to see his reaction.

He just stood there for a while, then I asked, "is it okay for me to finish what I was doing?" I held up the red pee bottle and said, "I have a back injury and it's hard for me to walk into to stores and restaurants every time I need to go." He returned my license and walked back to his car. I pretended to be using the bottle as he drove passed me.

It's pretty obvious there is a concentrated law enforcement presence in the area. It could be the missing girl, but I don't think so. The McFerrin's are obviously at odds with each other about the missing girl, and I need to be invisible until I can figure out my next move.

Tuesday—The surveillance of the church

The next morning, I got up early and packed up my surveillance gear. This would be one of those sitting in the woods all day situations. I packed food and drinks in a backpack along with my camera and note pads. The school is in a remote area, and it would not be wise to park my van anywhere near the surveillance from what I saw the day before.

I packed up my mountain bike and was wearing a bright yellow riding jersey and bike shorts. I figured I'd park far away and ride in. I'd make it look like a biker passing through then jump in the woods for a quick change. You don't see too many bicycles getting pulled over as suspicious vehicles as long as they are moving.

There is a store about five miles away. I went in and asked permission to leave my van, that I was mapping a route for a scout troop to do a ride soon. I explained that a GPS map doesn't show hills, and I wanted to be sure the younger riders could handle the route. The woman at the store said it would be okay, and off I went.

I was glad I chose this method. There was very little vehicle traffic in the area, but the same deputy passed me twice along the route. Before I left the office, I had pulled up a satellite view of the area and went in the back way. After leaving the road, I changed into dark clothes and had my leaf suit ready in case I needed to get up close and personal. I mounted the video camera on a monopod for long distant zooms and began my mile-long walk through the woods to the school.

I was feeling proud of myself when I reached the school and just happened to wind up near the bleachers of the athletic field. I couldn't see the residence from here, but I found a mobile classroom that had been converted into sleeping quarters surrounded by a privacy fence on the front side. I guess they didn't expect anyone to be in this part of the property.

This is where the new girls are staying and, obviously, they aren't your typical church schoolgirls. Two of them are sitting on the back steps. One of the girls looks to be about fourteen years of age, and she is crying. The other girl is around her late teens and maybe her early twenties. The older girl is smoking a cigarette and drinking what appears to be a quart size beer.

I was about a hundred yards away and zoomed in tight with my video camera. I didn't see the guy in the suit arrive until he was in view of the camera. The older girl held out her hand and the guy gave her something. She stood up, raised her skirt and pulled down her panties. She turned around and the guy mounted her from behind.

The young girl stood up as if to walk away, but the guy said something to her, and she sat back down and cried as she watched them have sex. I felt totally helpless since I was so far away and not sure I should intervene due to the nature of the situation. Turns out I didn't have to decide. He looked like he finished and zipped up to leave. The older girl didn't look too upset, and she sat down on the steps and counted the money the guy had given her.

I moved up closer to the field to see if I could get a better view of the school and parking lot. About a half hour later the guy in the suit and the Reverend walked out to the parking lot.

They stayed in the lot for about ten minutes talking and laughing before the Reverend went back inside and the guy walked out of sight around the building. A moment later I saw the black unmarked patrol car leave the parking lot driven by the same guy.

At the time I felt really uncomfortable shooting the video, but now I'm glad I did. This is a game changer, and I'll have to be super careful from here on out. I'm beginning to see why my client is being so secretive. I had thought she was just a nut case just giving me little clues in her text to run me around.

I stayed in the woods hoping Mrs. McFerrin would come out to the track for lunch, but she didn't. I moved around a few times trying to get a view of the school and church building to get a better feel for what was going on. I could see the students in their blue polo shirts come and go between the buildings every so often. From my present location the mobile classroom is not visible, and it appears that the new girls are isolated from the other students.

Around three the parking lot began to fill up with cars, and soon thereafter the students came out and left with their rides. I saw Mrs. McFerrin return to the school in a white passenger van. When she pulled up, I saw the Reverend and some man I hadn't seen before walk out to the van. I videoed as the Reverend searched his wife's backpack she was carrying as the other man got in the van and drove away.

The Reverend then entered the building with the backpack, and Mrs. McFerrin walked out onto the track. I was a good distance from the bleachers at this point. I pulled out my phone and sent a text to her number letting her know I was in the woods. I moved as quickly as I could without being spotted or alarming Mrs. McFerrin. I saw where she had hidden the phone, and she looked around when she read the text. I sent her another text and instructed her to take another lap. When she returned back at the bleacher, she should act like she twisted her ankle and sit down.

As Mrs. McFerrin was walking along the track I moved back toward the bleachers. I arrived just ahead of her and took a position close by. I have to say she did a great job falling down and crying out in pain as she landed on the gravel. I'm pretty sure she actually hurt her hand and knees during the stunt. She crawled over to the bench and sat down then removed her shoe to rub her foot.

I had changed into my leaf suit just before she arrived, and I was able to crawl up close enough I could talk in a low tone. I asked her what was going on.

Mrs. McFerrin said she couldn't talk right now; her every move is being watched. She directed me to go to Haven near Black Mountain. Find Robin, keep her safe until she can get there.

Mrs. McFerrin got up and limped away. I saw her husband walk out of the building toward the athletic field. I crawled back into the woods and headed back to my bicycle.

I made a quick pass by the trailer to see if anything was going on. There was no one in sight so I continued on. I reached my bike that was hidden in the woods, changed back into my riding gear, and headed back to the store where I had left my van. My heart was pounding from the events I had encountered. I rode hard as I could. I wanted to get out of there as fast as possible.

Wednesday—Black Mountain

I woke up early on Wednesday morning thinking about my new case. I laid in bed hoping I could go back to sleep, but that obviously wasn't going to happen. Developing a game plan is often an evolving process as new information is developed. I know this to be true, but this situation is baffling me since My only information is a name and a town to begin my search.

I finally gave up and got out of bed. I knew I had to tie up a bunch of loose ends on some of my short assignments in case I end up out of contact with my clients. That's always a possibility when working in the mountains. Cell phones and Internet connections are often in short supply in some locations.

The quickest way of doing this was to email all my clients and attach my current notes with a large bold heading indicating these are "NOTES ONLY" and in the body of the email I indicate the final reports will follow soon. I also advise them that my cell service and internet connections will be limited for the next few days. Since most of my clients are attorneys and insurance companies, they don't bother me for at least a week when I do this.

The timing of this case is pretty good. Everything I'm currently working on is long term, so no one should need anything for a few weeks. There are no court dates pending, so I'm feeling pretty good about my schedule at this point and can concentrate on the Black Mountain case.

I travel quite a bit and mostly stay packed in case a last-minute case pops up, or I get stuck out of town for an extended period of time. I have a tendency to over pack because of this. Not only do I keep a ready bag in my van but pack an additional bag for the case I'm working on.

I love the mountains and seriously hope I have some down time to do something other than work. I'm being optimistic so I packed some of my hiking gear just in case.

I'm packed and ready to go, but the uneasy feeling is still there with not having a clue what is ahead of me. I checked my phone hoping I had a last-minute text with further instructions. Just as I feared there were no missed calls and no text messages.

The three-hour drive to Black Mountain was pretty uneventful other than me placing a phone call to my favorite ex-client. For some reason this is a tradition whenever I pass through her town, I'm inspired to call and say hello. She was elected as Judge, so she no longer needs an investigator. I suppose I could call anytime, but something about passing through I feel compelled to call. I rarely ever actually get her on the phone, but it can never be said I didn't try.

Traveling alone is a pain. So often I eat on the run out of convenience and rarely go in and take my time to eat a healthy meal. Even when I do, I rush to get back on the road. I attribute this to my law enforcement days. Even though I've been out for some time now I can't escape the feeling that I have too much to do. There is always someplace else I need to be in a hurry.

I'm feeling this right now. I have no idea what I'm supposed to do when I get there, but I'm sure in a hurry to get there.

I arrived as instructed in Black Mountain and drove through town to check out the area stores and restaurants. I've been here many times before and there are new places every time I come back. I don't know what it is about the area. Places seem to come and go. I was glad to see one of my old watering holes was open again. As soon as I get a room I'll walk back and get food and my fill of beer. Hopefully, there will be live music tonight.

That's what I like about the town. Good places to eat, drink and some of the best bands I've ever heard well within walking distance to my motel.

As I'm driving around, I'm looking for some kind of sign or anything indicating a place called "Haven." I extended my search to the outskirts of town where there are several parks and religious retreats. There are also several rehab centers in the area. Nothing had anything associated with the name.

At this point I wasn't sure if I should overtly start asking around since this situation seems so secretive and having witnesses the scene at the trailer behind the school. I figured I'd just wait to see what happens. By now my client should assume I had either arrived or was at least on my way to Black Mountain. Surely, she would call or text with new information soon.

It was getting late in the day, and I was getting tired of riding around trying to figure out where to start. I checked in to my motel and just unpacked a few clothes and my work gear in case I needed to email anyone or update a file.

I dropped my bags on the bed, laid down to rest a bit and tried to think about the sequence of events leading up to this point. I can't imagine why the information was so scarce, or had I missed an important text or email that gave a better explanation or instructions.

As I was lying there, I checked all the text I'd received, then I opened my laptop computer. I checked all my email accounts and for the first time I checked the spam folders just in case an important message had been sent there. I couldn't find anything new and finally gave up.

The Well

The Well is a "Hole in the Wall" type of watering hole located nearby. In my travels, it's important that I have good food and a good drinking place well within walking distance to my motel. This place fits the bill well and is a regular stop when I'm in the area.

I rush all the time, but at the end of the day and I'm away from the office, I find the escape I need. When I walked in I recognized a few of the regulars even though I haven't been here in nearly a year. The place has changed hands, and I don't know the new owners. That may be a good thing since some of the old crowd knows who I am, and I don't want any discussion about why I'm in town.

I head down toward the far end of the bar and take a stool as far away from the other customers as possible. It's still fairly early in the evening, so there is no band set up yet and the dinner crowd should be filtering in soon. My bartender is a hippie type woman I'd guess to be in her mid-thirties when I got a closer look. She had dreadlock dirty blonde hair and numerous tattoos and piercing in various parts of her body. She introduced herself when she came to get my order. She had a very unusual name that I could not pronounce and would never remember if I could. She was quite friendly and continued to talk as she poured me a large draft beer and then entered my food order in a computer.

Normally, I'd love the attention, but I feel somewhat uneasy since my assignment here was a complete unknown situation and unfortunately several people in the bar are regulars that I've met before when I was in the area. I guess she is just being a good hostess and there aren't many people at the bar. Of course, when she asked what brought me to the area, I replied that I was there to relax and maybe do some hiking. The conversation changed to hiking and backpacking. She is obviously an avid outdoor lover and gave me a long list of places I should check out. I'm loving this conversation and truly wish I was actually there for an outdoor adventure. This woman must know every inch of the area and seemed to know exactly which trails to take depending on your skill level and time frame you have available.

I've worked and vacationed in this area many times, but I feel like I've never seen anything after spending a few minutes with her. I debated in asking her about Haven. I figured if anyone knew it would be her. Before I made my decision, a few more people came in and sat at the bar, and she went to talk with them. During this time my food arrived by one of the kitchen staff. I love bar food, and tonight I'm lustfully enjoying a huge, charbroiled cheeseburger and fries. I know this is killing me, but it's my weakness. Well, one of many, actually.

I'm feeling some jealousy since the crowd is rolling in, and I lost my bartender to her duties.

I turned my attention to fully enjoying my poison and occasionally glancing up to watch a baseball game on the TV. If it weren't for my love of bar food and beer, I'd probably never watch sports. For the next hour my only contact with my bartender was glances and a thumbs up, or I'd hold up my empty mug for a refill.

During one of our exchanges of distant communications she held up her index finger and mothed something I couldn't make out. I saw her approach two young hippy looking guys that entered the bar. I saw her approach them and point at me while she was talking to them.

I had a moment of "oh shit" but I'd just wait to see what happens next.

Both men came and sat down next to me. The guy closest to me mentioned the bartenders name and said, "I understand you're looking for some backpacking areas?"

I gave them both a long beer-induced stare, but finally broke the silence by asking, "How the Hell do you pronounce her name?"

I guess this was pretty funny since we all laughed about it, but I didn't get an answer. Our bartender came over and took their order, and asked how are things "Up Top?"

The guy closest to me said, "doing really well except we had to escort one down today."

Our bartender said, "sounds like somebody be misbehav'n up in Haven."

The guy next to me said, "yeah, but it gives me an excuse to come see you and get some real food.

The guy next to me introduced himself as Tony and his quiet friend was Madison. He said, "Her name is Orangejello."

Bewildered, I said, "What?"

Tony repeated, "Orangejello."

About this time, she returned to deliver our next round of beer. I couldn't resist but to ask again, "How do you say your name?"

Again, she said, "Orangejello." And walked away.

I wasn't actually asking anyone in particular when I said, "How the Hell do you spell that?"

Madison finally spoke for the first time and said, "Orange Jell-O...... O-R-A-N-G-E J-E-L-L-O. Like the stuff you eat. But her real name is Tammy. Don't you dare tell her I told you that."

We all got a laugh about that and went on to talk about the area. During our conversation I learned that Tony and Madison work for a resort village known as "Up Top." That wasn't the original name, but the name stuck after people kept saying they were going to hike *up top* of the mountain to camp. Every now and then they have a troublemaker they have to escort down the mountain.

I drawled out, "Guess that's what Orange Jello was talking about when she said somebody was 'misbehav'n in Haven.'"

Tony said, "Yep, same place, just a different section from where we normally work."

Their food arrived, and I decided not to ask any questions about Up Top, or Haven. My cover had been established, and I surely didn't want to give them the opportunity to ask me anything.

I paid for my tab and thanked them for the information. Just in case I encountered them again, I ended the encounter by saying, "Maybe I'll see you along the trails." I left The Well long before I wanted to, but I also wanted to put some distance between myself, Tony, and Madison for a while. I had a slight beer buzz and knew I'd better pace myself if I wanted to go back and watch the band later on.

I walked around town for a while looking in the shop windows. I've been here many times and have seen some really cool artwork, but I've never been here when the shops are open. Maybe I'll take a vacation and stop during the day like normal people do. The thought of normal people struck me funny for some reason, *What the Hell is normal?*

Glanced at my phone...9:17. I'm pretty sure the band should be playing by now, or at least very soon. My beer buzz was wearing off, so it was time to go back for a second round.

I went back to "The Well" since that was the only place close by that had live music tonight. The dinner crowd had left, and I was relieved to find Tony and Madison was nowhere in sight.

I went back to the same bar stool I had occupied earlier and Orangejello, made eye contact as soon as I sat down. She held up a frosty mug and gave me an inquisitive look. I responded by giving her a thumbs up, and my beer was delivered a moment later.

I took my beer and told Orangejello that I wanted to open another tab, and I was moving down near the band. The bar was slim tonight. The band was a jazz, blues, type of band. I guess that type of stuff doesn't work well with the mountain folks. Anything with a saxophone has my interest since I played a little myself. Not well, but I'm working on it.

The band did a lot of stuff I wasn't familiar with…mostly, I like blues and slower darker jazz and, of course, the standards. I wasn't hearing any of that here. I had my back to the bar watching the band. I made a half turn to put my mug on the bar. When I did, Orangejello was there sort of lounging with her arms crossed and resting her head on the bar.

I asked, "You tired?"

She rolled her eyes, "No, they suck."

I said, "I guess you don't like jazz?"

Orangejello said, "I love jazz, they suck."

I just shook my head in agreement, and looked back at her and said, "I thought it was just me."

She stood up and deeply sighed, "no, they suck. You want another beer?"

I just gave her a thumbs up, which had quickly become our way of communicating, and off she went to get me another beer. When she returned, she asked what type of music I liked.

"I'm more into Motown, Carolina beach, blues, and I like the more laid back softer, darker jazz styles like Dexter Gordan."

Orangejello gave me a strange look, "he's my favorite. I've never met anyone that actually knew who he was. Well, not around here, anyway."

Our conversation turned to our interest in music. Orangejello shared that she was a music education major, and regrets not doing performance, and spending more time on piano. She has been unable to find a job at a school. Her take on the situation was the lack of openings, but I'd think her hard-core hippy appearance, tattoos and piercings may be holding her back as well. I understand you can't judge people on appearance alone, but it is an indicator. I'd never tell her my thoughts on the subject. And, thankfully, she didn't ask.

My mind kind of wandered at the moment to something one of my friends told me. Jerry was a professional sax player that was helping me with my playing. He said he thought I was the biggest ass he had ever met, until he got to know me and found out I was a pretty nice guy. He continued to say he has met a lot of people that he liked at first and later found out they were not what they appeared to be. So, I guess if you had to choose, you're doing the right thing.

He will never know what an impact that had on me. I've always considered myself ugly as a bulldog, and I guess I come across as hard to approach, because I'm normally very quiet. The truth is I like to meet new people and enjoy learning about their interests. Jerry will never know because he died after only a few lessons.

Orangejello brought me back to the present when she asked about my music interest and playing. I had to tell her my story. My first interest was at a church function. My girlfriend and I were holding hands under the table watching her parents perform. Her mother was a singer, and her father played the tenor sax. My fantasy was that someday that would be us up on stage. Life gets in the way. We reached our teenage years and broke up. My parents were poor and couldn't buy me a sax.

I gave up the dream until I turned thirty. As a present to myself, I bought a beat-up alto in a pawn shop along with some method books. I had to use a pair of pliers to bend the pads back in place to make it work. I taught myself to read music and learned as much as I could. I did fairly well but developed some bad playing habits.

I told her about Robert. He was a middle school band teacher. I went to his school and asked if he would help me. We became friends and he worked with me off and on when he could. It was more off than on. We both had demanding schedules, and he played in several dance bands on weekends. He let me get up on stage a couple of times. It must have been bad; I think his band members got pissed. So, I quit doing that.

We lost touch for a while and when we reconnected, he had moved away and remarried. The sad part is he had cancer and had to quit teaching. Not long after that I learned through a mutual friend that he died. This friend wanted to know if I knew the details, which I didn't since we lived so far apart now. He wanted to know if it was true that Robert shot himself. I didn't know, and I never made an effort to find out. It was one of those things I was better off not knowing.

I looked at Orangejello and said, "Whatever you do, don't give me lessons." That lightened the mood.

She poured two shot glasses and pushed one over my way. She downed hers and said, "To us, we may suck, but we're still kicking."

I downed my drink and said, "Thanks, Tammy."

"Oh, shit!" She slammed her glass on the bar and demanded loudly, "what else did they tell you?"

"Nothing," I insisted laughing, "we didn't have time. I was more interested in hearing about the place you were talking about. The music came on, and I couldn't understand what they were talking about."

"Please don't be mad. Can I call you Tammy now?"

She gave me a stern look and responded, "okay, but not where anyone can hear you."

Normally, I'd follow through to hear her story, but I mostly wanted the information on Haven, or Up Top, as it is also known as.

Earlier, on my walkabout through town, I learned the area is a multi-use area. But Tammy went on to explain that it is mostly a wilderness camp that is used for drug rehab, and as a shelter for human trafficking victims. It's also run like a hippy commune, so It's hard to know who's who if you're not an insider. There are two ways to get there. One is by the sky lift that runs on Fridays. Or hike in. The sky lift is by invitation or referral. You can hike in anytime, but they keep a close eye on anyone that hikes in to be sure you aren't there for the wrong reasons.

Tammy gave me instructions on how to get to the trail head and a little about what the place looked like. Tammy couldn't give me any more than that since she had only been there once when she first moved to the area. She said she was invited up top for a drum circle on a Friday night. She was getting into the vibe and lit up a joint. She was escorted back to the sky lift and was given a ride back down the mountain and she hasn't been back since. She been invited many times but declined to go.

I hung out about another hour drinking beer hoping to find out more. The conversation turned back to hiking and music and some of her exploits. The more I learned about Tammy, I was sure she should pursue her playing or settle in as a bartender. She'd be fun to hang out with, but has no business being around kids.

I finally got out of the bar and walked the two blocks to my motel. I had to do some thinking and figure out my next move.

Thursday—Trip up the mountain

I woke up early despite my late night of beer drinking. I don't know what's the deal with motels. No matter how thick the curtains are, the sun seems to find its way in through a crack and the sun shines directly in my eyes. I never gave it much thought, but I always seem to get a room facing East.

After a quick shave and shower, I took an inventory of my backpack and did a shake down of supplies based on what little I knew about my hike up the mountain. It's about ten miles from what I was told. Being out of shape I figured it would take me five to six hours, maybe more if those ten miles was stated as the crow flies. Some people don't count the switchbacks as actual distance. I forgot to ask about elevation.

Even though meals are supplied at the camp, I figured I better pack for three days of meals just in case I can't get in. It would also help with my cover to be prepared. I had everything I needed except for the freeze-dried meals. I went to the local hiking supply store to stock up. They had a wide selection of pre-packaged meals and from the prices, they were very proud of their products. I guess that is to be expected when you're the only supplier in the area.

Normally, I'd just buy a lot of oatmeal and various foods from a regular grocery store for a couple of days in the woods. Since time was a factor, I grabbed a bunch of packages and hit the road to find the trail head. Tammy had never been to the trail head but knew its approximate location from the invitations to hike up top. I found the town park as described, then I needed to find a dirt road that looks like a driveway. There is nothing special about the driveway to distinguish it from all the other dirt driveways in the area, except when you enter you drive about one hundred yards and there will be an archway made from blue witch bottles.

I pulled into five driveways but there were houses just beyond. On my sixth try, the narrow rutted out driveway opened to an area covered with flowerpots, and an archway made from wrought iron and had blue bottles sticking out at all angles. I drove through the gate and saw an old house just to the left of the dirt drive. I had no idea what I was supposed to do from here.

I sat there in my van looking around for several minutes, before an older woman came out of the house wearing a witch's hat and carrying a broom. She approached my van, pointed at me and said, "state your business young man!"

I stuttered my response, that I was looking for a way to go to Haven.

The old woman gave me a stern look and said, "you have to go to church if you want to go to Heaven."

I repeated, "no, a place called Haven."

The old woman gave a loud laugh and pointed to a white fence and said, "through that gate is a long journey. At the end of your journey you will meet an old man at the top of the mountain. This man will answer all the questions of the universe. "Tell me, young man, what wisdom do you seek?"

I was stunned with her question and didn't have an answer.

The old woman laughed long and hard. I was about to turn around and run, when she regained her breath and said, "I'm just screwing with you, I love doing that. I've got a camera posted right there in case you want to see the look on your face. I can print you off a copy if you want one. You know, like they do at the amusement parks when you ride a roller coaster."

Damn, I was still speechless.

She pointed to a gravel space, laughed again and said, "I'm Mattie. Park over there, and you can leave it as long as you'd like." She walked away still laughing at my expression, and said, "I'll be out back, come see me before you head up top."

I parked my van and got my gear together. I was still in shock, but then again, that was damn funny when you think about it. I added a few more things to my pack. I put my 9mm, extra ammo, and a bottle of Crown in the pack. I better keep these out of sight if I get in.

I walked to the back of the house to see the woman tending to some herb plants. There were cats and dogs all around. Several of them came over to greet me. One dog, a black lab seemed to be the friendliest.

The woman said, "that's Merlin. Don't be surprised if he hikes up with you, unless you don't want him to. If you don't want the company, I'll put him in the house until you're gone."

I said, "I don't mind, if you don't mind."

The woman shrugged and said, "why would I mind? He's not my dog. He just shows up from time to time. Oh, and he likes turtles. Dang dog is always bringing up turtles. I swear I spend half the day turning them back on their legs."

She continued, "hang on, if you don't care."

She disappeared into the house and came out a few minutes later with a small tote bag. She gave me the tote bag, and said, "this is for Merlin, in case he gets hungry." Inside the tote was a plastic bag of dry dog food, some treats, a bottle of water and a collapsible bowl.

Mattie said, "he'll start nipping at the bag if he gets hungry or thirsty."

I attached the tote to the frame of my pack. Merlin came over and sat down beside me, he looked at me and shuffled around like he was excited and ready to start our journey.

Mattie laughed, "looks like you have a hiking buddy. Don't worry if he disappears. Sometimes he comes back and sometimes he don't. Crazy dog showed up here a couple of years ago, stays gone about half the time. Ya'll better get going, and whatever you do, don't walk backwards as you pass through the gate."

Innocently falling into her trap, I suspiciously asked, "why's that?"

Mattie laughed again and said, "because you'll fall on your ass. You better get going, just follow your nose and stay on the trail. You'll get there sooner or later."

On the trail

As soon as Merlin and I crossed through the gateway the air seemed to change, I paused for a moment to look out through the forest and think about what may be ahead. Merlin had continued down the trail; he turned and gave one quick bark to get my attention and continued on. There was no reason to try and figure this out now. I better get moving.

The trail was mostly smooth from the heavy foot traffic. The area was a beautiful dark green and the trail up ahead can be seen as it descends toward a stream after several switchbacks. On the other side I could see the trail as it climbs the ridge in a zig zag as it climbs the steep slope.

To a real hiker, this would be a majestic sight, to me, I was thinking… *this is going to kick my ass*. The descent down to the stream wasn't too bad, but it's pretty obvious I'm out of shape. I tried to pack as light as possible, but I'd swear the doggie bag was as heavy as my pack and having it dangle from an exterior D ring on the lower portion of my pack wasn't working.

I made it to the bridge that crossed the stream at the bottom of the trail. Luckily there was a bench on the other side of the bridge. I crossed over, but Merlin went in the water and laid down. I rearranged the doggie bag, so it was higher up on the pack and tied it down to keep it from swinging. Merlin was enjoying himself as he began to run back and forth in the stream.

I heard Ms. Mattie laugh out loud. I have no idea what she was laughing at but sitting here in the woods and thinking about her witch act was sort of spooky. I wanted to get moving before Merlin had the chance to come shake the water out of his fur all over me. I'm already sweating. I surely don't need to smell like a wet dog on top of it. I reached the first switch back before Merlin rejoined the hike. I guess I should be lucky he got most of the water off before he reached me, but sure enough, he had to get in one more shake to get rid of the rest of the water. I was able to take a couple of steps back and avoided most of the doggie water. I half expected to hear Ms. Mattie laugh, but I didn't. I looked back to see how far I'd gone so far. *Holy crap*, I can still see the roof of Ms. Maddie's house, and I'm already tired.

I made sure to take small steps. At least I remember this from my Boy Scout days. It's better to take a lot of smaller steps than big strenuous steps when hiking on steep terrain. It seems to be working. I made it to the next two switch backs without too much effort. The trail seemed to level out and Merlin ran ahead out of sight. When I reached the crest of the hill the view was amazing. I could see nothing but wilderness as far as I could see. No buildings, no cities, nothing. I had to stop for a moment to admire the view. I really want to drop the pack and hang out, but if I keep stopping, I'll never get to Haven.

I came to a rocky area and seemed to lose the trail. Merlin was nowhere in sight. I called out and heard him bark. He seemed to be lower on the ridge. I crept to the edge to look over, and my vertigo went into overtime. Merlin was standing on a ledge that ran along a cliff. I could see a cable attached to the cliff. I was feeling sick at the realization I had to walk along the ridge holding on to the cable. I stepped back looking around for an alternate route. Unfortunately, there wasn't one. I wondered why the trail didn't follow the upper ridge. I went up a little further and got my answer. There was a large gap between the ridges, and it was painfully obvious the cable route was much safer.

I went back to the area where the cable began. I got down on my knees and took hold of the cable on the ground. I slowly crawled around the rocks until I was able to stand on the ledge. I'm sure most people would say the ledge is two feet wide, but it feels more like six inches.

I tugged on the cable to test the slack and be sure it was firmly secured to the cliff. It seemed secure, and I didn't see rust on the connections. I was glad to see Merlin was on the other side and thankfully he didn't feel the need to come back and help me along. This was hard enough without having a hyper dog along the edge. I wanted to look down, but I decided that would be a very bad idea. I have ear issues and tend to have vertigo. This would not be a good time for that to kick in. I kept my eyes toward the rock face and felt along the cable while scooting my feet side to side, careful not to trip and testing every footing before I committed my weight to that foot. Merlin was barking, and I could see him out of the corner of my eye as he seemed to be chasing his tail and barking. I guess he was telling me to hurry up. I didn't dare look toward him in fear I might accidentally look down. I looked closely at the rock wall noticing details I'm sure no one else has ever noticed. This helped me to concentrate as I inched my way along the cliff.

I finally made it to the other side. I took off my pack and sat down to rest and have a drink. I also took out the bowl from the doggie bag and poured Merlin a drink too. I was beginning to think I should have waited until Friday and try to get an invitation to the lift. I know that would have been a long shot, but it sounded good at the moment. I asked Merlin if there were any more surprises? Merlin didn't answer. I repacked the doggie bag and hoisted on the pack. The trail in this area is elevated but free of obstacles. I continued to baby step my way up the trail. Merlin and I walked about an hour at this pace and came to another peak. The view from here was similar to the last but not quite as far since it looked out toward other mountain peaks.

While I could see that the trail descended again, I couldn't see far because of the thick trees. I took off the pack and Merlin and I had a small snack and another round of water. I had no idea how far we had walked or how far we had to go. There was no cell signal, and I hadn't worn a watch in years, so I had no idea what time it was. The sun was still high in the sky so I'm sure it was just a little past midday. I should have paid attention to the time we entered the trail, but I guess we walked about three hours. I'm no average hiker so I'm sure I fall well under the average two mile an hour suggestion. My best guess is that hopefully we're about halfway there.

The trail was a manageable downward descent. The views were amazing. The thick lush forest is beautiful. Even the fallen trees on the steep mountains add to the wonder of this place. Most are moss covered and surrounded by bright green ferns in contrast to their dark wet trunks. There are large gray boulders peeking out every so often to add to the contrast. Just below the trail a small stream originates beside a large gray moss-covered rocky area and flows down toward the same direction as the trail. I can smell the water. I wasn't sure if it was the small stream or a larger body of water ahead.

I was beginning to enjoy being here and almost forgot my mission. I seriously wish I could be one of those in the moment people. Merlin ran off out of sight further down the trail. The smell of water was getting stronger, and I could hear the faint sound of moving water.

I hiked on for what I think was another mile by myself. I found Merlin sitting in the water. Of course, he came out to greet me when I arrived and performed the customary doggie shake. I was not as quick this time and now I smell like a wet dog, which by this time probably doesn't matter. This seems like as good a place as any for another break. Merlin was nosing at the doggie bag, so I opened a plastic bag of food and poured some in bowl and another with water. I elected for a protein bar, water and an apple.

I could hear the rush of water like a waterfall nearby. I'm hoping we will come across it along the trail. Merlin and I finished up our meal. I packed everything away and munched on the apple as we walked. About a half mile later I found the waterfall. We were near the top of it. The stream we had been sitting beside was just a small portion that joined a much larger river that flowed from above. I could see the water high above where we were standing, and it gathered into a pool before falling again on the far side of the pool. I looked around hoping to find another trail that would provide a better view. The terrain was steep and slick. There were no other trails in sight. Merlin was no help, he just sat there beside me looking at me like I knew what to do.

Frustrated, I turned to hit the trail, and Merlin took off further up the trail, but he stayed in sight this time. Before long we came to an opening and a small pond between the rock faced ridges. The waterfall we had seen was from this pond. I couldn't see what was feeding the pond. It must have been the mouth coming up from under the rocks. The area was steep and rocky. Merlin stayed away from the edge, and I took this as a good sign to do the same. Merlin had walked further up the trail away from the pond. Although it was an excellent sight, it felt dangerous, so I followed Merlin up the trail away from the pond.

Once we were away from the pond Merlin seemed to perk up again and seemed happy to be away from the area. I called Merlin to come over. He came and sat down beside me. I asked Merlin what was wrong with the pond? Merlin didn't answer. He doesn't talk much, but he's still good company. I'm glad he came along.

A little further up the trail we came to an opening that looked out on a field of yellow weeds. It looks like it could have been farmland at some point. There were a few trees among the open field, but it was mostly open. I caught the faint smell of wood smoke but did not see or hear anything. Being this far away I'm hoping this is an attended fire, and a sign we are getting close.

The trail descended again back into the lush forest and seemed to be going away from the smell of smoke. We descended further down the trail and the smell was completely gone.

It seemed to be a mile before we hit the bottom of the trail and looked up the opposite ridge as the trail is visible with multiple switch backs zig zagging toward the top up the steep mountain.

Merlin looked like he needed a break before we tackled the journey up the next level. Merlin laid down next to my feet as I prepared our water. He didn't seem hungry, but he gladly drank from his bowl. I sat down against a tree drinking water and chewing on jerky. Merlin came over and sat down facing me. He didn't come right out and ask for it, but I'm pretty sure he wanted some jerky too. I gave him the rest of it, then poured him some more water.

I couldn't see the sun since we were deep between the ridges, but I'd estimate we should be getting close. At least I hope we are. I was tired and in a lot of pain. I'm not sure I've ever hiked this far in my life. I was so tempted to set up camp and just stay here for the night. I got up to look for a suitable place to set up a tent. I reach for my pack and Merlin got up and ran up the trail… *Well damn*, I watched as Merlin run to the first switch back. I could barely see him in the distance, but he stopped and looked back at me before he started running further up the trail.

It's obvious he's not coming back. Mattie said he runs off sometimes. I wonder if this is one of those times, or do I need to follow him. I heard him barking as he ran up the second switchback and he was quickly out of sight.

Every muscle and joint is screaming in pain as I hoisted up the pack. I started up the trail. By this time my baby steps are even smaller baby steps. I can only imagine what I'm going to feel like in the morning. So far, I've been amazed by the views. This is still nice, but I find I'm just looking at the ground wanting this to be over. Baby step after baby step…I didn't want to look and see how much further to the top. Baby step after baby step…I counted four switchbacks. I smelled smoke. I looked up to see two more switchbacks before reaching the top of the trail. I swear I'll cry if I see more trail at the top.

Haven

I emerged from the woods to find myself standing in front of a large wooden gateway. Beyond the gate I could see a bright green grass field about the size of a football field. There were small wood buildings recessed a few feet back from the field. The buildings were about twenty yards apart, and each had a wooden walkway leading out to the tree lined field.

There were children playing at the far end of the field kicking a ball, and there were people sitting on the ground along the edge of the field in front of some of the small hut-like buildings.

For some reason I feel like I've been here before. I know that was not possible. I would surely remember taking such a long hike having to get here. There was something strangely familiar about this place. I've either seen it before, or I've dreamed about it in much detail. I remember when I was young, I could dream about places I'd never been to and would go there later on and know where things were and know some of the people there. This ability was very troubling to me, and no one believed me when I talked about it. By the time I was eighteen years old I was sure there was something wrong with me, I fought the dreams and dismissed the predictions as nothing more than craziness.

There was one dream that was vastly different. This place was dark, I could feel nothing. I had no form. I was like a floating energy, but it was still me. I remember that I was connected to everyone that ever lived in the past, and I could read their thoughts just by thinking about that person. It was very strange that I was able to freely access all the knowledge this person ever knew.

I suddenly woke up and still retained a brief access to the ability to communicate with other people. It scared the Hell out of me, and I was in a panic. I heard the voice ask, "do you want to give this up?" I recall silently screaming, "Yes!" I was crying, "please go away. I want to be normal!"

The bedroom light came on, and my door slammed shut. The dreams stopped after that. I had not experienced that feeling again until just now standing at the gate.

I saw a slender red-haired girl running toward the gate waving her arms above her head calling out, "I've been waiting for you."

I looked around to see who she was talking to. I was the only one standing there. She came over, hugged me and said come on in. She knelt down and started untying my dirty hiking boots. I really felt uneasy about this, especially since I had been on the trail for so long. I protested and she stood up and unhooked the buckle on my backpack straps. She said just leave the pack and shoes here. Someone will take them to your hut.

I told her that I wasn't staying I was just passing by. She just laughed and took my hand and said, "no one just passes by up here. You are either coming in or going out. I will take you to the big hut so you can check in."

At first glance my guide appeared to be in her twenties. I really could not tell. Up close she looked a little older but moved and talked with the energy of a chatty teen. She pulled me along, and I'm sure we would have been running if I'd let her. She led me to a cabin located to the left of the gate and told me to have a seat on the porch and she'd go get Sensei Mike.

I sort of chuckled to myself, "Sensei Mike." *What have I gotten myself into?*

I sat down in a rocking chair and waited to see the Sensei. I looked out onto the grass field and watched the activity. Mostly it was kids playing a game I couldn't figure out, kicking a ball around with no apparent goal. Most of the adults were sitting around near the entrances to the huts talking. There were others coming and going from the area and appeared to be workers.

I felt tired and drifted in and out of sleep. I wasn't sure if I was awake or dreaming, I saw the familiar place again and it was much like the one I was in now or am I back in the place that I dreamed about? I was too tired to figure it out and then fell asleep.

Sensei Mike

I don't know how long I'd been asleep, but when I woke up my guide was sitting beside me holding my hand. She was calm and quiet and whispered "did you have a good nap" Mike can see you now."

She led me into the cabin and then she left. I was alone in the cabin and was expecting a hippie guru type with long hair and a beard dressed in a white robe to come greet me. I was completely surprised when a man in his seventies or older, dressed in khaki pants and a checkered blue shirt enter the room and introduced himself as Mike the manager of Haven.

Mike is a well-groomed man and appeared to be very friendly and educated. Mike invited me to have a seat and talk about my desire to enter Haven. I wasn't sure what I should do at this point. I was afraid that if I told the truth I'd be escorted out of Haven and then I'd never be able to work the case. I also realized that I didn't have my shoes or pack. Walking down the mountain without them was not a good idea. There was one half-truth and that was what I said. I told Mike that I was hiking and just came across the entrance.

Mike gave me a strange look and said that was very adventurous to be hiking in the area without a plan. He looked at me for a period that seemed to last forever. Then he said no one simply arrives at Haven. Then he watched me again as if he were reading my thoughts, or my reaction. Neither of us moved as if we were playing some sort of game where the first to speak or move would be the loser. The truth is I was just too scared to speak or move since I'd be put out if I lost.

Mike laughed, rubbed his well-groomed beard and looked at me over the top of his glasses and said, "you are welcome here, but I must warn you that everything you think you know will be challenged. Your purpose here will be exposed and when you leave here you will have a very different outlook on yourself and others."

As if on cue my guide appeared to escort me to my cabin. My guide introduced herself as Sam; I guess that would be short for Samantha. We didn't talk much as we walked across the large grass field and then entered the woods at the far end of the field. There were additional cabins scattered throughout the area in every direction. Sam walked ahead of me not talking and was walking fast. It was kind of hard to keep up with her, but I managed. We walked down a path leading toward two cabins.

We reached a fork in the path and Sam spun around and looked me straight in the eye. She said, "I'm sorry if I seem cold, I thought you were someone else, but I was wrong. I'm still glad you're here, and I'll be glad to assist you with whatever you may need during your stay here."

Sam pointed toward the two cabins and said there're both empty, take which one you want. She then pointed across the path and indicated that cabin was hers. "Just yell if you need anything."

Sam walked toward her cabin, then she stopped and said, "oh yea. The bath house and chow hall are down that path." She spun away and walked the rest of the way to her cabin. I walked toward the two cabins and found my backpack and shoes in a wood chair between the cabins. It looked like someone had searched my pack. I was really glad I had my ID and gun on me at the time. Thankfully, Sam didn't notice the gun in my ankle holster when she untied my boots.

I checked both cabins and found them to be identical, one room structured with a double bed on one side, a bunk bed on the other, one chair and a table attached to the wall. There was a window and a small propane heater. No air conditioning and no electricity. I took the cabin to the right since they were the same, and I was already in this one. I put my pack down and sat on the porch. I looked out across the woods toward the other cabins. There was no one in sight. I could hear people off in the distance. It reminded me of summer camp many years ago. It was nice to be here, but the big question was... *what the Hell do I do now?*

I sat on the porch for about an hour, I would have guessed. Funny thing is I realized that I had been there for some time and had not checked my phone the entire time. I took out my phone, turned it on and checked to see if I had a signal. There was no signal. I was not surprised since I hadn't had a signal since I left town. I turned off the phone and put it away. The first few hours of the trip up the mountain I checked my phone every so often looking for a signal. This was the longest I've been away from contact in ten years. I was uneasy about it at first, but it seemed to be growing on me.

I got my soap, small backpack towel and a change of clothes together and walked toward the bathhouse and thought, *if I'm going to be around people I better get cleaned up.*

The bathhouse and chow hall were next to each other and apparently the only buildings in Haven with power. I hadn't noticed if Mike's place had electricity or running water.

I entered the bathhouse and found it fully equipped with everything I needed. I shaved my head and took the longest hot shower I've ever taken in my life. My mind was racing about my mission; I was still unclear what my mission was. You would think having nothing else to do, I'd have it figured out by now. *If I found Robin in Haven, how was I going to convince her to go back home?* I just arrived here, and I wouldn't go back. Not after what I saw her home to be like. If she is here, I wonder how she found this place.

I was deep in thought when I heard a bell ring. That was followed by sounds of children running and yelling. It was pretty obvious that dinner was served, and the kids were first in line since they were the fastest. I walked out of the bathhouse and looked toward the chow hall watching as the kids raced inside and the adults coming into view from the field. As I was standing there a woman in a multicolored tie-dyed dress passed by me leaving the same bathhouse area.

She smiled as she passed by and said, "come on if you're hungry."

I was embarrassed and hoped I hadn't just made a big mistake that would get me kicked out of Haven on the first day.

I walked into the dining hall with a large group of people. I was trying to not be noticed but most of them were dressed in what I'd call bohemian style, and I was dressed in modern hiking clothes in comparison to their worn-out jeans, shorts and t shirts. There were a few exceptions. Some of the women were better dressed. The styles ranged from the same worn-out clothes to pretty summer dresses like the one Sam was wearing.

As soon as I entered the chow hall, I noticed a line of about thirty people waiting to go through the serving line. A group of six kids ranging in age from I'd guess around six to ten years old came running toward me. They surrounded me and all wrapped me in a group hug. The two older girls took me by the hand and pulled me to the front of the line. One of the girls indicated, "new people go first here."

I guess I'll never get lost here; someone is always leading me around.

I was looking for Sam. Since she was my first contact, I guess I felt a connection somehow. I saw Mike enter the chow hall and the room fell silent. All eyes were on Mike. He raised his hands in the air, and I expected to hear a little Hell fire and brimstone. All I heard was Mike say, "for all we have, we give thanks." The room cheered and the servers began filling plates.

The kids pushed me along the line toward the front where I was to receive my plate. I guess this is one of those places where you take what you get. It's been a long time since I had an all-vegetarian meal. It all looked really good, but I couldn't help but remember the scene at the bar watching the couple devouring a meal of a huge cheeseburger, fries and pint of beer. I wonder how long I'd last before I took the plunge down the mountain to get my fix.

I walked to a table toward the back of the chow hall and sat down. I was still hoping that Sam would come in. I was busy looking around for her when I saw Robin.

Robin was easy to pick out with her long curly blonde hair and the striking bright blue eyes. She looked like her sister, and mother, but she was much brighter, she didn't have that drab down-and-out-look. She went to a table where several other young ladies were eating, and she joined them. A few moments later Sam entered the chow hall and sat down with Robin. Sam didn't even look in my direction, but Robin did. In fact, she looked right into my eyes as if she knew who I was and why I was there. I felt a panic attack coming on. I wasn't sure what to do or how I'd react if she made a scene here. I was totally out of my element.

Sensei Mike came to my table and sat down. He asked how I liked my accommodations and if I'd had a chance to look around Haven. I told him that I hadn't and this was the furthest I'd ventured out. I asked him what was expected of me during my stay here. Was there a charge for my cabin and meals; was I to work, or what?

I addressed him as Sensei Mike, and he laughed and said you don't have to call me that. I'm just Mike; some call me Sensei because I'm a teacher of sorts. I lead many of the groups here. Mike told me that I was welcome to join in. There are no requirements during the first week. If you feel like joining in the work groups, go ahead. If you feel like teaching something in The Commons area, go ahead. If you're still here after a week, you'll be assigned to the work rotation. There are seven work groups. Each has a work detail and they rotate each day, so that everyone shares the same duties. There are the gardens, the landscaping, the childcare, the kitchen, clean up, and a few others, you'll catch on pretty quick. Those that have special skills will teach in The Commons. That is the area you saw when you arrived. The Commons are the huts located next to the field. Each hut has a different theme. Some are art, some are music, and some are counselors that volunteer their time here.

Mike reached across the table and took hold of my hand. He wanted to be sure what he was about to say had full impact. Mike said, "you are an observer. Observe with your heart as well as your eyes and you will find everything you are looking for, and more. Just observe for now." Mike got up and went to the chow line, he didn't return to my table.

A bunch of the kids came and sat down with me. They asked me a hundred questions each. Mostly they wanted to know my name, and why didn't I have any hair? Did it hurt to be bald? Could they touch my head and so on? When it was obvious that I'd finished eating one of the boys grabbed my tray and took it to the kitchen and the others began cleaning up. I figured I might as well help too. This again reminded me of my time at scout camp and that's what I talked to the kids about while we were cleaning. We made pretty short work of wiping down tables and sweeping. Next thing I knew I was standing alone. When the kids were done, they ran outside. Guess my scout stories didn't hold their interest.

I wasn't sure what I should do next. I ended up on the front porch of the chow hall sitting in a rocking chair. I could hear the faint voices as the children were playing in the distance. There were the sounds of nature and the sound of the rocker as I rocked back and forth.

The next thing I knew Robin was standing right in front of me. She sat down and said, "thanks for coming. Mom sent me a letter and told me that you were on your way."

Completely puzzled, I said, "what do you mean she sent a letter? I thought you were missing. Did she know you were here all along?"

Robin replied, "yes, my mom sent me here."

Robin went on to tell me that was not her real mom; her real mother was killed in a car wreck shortly after she was born. The woman I met was her aunt. "She's the only mom I've ever known, and I don't know anything about my father. She met the Reverend at some church thing. He wanted everyone to call him Reverend. Later on, they hooked up again. He was a religious freak, and mom is too weak to go against him.

She was young and did her best to try and raise me on her own, but she took the path of least resistance, we ended up at the school, and they got married."

The Reverend has everyone convinced that he is the next best thing to God himself, and mom is scared that she can't survive without him. The only job my mom held was a waitress before working at the school."

Continuing, Robin explained that her mom had been skimming money off the school for years, "she planned to send me here when I turned eighteen."

I had to stop her there. I asked her, "are you eighteen?"

Robin responded, "yes, and I will bet the Reverend told you I was younger."

Perplexed with our conversation, I asked Robin, "why am I here if your mom knows you're here? Why did she hire me?"

Robin was quiet for a moment then continued, "mom is planning an escape from the Reverend, and she says there is some kind of big secret she will tell us about it when she is free. She told me that she was sending a man to Haven. She told me to keep you here until she arrives. I guess you are the one she sent?"

Robin handed me a note. "This one is for you."

The note was short. It just said, "Stay close to Robin. Keep her safe. I should be there in two weeks. I'm sorry I can't tell you what this is about right now. Please forgive me; I had to keep the secret until the time was right."

I asked Robin if she knew what the secret is, and why I was there.

Robin shrugged, "no. About a year ago Mom started talking about a family secret and started making a plan for me to come to Haven. I want to go get my little sister and bring her here too. I hate the Reverend so much; I want someone to kill him."

Robin was full of rage and the tears flowed. She jumped up and ran away. I started after her, but Sam stopped me. I had not noticed her sitting at the other end of the porch.

Sam quietly said, "let her go. She needs some time to herself right now. I know where she's going, and she'll be fine. I'll check on her in a bit."

I wanted to go find Robin but had no idea where to look. I looked out in the direction where Robin had run, but she had run into the quickly darkening woods, and I had no idea which path she took.

I sat back down, and Sam came over and sat down beside me. I asked if she knew what was going on.

Sam said, "no, not really. She hates her father, Reverend, or whatever he is. She's told me a few things but I'm not in a position to break a confidence. I talked to her mom once on the phone the day Robin arrived. I only know that you are here to keep Robin safe until she gets here."

I asked, "there is a phone here?"

Sam said, "yes, but I can't tell you where it's at. Only Mike has access to it."

I asked Sam why she changed her attitude toward me.

Sam said, "I heard the conversation between you and Mike. I wasn't sure if you were here for Robin or sent here by the Reverend to kidnap her and take her back."

"So, what do you think now?"

Sam hesitated, "I'm not sure yet. I'll be watching you. Besides, you'd have a hard time, calling for back up or getting her off this mountain."

I asked, "so why are you talking to me now?"

Sam said, "you didn't have to help the kids clean up. You could have followed Robin out, but you didn't. Me and Robin sat out here and watched you. Robin says there's something about you that she trusts and thinks you're the right guy. I'm not sure yet, I'll be watching you."

Sam got up and walked away. I really wanted to talk with her more and convince her that I was the right guy, but I kept my seat and thought about it for a while. *I guess I can see her point. I don't even know why I'm here. I wonder if Mike knows who I am?* I dare not ask until I talk to Sam and Robin again.

I have no idea of what to do now. I'm sitting here at the chow hall. No place to go, nothing to do, no phone, no computer. I got up from the steps and went over to a row of rocking chairs and sat down again. I wish I had a book to read, I'm sure there is a library around here somewhere. Maybe I'll put that on my to-do list for tomorrow. I thought about that for a moment. If I'm this bored now what was tomorrow going to be like.

I sat on the porch for a long time, just thinking. This whole situation is so strange. I can smell smoke from distant fires and the sounds of people laughing and singing. The sounds were coming from different directions. It's dark, and I have no idea how to get around. I know my cabin is to the right of the bathhouse, and I didn't bring a flashlight to the chow hall. I found the bathhouse with no problem, but the trail was a different story.

I heard a little voice close by asking, "are you lost?"

I turned to see a little girl standing there.

She said, "I can show you the path."

I asked, "are you out here alone?"

She said, "no, mom is back there." A moment later her mother showed up with a flashlight and led me to my cabin.

The little girl cheerfully chirped, "I'm Andrea, and my mom is Cassie, I hope you have a good night."

They walked away into the darkness. I made it inside my cabin and fumbled around in the dark and finally found my pack. I dug around until I found my flashlight. Part of me wanted to go explore, but dang, I'm sore. I located an oil lamp attached to the wall and a lighter on the table. I hadn't noticed these before, maybe I just wasn't paying attention. I was kind of surprised they allowed flames in such a remote area. I lit the lamp and dug to the bottom of my pack to find the bottle stashed inside my sleeping bag. I turned the light down low and went out onto the porch and sip whiskey. It's fairly quiet close to the cabin, but I can hear people off in the distance. They sounded like they were having fun. Somewhere further out I can hear drums beating. I held my bottle up to see how much was left. I guess I better conserve some of this, I don't know how long I'll be here. I was tired and went in my cabin and fell asleep fast.

First full day—Friday

I woke up to a pounding on the side of my cabin. Not the door, but right next to my bed. Someone called out for me to get moving if I wanted breakfast. I laid there in thought. *What would I rather do, eat, or just lay here?* A few minutes later I heard the chow hall bell ringing. I figure since I was awake, I might as well go eat. One thing I was grateful for was the fact my door and window did not face East. Maybe I can find something to make a do not disturb sign for the side of my cabin.

Being late has its advantages sometimes. I had the bath house to myself and the line had cleared out by the time I made it to the chow hall. There was plenty of food left, and I was able to get everything I needed. *Maybe I'll be late every morning.* That thought vanished when I went to get coffee and found there was none left.

Someone passing by saw my momentary distress and reassured me, "the canteen will open in a half hour, if you can wait that long."

Grateful for that detail, I said, "thanks!" I walked to a table on the far side of the chow hall far away from everyone else. I'm not trying to be antisocial, but the truth is I've never been comfortable exerting myself into crowds of new people. Plus, the fact I am not sure if I'm undercover or not. This whole situation is so bizarre, if this had not been a generous cash retainer, I'd just walk away from it. But, *what the heck, I might as well enjoy the views and hang out. From what I have seen so far, I am being paid to go on vacation.*

I am feeling content to be by myself, but Andrea and Cassie came over and sat at the table with me. A few minutes later, Mike came over and brought me a cup of coffee. I don't mind the company. Mike brought coffee and Cassie and Andrea are a visual pleasure. Both are quite different than anyone here. Most of what I've seen so far is something like a hippy commune where these two are elegant and just pleasant to be around.

Andrea took two apples from her tray and put them in a cloth bag. Mike gave her a look over the top of his glasses which seemed to indicate something was wrong. Without a word from Mike, Andrea said, "I need these for a lesson today."

Mike said, "I'm sure I'll hear about it later."

Mike gave me a booklet and told me where to go to get more information and where to sign up for events and post items of interest. Then he left. I didn't see Robin or Sam at breakfast, and I had no idea where to start looking.

Andrea asked if I had plans for the day. I told her, "no, I figured I'd just walk around and see what this place is all about."

Andrea happily explained, "you'll find something interesting everywhere you go. Just be open."

Cassie got up and cleared the table. Andrea started to walk away, but she came back and said, "it will hurt for a while, but you'll be fine. It will all work out in the end."

Perplexed with her comment, I asked her what she meant?

Cassie took Andrea by the hand and said, "we need to get to class."

I watched as they walked out the door and wondered what she meant. Andrea is just a child, but she commands your attention for some reason.

I walked out to the porch planning to do so rocking chair time and do nothing but think. Robin and Sam were sitting on the porch. They were waiting for me.

Sam said, "I see you met Andrea?"

I replied, "yes, I met them last night. They escorted me to my cabin. Otherwise, I'd have been lost all night."

Sam warily said, "Andrea scares the Hell out of me."

It took me a moment to process what she had said.

I asked, "why?"

Sam said, "That little girl knows things, she's like psychic or something. Watch and you'll see what I'm talking about."

I resisted telling them what she had said to me, and I figured it was all because they were different than everyone else there. I was curious nonetheless and so far, they have at least made an effort to be friendly and helpful.

I sat down in a rocking chair and asked, "What's on the agenda today?"

Sam said, she was going to work in Mikes office. Robin said, "I'll be in the library this morning and the music room this evening."

I asked Robin if I could go with her, she said it would be fine If I drop by, but she made it noticeably clear she did not need or want a babysitter. She said it in a way that was close to a threat to give her space. I didn't reply and wanted to process the situation. I guess I would feel the same way if I had people controlling my every move my whole life and suddenly found a way to break away. The last thing I would want is someone watching over me.

I leaned over so we could be face to face. I looked into her eyes and said, "If you have any sailing adventure books, bring me one to lunch."

I got up and walked in the direction Andrea and Cassie were last seen.

After I left, I realized I hadn't even said bye to either one of them. I will apologize later. This situation is confusing. My job was over before it started. Robin is not missing. *So, am I here to be her bodyguard or what?* Clearly, she is of age to decide and declined. If I crowd her, she could complain to Mike, and I could be asked to leave Haven. I have no idea what I'm doing, but at least I know where I can find her if I need to.

I walked out to the edge of The Commons and walked around the outer gravel pathway between the grassy filed and the little huts. I found them sitting out in the grass near a hut at the far end of The Commons. A chalk board next to the path read, "Religion, Helpful or Harmful?"

I took off my boots since that seems to be the thing you do before stepping out on to the grass. I walked around toward the back. I tried hard not to be noticed, but that didn't work, seemed like everyone looked at me at some point. Sitting on the ground was not comfortable at all. I don't see how anyone does this. Cross-legged on my butt hurts, so I leaned over, and sort of half laid on my elbow resting my head on my hand. The discussion seemed unstructured. The audience posed questions to a moderator, and she asked the group to give their opinion before she would provide her take on the subject. They were in a discussion about homosexuals attending church, and somehow alcohol was mentioned near the end of the discussion. I got there late, so I really don't know what they decided. Someone posed the question about paying the church vs good works in the community.

Andrea stood up and walked to the front of the group. She held up the two apples. She didn't say anything at first. She just stood there until everyone stopped talking and every eye was on her. There was a small boy sitting in his mothers' lap crying. Andrea walked over knelt beside the boy. She brushed the hair out of his eyes and gave him an apple. The boy stopped crying and smiled before he buried his head in his mother's chest. Andrea walked slowly to the front of the group and held the apple up toward the sky, then she held it close to her chest and looked at it as if she were praying. She turned and threw the apple out into the woods.

Andrea turned to the groups and said, "which pleases God?"

Andrea walked away from the group and left on the gravel path toward the buildings. Cassie followed her. The group remained silent for a moment.

The moderator was the first to speak and said, "Well damn. Anybody got anything to say about that?"

I watched as Cassie and Andrea walked away. Part of me wanted to go with them and part of me wanted to stay here. I've had so many bad experiences with church, not to mention my short dealing with the Reverend and his followers. I was lost in my own thoughts and didn't hear the next topic. It seemed to shift to the lack of forgiveness in the church and how people were left to feel unwanted.

One young girl shared she was addicted to drugs and worked as a prostitute to support her habit. Only when she hit bottom and was gang raped and beaten did she decide to get help. She turned to the church. Since she was only fifteen, she was referred to their youth pastor. He told her not to make friends with the other kids because he did not want her to influence them and lead them in the wrong direction. She said, "I never went back. Luckily, last summer one of the scouts found me and brought me here. Here none cares about your past. I wish the whole world could see what I see here."

The moderator encouragingly said, "this has been a great session so far." No one seemed to have anything else to add so the group gathered around the girl that had just spoken and they hugged her and talked with her.

This session seems to be over, so I wanted to walk around and get to know the area. I checked the booklet Mike had given me. All the buildings were numbered, and trail heads were named and color coded on difficulty levels. Most of the trails seemed to be loops. Only two seem to have actual destinations. One was the trail from Black Mountain, the one I hiked up. This trail was marked moderate. *What the Hell, moderate! How is this moderate with all the switch backs, cable cliff and a killer pond? What is on the difficult trail?* The difficult trail showed it joining another trail. It didn't list a destination. It showed the joining trail from the left of the map running the length of the map out to the right. There was no description or destination in the book that I could find.

I walked down the outer gravel path toward the buildings, but I didn't see Cassie and Andrea. The first building I came to was the library. I didn't want Robin to think I was stalking her, so I kept going. I found the music building. There were several people there playing guitars and drums. They didn't seem to be playing together, mostly just there doing their own thing. I turned to walk out and spotted a tenor saxophone on a shelf. It was beat up and the pads looked bad. It smelled musty and the keys were sticking. I asked if anyone knew anything about it, and no one seemed to have an answer. I didn't see a mouthpiece, so I was out of luck anyway it would seem.

I left the music building and took the first trail behind the chow hall. The trailhead had a drawing of logs on fire. I walked a short distance along a wooden walkway then it opened up to another gravel path. This path led me to a large amphitheater type of area with a large fire ring near a stage behind it. I walked down to the fire pit area and sat on the stage. I noticed how quiet it was here. It's just a short walk from the buildings and The Commons, but I guess it being down in a bowl-shaped valley surrounded by trees muffles the surrounding sounds. I hope this works in reverse as well. This would be a great place to play the sax if I can get it fixed.

I went back to the music room, and everyone had left. I started searching through the boxes and found the case, mouthpiece and a box of reeds. I took the neck of the sax and put it in the case and put it back on the shelf. I'll have to ask Robin this afternoon.

I didn't want to get too far away since I had no idea what time it was and to miss lunch. I suspected I had killed a couple of hours since breakfast. I went back to the path around The Commons and checked out the huts. I didn't stop in to check out the sessions, but it looked like the one I had attended with Cassie and Andrea. All the people sitting on the grass and a moderator up front. I wonder what they do when it rains.

As I was passing Mike's cabin, I saw Sam sitting on the front porch. When she saw me, she got up and walked out onto the path and asked if I wanted some company.

I smiled and said, "I'd love some company, I'm pretty much a loss of what I'm doing here."

Sam took my hand, and we went walking out toward the opposite end of The Commons. I didn't feel like Sam was being flirty, I think she just liked to lead me around.

I told Sam about the session and Andrea's stunt, or lesson, whichever you want to call it.

Sam thoughtfully responded, "Andrea is something special, she knows things. I do not know why, but she seems to know what people need to hear."

I didn't tell Sam about Andrea telling me it will hurt, but I'll be okay in the end, or something like that. I really hadn't given it a lot of thought, but this seems a bit concerning.

We walked out to the edge of the field where the Earth seemed to drop off. I can see a mountain range far off in the distance. Sam explained, "this area is called The Point, because of the rock at the edge of the field, it a great place to climb and look out over the valley below."

I see a large triangle shaped rock with its peak coming to a point, beyond that all I can see is sky. Sam started leading me toward the rock. I stopped and said, "I'll just look at it from here." I didn't need to get any closer, I could feel my vertigo kicking in just being this close.

Sam tried to pull me along, but I resisted. Sam seemed to think that was funny and teased, "what's wrong, tough guy afraid of heights?"

I tried to tell her about my ear issues which caused me to get dizzy and it might not be safe.

Sam continued to taunt me and didn't hear anything I was saying. Sam asked, "would you rescue me if I was about to fall?"

Sam kicked off her shoes and ran up to the top of The Point. It became clear Sam was a dancer as she stood at the peak on one toe like a ballerina. Sam had to top that move by leaping into the air then spinning around. When she stopped, she motioned for me to come closer.

I was scared, my heart was racing, and I felt dizzy. I'm sure I screamed like a little girl as Sam fell backward off the rock. I hope someone heard me and would come help. I ran up the rock and looked over. Sam was a few feet below on a path not visible from the field. She was rolling around laughing. I have no idea what she said after that. I slid down the rock and walked back across The Commons. I didn't even stop to remove my shoes either.

I made it all the way across The Commons before I looked back, Sam was nowhere in sight. I was glad, I didn't want to talk to her. I didn't want to go to my cabin in case she came there looking for me, so I headed down one of the other paths behind the chow hall. At the trail head there was a sign with a hammer, saw and a wrench painted on it. The short path led to a workshop. There was one man inside working on an old Jeep. When he saw me, he said, come on in, you need anything?"

I said, "no, I'm just out exploring, I arrived yesterday."

He gestured around the workshop and said, "feel free to hang around."

I spoke up and said, "thanks Henry."

He laughed and said, "I'm Randy. There's a big box of donated clothes in the basement. I don't like to do laundry, and no point in getting my own stuff dirty. Got a bunch of old garage uniforms down there."

I thought that was funny on many levels. I was worried about people finding out who I was. Hell, nobody uses their real name around here.

The workshop was well-equipped with plenty of supplies. I thought about the old sax and maybe I could bring it up here and work on it.

I said, "tell me Hank, can anyone come in here and work on stuff?"

I could hear him chuckle a bit. He didn't stop what he was doing under the hood and said, "go for it!"

I peered out the door to be sure Sam wasn't around. I'm all for a joke, but that scared the Hell out of me. Maybe I was just overreacting, but right now I have a mission to accomplish. I went down to the music building and got the sax and took it back to the shop. I announced my arrival.

Randy didn't look up and said, "okay."

I started working on the horn trying to get the keys unstuck and bending the keys to seat on the tone holes. I'm aware this is not how you are supposed to do this, but I was more afraid to take it apart and reassemble it. I'm sure it would never play again if I attempted it. I slid a light down the bell and kept bending the keys until I could no longer see the light leaking from the tone holes. I glued cardboard where the corks and felts were missing. I used some fix-it-all duct tape to replace the missing neck cork and to seal a few cracked pads.

I slid a fresh reed onto the mouthpiece and forced it onto the neck. I fingered the keys from bottom to top and got a pretty solid pop as each key sealed. I took a deep breath and attempted to test my work. What I got was a loud squeal which got Randy's attention, and he bumped his head as he was looking for the source of the offending sound.

I readjusted the reed which had worked sideways on the mouthpiece. I made another attempt and actually made it work from bottom to top, even though I had to power down on some of the keys to make them seat against the tone holes. I played through a few scales as Randy stood by and watched. He came over and looked at the horn and asked if he could look at it. I handed him the sax. Randy turned it in all directions and looked it over.

Randy said, "that's amazing you made this thing work. I wish I'd have known what you were working on."

I asked him why.

He replied, "some other guy had one in here a couple of years ago. As far as I know, it is still in the storage room where he kept it. I'll look for it after lunch."

Randy and I left the garage and headed toward the chow hall. The bell started ringing as we approached signaling it was lunch time. I half expected to see a stampede like my old Scout camp days. We entered a nearly empty building and entered the line.

I asked, "where is everyone?"

Randy said, "lunch is pretty laid back. Folks will drift in over the next couple of hours."

I was more interested in Sam and Robin.

Randy and I sat together and talked about Haven. He was one of the hired crew and pretty much does whatever need fixing, running the lift, supplying the work crews, and sets up for the Friday night fire. I guess if I need to know anything about the grounds, he will be my go-to guy. Beyond that, he seemed reluctant to talk about the people and functions of Haven. He mentioned how he likes to keep to himself, and from the way he looked at some of the Haven participants, I have the feeling he doesn't approve of their lifestyle.

This would deter most people, but I see this as an opportunity if I can gain his trust. I had finished my sandwich, and I was about to leave when I spotted the salad bar next to the back wall. I told Randy I wanted to check it out and I'd be back at the shop later today.

I went over and found one heck of a salad bar, and I filled a large bowl. Not only was I still hungry, but I was hoping Sam and Robin would come in.

I was trying to kill time, and I think that's the longest lunch I've ever had. I heard a small voice behind me asking, "Do you think they got the message?" Andrea sat down beside me, and a few minutes later Cassie came and sat down on the opposite side of the table.

I told Andrea, "I hope so, I did anyway."

Cassie is very quiet and smiles a lot in kind of a shy way. Whenever she speaks, she seems to speak to Andrea although the message was actually meant for me. Normally I'd try and engage her in conversation, but I thought I'd give Mike's advice a try and observe and see what happens. I turned my attention to Andrea and asked her what inspired the lesson.

Andrea said, "There was someone there needed to know she was doing the right thing."

I started to speak again, but Andrea took my hand, looked at me sternly and said, "I just know."

Cassie smiled and said, "she knows."

I decided I had all the evidence I needed that Andrea may have ESP or something. I will just keep my eyes open and see. I was curious about why I keep running into her and Cassie. I wonder if she knows what I'm thinking right now. I wanted to lighten the mood, so I asked her about what she does for fun.

Andrea said, "I like to run and play like all kids, but they are afraid of me. That will change soon. I like to swim too! We're going right after lunch."

Andre looked at her mother and asked, "can he come too?"

Cassie said, "yes, if he wants to."

I said, "I didn't bring a bathing suit."

Cassie said, "nobody cares what you wear around here."

I said, "I see that, but you two seem to dress very pretty."

Andrea jumped up and spun around showing me her dress, and exclaimed, "I like being a girl, and I like to be pretty!"

I said, "I can see that." I was more interested in the other sax than going swimming.

Cassie and Andrea were still eating so I excused myself and went to the shop. Randy wasn't in, and I had no idea where he could be. I guess I'll just have to be patient and see if the other horn turns up. I picked up the project horn and gave it a blow. I was able to make sounds on every key, but it was obvious it was leaking, and I had to press hard to make the pads seat.

I kind of lost interest in the project sax in hopes of getting an actual sax to play. I left the shop and went looking for the swimming hole. I was pretty sure I remembered the general direction from the book Mike had provided, I guess I should carry it until I get the hang of things. I walked about fifteen minutes and found the sign with a picture of a swimmer with squiggly line to represent water. I followed the path toward the sound of running water.

I arrived to find a large pool of clear water just below a waterfall. There were large rocks and beach areas on both sides of the pool. The water continued and a second waterfall just beyond the pool area. The upper fall was about forty feet and the second was only about ten feet and it sloped like a natural water slide.

I was the only one there. I guess the others were still in sessions or work crews. I wasn't sure I was in the correct spot, but seriously didn't mind being there alone. I sat on the ground leaning against a rock facing the pool. I was sort of dazed and wasn't sure if I heard voices or not. I was feeling too lazy to turn around and see.

A moment later Andrea ran past me totally nude and squealed as she jumped into the stream. She turned and said, "You want to come in?"

I didn't have a chance to speak and wondered where Cassie was. I stood up and Cassie was standing next to the rock, nude as well and smiled as she walked into the water. Andrea swam across the stream and turned every few strokes to look back. Cassie turned toward me and gave me the one finger come here sign. I was seriously thinking about joining her, but wasn't sure her thoughts were the same as mine since Andrea was close by.

The thoughts were dashed almost as suddenly as they started. Sam and Robin showed up at the swimming hole. I was feeling awkward and wasn't sure if I should leave since Robin was my mission and if she dropped her clothes, I'm sure that would be out of bounds in this situation.

Sam came over and kissed me on the cheek and said, "I'm sorry about scaring you at The Point."

Sam kicked off her sandals and dropped her dress while standing very close to me. She stood there a moment longer and again said, "I'm sorry." Sam turned and entered the stream.

Cassie was watching the entire time. I'm sure she didn't hear the conversation, and she didn't know about the incident at The Point. She looked hurt and swam away. At this point I didn't owe anyone an explanation, and I finally looked over to Robin. I think the situation was obviously awkward and Robin asked if I wanted to go for a walk.

I looked to Robin and said, "yes, that would be wonderful, I never would have dreamed I'd rather go walking than look at naked women."

Robin just laughed and said "yes, we saw Cassie flirting with you. I guess Sam couldn't let Cassie win."

"Win?" I was confused.

Robin took me by the arm and said, "come on detective, I'll explain it to you."

We walked further down the trail away from the main complex not speaking.

I said, "win?"

Robin said, "Cassie and Sam both like you. And, if you hadn't noticed the men here are either gay, weird, or already hooked up. So, you're prime real estate in these parts. Not to mention, you actually take showers."

I had to laugh at that. I never thought a short fat guy was prime anything.

Robin tugged on my arm and said, "lets walk, no talking for now."

I had a million questions for her, but respected her wishes and we walked about a half hour down a smooth manicured trail. The views here are as beautiful as the trip up except this time I was mostly looking down. We came to an area where the trail took a dip down the side of the mountain. The trail went off to the right and there was a bench next to the trail. Robin sat down and patted the seat next to her for me to come sit.

I sat down next to Robin and gazed off into the distance. The views here were excellent, and I was amazed that no matter which direction I couldn't see distant towns or buildings.

"Well damn," Robin said, "I forgot to look for your book."

I said, "that's okay. How does it feel?"

Robin looked confused and asked, "how does what feel?"

"Cussing and no one no one correcting you?"

Robin laughed, "it feels pretty damn good."

I asked, "did I interrupt your swim time?"

Robin replied, "no, it gets busy down there, and I'd rather be alone. The school was always crowded, and the weekends were a pain. Saturday was cleanup day, and Sunday was a bitch. I lived in a zoo. It was so fake. The Reverend is a drug dealing pervert that got caught screwing a little girl and everything went to Hell after that. I really don't know much, only that I was restricted to certain building and could never go near the new dorms."

Robin stood up, walked over the edge of the trail and screamed, "fuck you, you ass hole, I hate you so much!" Robin sat back down, smiled and said, "yes, that feels pretty damn good."

I just hope no one heard that and thinks that was meant for me.

Robin took my hand for attention and asked," who's it going to be?"

I am sure I looked confused. Robin said, "Cassie or Sam? I'd do Sam if I were you."

I had to ask, "why Sam?"

Robin said, "Cassie would be better in the long term, but screw that, go have some fun. Live in the moment. Sam would be more fun, and she's not tied to a kid. I had to admit I have thought about Sam a lot since I arrived and never thought Cassie was interested until today."

I gave Robin's hand a squeeze and said, "right now, I need to find out what is the deal with you and your mom."

Robin was quiet for a long time staring out toward the hills and valleys. Robin finally spoke up and said, "I really do not have a clue. I'm no dummy, I saw a lot of things going on at the school. Mom kept to herself as much as possible and told me I was better off not knowing what was going on. She told me we would escape soon and never look back. I've known for a year now that something was going to change. I thought mom, my sister and me would all run together. A few days before my birthday mom sent me here and since I was not the Reverend's biological child, he could not make me come back if I got caught."

Just before I left Mom told me a plan had been put into action, and I was not to come back to the school no matter what. She told me to go and be whatever or whoever I wanted to be and not be ashamed of my choices. The last thing she said was she wanted me to be wild and free."

Robin went on to tell me that she had been here a few weeks. "It's mostly been fun, but so different. I think mom sent me here to be around wild and free people, but this is also mostly a lie, very much like the people at the school but in a different way. The school people looked for a god to swoop down and give them a better life or the promise of a better life after death. These people are looking for some magical thing that will give their life meaning. Then there's the druggies that just live to get high."

I asked, "Where do you see yourself in this picture?"

Robin was quiet again and said, "I'm not sure, but if I had to compare myself to anyone, in the future I'd like to be like Cassie, dedicated to someone and sweet like her. Sam is more of a hard worker during the day and a bit of a fun girl at times. "

I didn't ask out loud but gave Robin a look that begged her to explain.

Robin blushed a bit and hesitated before explaining she has stayed at Sam's a few times and Sam masturbates a lot and is very verbal about it. She also knows that Sam and Gladys that works in the laundry are having sex.

I asked, "So, why do you think Sam should be my choice, as if I have a choice?"

Robin stood up and said, "crap it's almost time for my shift in the music building."

Robin had a good lead on me before she turned around and motioned for me to come on. We did not have the in-depth conversation I would like to have had with Robin, but I glad we were able to connect and spend a little time together. I'm fairly sure this wasn't the conversation she would have wanted either, but the previous circumstance seemed to point us in that direction.

Robin walked at a rapid pace on our return trip, I didn't put much effort into keeping up. I just called ahead and said, "I'll see you at dinner." There was no reply, only a wave, and she broke out into a trot. I stopped off just before the swimming hole. I didn't go all the way down the path. I was sort of hoping to see Sam or Cassie, but a part of me was relieved that neither one was in sight.

I went back to the shop and Randy was there working on the Jeep again. I told him I had dropped by, but he wasn't around. Randy pointed toward the work bench and there was another case present. I opened it up to find an old King tenor sax. It was kind of on the ugly side, but sometimes the best players are like that. I picked it up and slid on the mouthpiece and gave it a shot. *Holy cow,* it played on all keys without fighting it.

As I was walking over to the Jeep to thank Randy, he asked if I had ever been a Boy Scout?

I said, "yes, why?"

He asked if they taught me to build a fire.

I grinned and said, "well, yes, that's part of it, why?

He looked up and said, "good, you're the new fireman."

I thought about the oil lamp in my cabin and wondered about fire hazards. I said, "yeah, I was surprised there was an oil lamp in my cabin."

Randy stopped what he was doing, "so, that's where that got off to." You'll need to take that to the quartermaster."

I was speechless for a moment and felt awkward about it, but it was obviously there when I arrived. I assured Randy I would take it there today. I questioned him if there were a lot of fires, since I was the new fireman and wanted to know what I needed to do.

Randy said, "listen up tenderfoot, you are building the fire."
A bit confused, I said, "oh, I guess I wasn't following the conversation."

Randy informed me that I would be responsible for the Friday night fire at the pit. I was to get enough wood from storage, transport it by wheelbarrow to the pit, light it right after supper and be there until it was cold out. Randy looked at his watch and said, "you better get moving."

I said, "okay, can I take the horn to my cabin?"

Randy said, "sure, just bring the lamp back with you."

I wasn't happy about losing the lamp, but I was really happy about the sax. I guess I'll take the good with the bad. I made the round trip and checked in the lamp and checked out my stuff to haul the wood to the pit. I was informed by the quartermaster that I also had to fill the fire buckets with water be sure there was a good supply of sand behind the pit. The water supply and extra sand was behind the shop.

Oh my gosh. I hope the water buckets are full and there is a good supply of sand. If not, I'm going to be one worn out puppy by supper time. I made it to the pit to find all ten buckets empty and maybe a half a wheelbarrow of sand on the ground. The pit had a lot of half burned logs remaining from the previous fire. I tried to calculate a way to get everything I needed in the fewest steps. Nothing came to mind, and I had no idea what time it was and when I had to get this ready.

I found the sand pile and water spigot as described and filled the wheelbarrow with sand. As soon as I dumped it, I was already breathing hard and was not happy since I didn't get the first week off as indicated. I wasn't going to complain. As far as I know this is a one day a week job, but I could be wrong about that. Either way, I got a horn out of the deal.

I forgot to ask how big of a fire was needed, but I wasn't going to stop and go ask. I took six loads of wood to the pit and built a tee pee around the old wood. I had to go find tinder and kindling from the surrounding area. I wasn't sure if it was available, and I'm sure time is getting short. Six trips to the shop, and I was able to get the buckets filled. I was wringing wet with sweat and in pain.

Wondering if I had time to shower before supper time, I headed toward my cabin. I could see people moving toward the chow hall. I picked up the pace and decided a shower was more important at the moment. If I miss chow maybe the canteen will be open later. I passed Sam, Robin, and Mike as I passed the chow hall. Robin held out her hands in a gesture of "what's up."

I said, "I'll tell you later and kept walking." I'm sure I heard a bit of a chuckle from Sam, but I didn't look to see.

I grabbed my shower stuff and a change of clothes and headed for the showers, people were still walking to the chow hall, so maybe I had time.

I made short work of a cool shower which revived me enough to make me feel alive again. A quick trip back to the cabin and then I'd head for chow. Luckily, I didn't turn in the lighter when I took the lamp back. I had made it about halfway to the chow hall when I remembered I needed a flashlight to get back tonight. One more trip back to the cabin and I'm starting to sweat again.

I'm either going to get in shape or this assignment is going to kill me. *How did this happen, so far nothing has gone like I had expected?* Not that I knew what to expect, but this was not it for sure. I headed straight for the drink table and downed a large glass of water. I felt a presence behind me and turned to see Robin standing very close.

She whispered in my ear, "how was your first day at work?"

I said, "funny, what the hell did I get myself into?"

Robin said, "I have a tray for you, come on. There's normally a crew that sets up for Friday night, but something came up at the landing. Mike told me something about a problem with one of the new people and a bunch of the workers went down to check on it."

I was thankful Robin was looking out for me. She said, "I hope this makes up for me leaving you behind."

Sam came over and gave me another glass of water. I said, "It was really nice seeing you earlier today."

It took her a minute, but she finally got the reference and said, "It was nice being seen by you."

I think we've all made up now.

Mike came over and joined us which gave me a chance to find out what I was supposed to be doing tonight. Mike informed me I was to light the fire about an hour after dinner and put it out when the people leave. Mike also said we could just hang out until it dies down if we want to.

"Go have fun and don't burn the place down." Mike didn't hang around long, and he seemed to have something on his mind.

After dinner, I went to the canteen and picked up a couple of drinks since I didn't know how long I was going to be at the pit. I could see people were beginning to arrive at the lift. There was a lot of people hugging, and they seemed to be upset. This was not the scene I had pictured when the new people arrived.

I figured I should go ahead and start the fire, I'm sure I'll find out later what's going on. I started working on the fire and wished I had some paper to get it going. I went out and scooped up a bunch of pine needles and pinecones. Thankfully, it's been dry, and this did the trick right away. The smaller wood was burning as the people began to filter in.

Once again, I wish I had my book with me to see if there was anything on the schedule for tonight. Once I saw the fire was taking shape, I sat down in the second row across from where the crowd was coming from. A few minutes later, people with guitars and other music instruments came over to my side and sat down. Mike, Randy and a bunch of workers I recognized came over to my side and sat closer to the center.

After the crowd seemed to be settling in, Mike walked out to the other side of the fire closer to the other seating area and got everyone's attention. Mike performed what I later found out was a safe space blessing for all that came together.

Mike pointed toward the East and said, "as the sun rises and moves across the sky to set in the West, each day holds lessons. We are to observe and learn. We are here to embrace each other in compassion and forgiveness. From the North, South, East and West we give thanks for the elements of Air, Fire, Water, Earth and Spirit. We ask the ascended masters to be with us, to guide us along the path we choose. Be with us and bring peace, joy and happiness to all that gather here."

He then made an announcement about one of the prospective members committing suicide prior to his arrival at the landing.

Mike went on to say, "we all have weaknesses, and we should all love and support each other before, during and after a crisis. Haven was formed to bring people together and help them overcome the things that seem to overpower them. We try hard to identify people in need through our referral and rescue teams. Words cannot express my sadness when someone cannot see beyond their current situation and gives up. Here is a place to start over. Here is a place to unburden your soul, here is a place of love, compassion and forgiveness."

The crowd was quiet, but that was interrupted by a loud siren. Everyone covered their ears. Thankfully it only lasted a short time. One of the workers motioned for everyone to sit down. There were workers carrying signs for the sleeping quarters. A dorm, B dorm, Cabins, Wilderness, Crew. The workers scattered out to different section of the bleachers.

The announcers said, "That was a demonstration of their alert system, if you hear that any time you are here, you must report back here and go to your assigned area. Be sure you sign in and out of camp, so we can account for where you are."

The music began to play, and Mike walked away, not to be seen again for the rest of the evening.

The mood quickly changed to a party atmosphere. People were dancing and drums were beating from everywhere at once. It was a little busy for my taste, so I moved further up the bleacher away from the crowd. Cassie and Andrea followed me, and we all sat near the top and watched the party unfold. I kind of imagined I had gone back in time landed in the land of the hippies from the sixties. It was fun to watch, I just didn't want to be in the middle of it.

Sam and Robin came up too. Sam opened her backpack and passed out plastic cups. she pulled out a box of red wine and started filling cups. I thought about the story Orangejello told and wondered if this would be a problem. Randy and some of the other workers were doing the same, I joined in. If I'd have known I would have brought the bottle of whiskey I had hid in my pack.

The crowd was wild, dancing and yelling. People with hula hoops and sticks with streamers running around.

This went on longer than I would have liked, but it's not my circus. I was glad I had moved away from the crowd. Several of the workers had moved up too. After a while, the drumming stopped, and the crowd was instructed to return to their seats. A group of people stood in front of the crowd and began playing and singing. I could not hear them since we were too far away, and they were facing away from us. I had considered moving down, but Andrea crawled into my lap and was about to go to sleep.

Cassie tried waking her so they could walk back to their cabin.

Andrea said, "I can't walk, you'll have to carry me."

Cassie pleaded with Andrea and said she could not carry her that far.

I asked Andrea if she could hang on, I'd give her a piggyback ride to her cabin. Andrea agreed and off we went.

The air was much cooler as we ascended the path away from the fire. Cassie draped a blanket over Andrea and me. We were mostly silent on our walk. I wanted to learn more about them but wasn't sure if I should ask. Cassie seems shy or maybe she just wanted to avoid revealing anything about herself like so many other do here.

When we reached the cabin, Andrea went inside and closed the door. Cassie turned to me and said, "Andrea really likes you."

I said, "I can tell, but I wasn't sure why."

Cassie said, Andrea seems to know when people need something.

This shocked me, and I thought back to her statement about it *hurting, but I'd be okay in the end or something like that.* This changed my mood, and I was silent trying to process what was being said.

Cassie must be able to read minds herself. She kissed me and said, "I like you too....but."

There was that "but" thing.

Cassie said she was not able to allow anyone into her life right now.

I didn't speak as much as I wanted to. So many things were going through my mind, and I could not process them fast enough to form how I really felt, other than the obvious disappointment.

My mission here was strange and somehow should accept this as part of it. I have no idea what tomorrow will bring, and I should not start something I'm so unsure of.

Cassie seemed to read my mind and spoke. "You need to take advantage of the offering of Haven. I have noticed I'm not the only one hanging around you."

I agreed, "yes, I've noticed too, but I'm not sure if it's me, or she needs to be in control?"

Cassie said, "maybe you should let her try. She's hot in case you haven't noticed."

I stuttered a bit, "I, I noticed."

Cassie kissed me on the cheek, "good night," and she went into her cabin.

I walked back to the fire thinking about the situation. I passed a lot of people walking away from the fire area. When I arrived, most of the crowd had left. Robin and Sam had left too. I went back and sat down closer to the fire. I was in no hurry to go anywhere, and it would seem I'm in charge of putting the fire out. There were small groups on the opposite bleachers talking. There's no point in ending their fun, so I just sat back and watched the flames.

About an hour later Sam and Robin came back to the fire ring. They were both unsteady on their feet. Robin kept her distance and seemed to be trying hard to hide the fact she was drunk.

Sam sat down beside me, well actually, she pretty much fell on me. I motioned for Robin to come over. She hesitated at first, but finally came over and sat down.

I looked at her and said, "I am not going to lecture you on underage drinking. I am not your father."

Robin, said, "I wish you were," as she moved close to me. "I'm cold."

I put my arm around her and pulled her close. Sam pulled a blanket out of her pack and handed it to Robin.

I looked at Sam and said dryly, "you're well prepared, what else are you carrying?"

Sam produced another bottle of wine and a bunch of plastic cups. She handed me the wine and gave the cups to Robin.

Sam said, "I need to go potty," and walked away.

Robin wrapped the blanket around us and put her head on my shoulder, "that girl isn't going to come back, is she?"

I said, "Sam?"

Robin said, "No."

"Cassie?"

Robin said, "No, Andrea, she is always sitting in your lap."

I said, "no, not tonight."

I pulled Robin closer, and we watched the flames. We sat in silence for a long time. There were so many things I wanted to ask her, but I kept hearing Mike tell me to observe. This was totally out of my element, but I wanted to give it a try. I felt I should just be there and wait to see if she would open up to me.

The crowd had died down to just a few people on the opposite side of the arena. One guy picked up a log and started toward the pit. I spoke up and told him I was about to hose it down for the night. He wanted to argue but that ended quickly when one of the workers went over and knocked the log out of his hands and got up in his face. I didn't hear what he said but the guy left in a hurry. His friends left behind him.

The worker said, "the hose is behind the building." He pointed toward a small shed.

I walked around and found the hose attached to pipe coming out of the ground. I was glad I didn't have to use the buckets and sand.

Robin remained on the bench while I sprayed the fire until no embers were glowing. The arena was dark without the fire. I looked up and saw the smoke rising up to the night sky. I must have stood there for several minutes. I was amazed by the stars. The sky was filled with them. I've never been so far away from light pollution and the clear sky had more stars than I'd ever seen in my life.

Robin came over and took my hand. She said, "come on, I want to show you something."

We walked the short distance to The Commons. My eyes were adjusting to the darkness by the time we arrived. I could see people scattered out among The Commons. There were no sounds. I could see them on blankets looking up at the sky.

We kicked off our shoes and walked out onto the soft cool grass. Robin spread the blanket out on the ground and laid down looking up at the sky. I joined her on the blanket.

I said, "this is amazing."

Robin whispered, "no talking during the gazing."

I settled in and watched the night sky. I could see clusters, and I wasn't sure if I was seeing the Milky Way or clouds. There were colors I'd never noticed before and occasionally a falling star.

We stayed for about a half hour I would have guessed, and probably would have stayed longer except the night air was much colder than sitting next to the fire. The dew was settling, and I noticed we were getting damp. The gentle breeze was cold from the moisture and the blanket was useless at this point.

When we reached the edge of The Commons, we stopped to put on our shoes.

I asked Robin if she made a wish on the falling star.

She replied, "yes, but if I tell you, it will not come true."

Robin was still a little unsteady. I offered to walk he back to her group cabin, which was in the opposite direction.

She said, "no, I'll stay at Sam's tonight. She will not mind. I stay there about half the time anyway."

Robin was leaning on me, not so much for support but she had something on her mind.

I asked, "what's up?"

Robin started laughing and asked if I had made up my mind?

I gave her a puzzled look.

"Cassie or Sam?" Robin exclaimed as if we were just talking on the subject.

I asked Robin, "why are you so interested?"

Robin explained, "Sam has been really nice to me since I've been here. We talk a lot, and I think she is lonely. I know she's horny, I hear her playing with herself a lot."

I asked about Gladys.

Robin was silent for a bit, then said, "I know they've been together, but I don't think it's an ongoing thing. You know, Haven kind of has an effect on people."

I asked, "aren't you concerned she's trying to get in your pants?"

Robin let go and walked on her own the rest of the way to the cabins.

When we approached Sam's cabin, Robin stopped and said, "truth is, I was trying to distract both of you. I've always had someone watching over me. As long as I can remember, someone has watched over me. When I arrived here it was like I had a built-in babysitter. Sam goes out of her way to be around me. Don't get me wrong, she has been a great friend, and we talk about things, and she doesn't judge me. Then you show up, and I'm being watched again. I'm a big girl, and I'm glad you're both here, but I want to make the most of my time here. I really need to experience life for a change."

"So, here's the deal, either you start sleeping with her, or I will." Robin stormed off towards Sam's cabin and slammed the door.

I walked over to my cabin and felt my way around until I found the bottle of Jack stashed in my pack. I went out and sat on my porch sipping from the bottle. Mixing wine and jack probably wasn't the best idea, but it had been a couple of hours in between, I kept on sipping.

Haven sounds like a festive place at night. Off in the distance I can hear people whooping and hollering along with the drumbeats. These people must love their drums. I mean it was fun to watch for a while, but it got old fast. I did enjoy what little I heard from the girl singing and playing the guitar. If I'm still here next week, I'll make it a point to stick around a little longer. Maybe if I practice all week, I could play the sax. Maybe, maybe not. The Jack is working, and I'm kind of buzzed. I'm mostly a beer drinker, but I don't think I could have hauled enough beer up the mountain to have been worthwhile. Not to mention I was a bit gun shy because of the Orangejello story. I'll have to ask someone about that.

The drum sound finally ended, and I could hear nature all around me. At times, the sounds were almost as loud as the drumming. Then all at once the sounds would end. It's funny how nature communicates. I looked up at the stars and wondered why our world was so messed up. We are this tiny speck of dust in all of the cosmos and somehow, we think we're so smart. Funny the things you think about while you're sitting in the dark, drunk and nothing else to do.

I really wanted to go over and talk to Robin, but even as drunk as I was, I knew that would be a bad idea. I tried to think about Cassie, but discovered it was a forced thought. She is beautiful in every way possible. Even without the conversation tonight I realized this would be the wrong time and place for someone like her. I have to admit Sam is sexy as hell. I love her slender athletic shape, amazing legs, bright blue eyes, and her long red curly hair drives me nuts. I never dreamed someone like her would ever be interested in me.

Yet, here I am, thinking about this as if I'm in charge and the decision is all mine. Come to think of it, Robin seems to be the only one pushing us together. Not that I mind. I held the bottle up to the sky in an effort to see how much was left. It looked like one good shot. I took it and leaned back against the railing. My biggest decision at the moment was whether to get the other bottle out or conserve it for another night. Sam seemed well-prepared, but I wasn't sure how. After a minute or two, what the heck I went in and dug it out.

Sam

I was about to sit down with my fresh bottle of Jack when I saw a flashlight coming down the path. Swing from side to side, up and down then it was on the ground. Then I heard Sam cussing at the top of her lungs, then crying.

I called out, "are you okay?"

I got a reply.

"I always yell fuck when I'm happy, what do you think?"

As I stepped down off the porch, I realized I may not be in much better shape than her, and I didn't have a light. You know my Boy Scout days are not helping much right now. I was navigating mostly by memory on how to get back out onto the path. From there I should just be able to go toward the light. I told Sam to point the light down the path so I could see where I was going. The next thing I knew I was standing in the dark, and I could hear Sam laughing.

A moment later Sam was mobile again and laughing out loud as she approached me. She wrapped her arms around me, and we both nearly fell to the ground.

I asked, "do I help you to your cabin, or do you want to help me find mine?"

Sam took me by the hand which was still holding the bottle. Sam said, "hey, what, you got there? Let's go to your place."

We fumbled our way into the cabin, and Sam kicked off her shoes and pulled off her dress. We fell on to the bed, and I ran my hand through her long soft hair.

The next sound was Robin banging on the side of my cabin yelling, "you guys going to breakfast?"

The sun was up, and I was still dressed. Sam was lying there naked, drooling and snoring.

I tried to wake her up, but that wasn't happening, So I covered her up right after I took a good long look at her. *Damn, she's beautiful.*

Robin banged on the cabin again. *Hell, I'm dressed, might as well go.* I went out and sat on my porch to put my shoes on.

Robin asked, "how was it?"

I couldn't bring myself to tell her the truth, so I just told her to ask Sam later on.

Saturday

After a quick trip to the bath house to make myself reasonably presentable, I made my way to the chow hall. Breakfast on Saturday is a big deal I came to find out. All the new people, workers, guests are all there. It's loud, crowded, and I'm hung over and wish I was still in bed with Sam.

Robin informed me the early breakfast was her favorite part of Haven.

I said, "early breakfast! You mean I could have come later?"

Robin seemed to shrink and said, "yes, but it's not as good as the early breakfast."

"How so?" I demanded.

Robin informed me it was only cold stuff if you come later. And you don't get to meet all the new folks.

I had to think about this a bit. I took a deep breath and decided this should be another one of my observation moments. *Right now, I'm thinking a cold breakfast, and a hot woman would have been much better.* But Robin is my main objective. I'm also observing for someone that wants to be left alone she sure seems to be seeking me out to spend time together. If I'm right maybe she has never had the option to just be alone.

I look around and sort of realize her home life may have been somewhat like this but on a smaller scale. Schedules and surrounded by people all the time. When one moves, they all move. Even though these people seemed to be the free-spirited type, you can't help but notice most of them follow a certain clothing style, hair and mannerism. *So, how do you express yourself as an individual if you look and act like everyone else?*

I must still be drunk or hungry, normally I don't think like that, why would I care. In fact, the only thing I really care about is whether they have real bacon this morning, and coffee.

I thought I'd try something. Robin was talking to some of the younger kids, so I headed toward the serving line and left her behind. I scanned the room and spotted Andrea and Cassie seated near the exit on the other side of the room. I made it a point not to look back toward Robin and see what happens.

I made my way through the line to get my tray. I spied the large tray of bacon as well as all the other traditional breakfast foods. I sort of felt guilty about leaving Robin, but I needed to see what she would do. I wanted her to feel independent, but not alone. When I got my tray and started toward the area where Andrea and Cassie were seated, I stopped and made sure to make eye contact with Robin. I sort of nodded in the general direction to indicate where I was headed. I wanted to see if she would come over or not.

Before I could reach Andrea and Cassie, the table was mostly full of kids. I do not think my head could handle that this morning. I headed a little more to the center and found an empty table. I sat down and a few minutes later Robin joined me.

Robin seemed a bit smug and said, "I figured you were headed to your girlfriend's table."

I didn't offer an explanation. I asked about Saturday activities, and asked recommendations of things I could do to.

Robin replied with a list of activities such as hiking, reading, and attending the hut sessions.

I said, "I didn't think they had classes on Saturdays."

Robin replied, there are no scheduled classes, people hang out at different huts and do things together. It's really no different than the weekdays other than the schedule part.

Robin leaned in closer and sort of whispered, "you can always go swimming."

I had to laugh at that one.

About this time, Mike came over and sat down with us.

He said, "I hear you have a job already?"

I said," yes, I do. I was sort of tricked into it, but that's okay."

I paused and looked at Mike. "It is just the Friday night fire, isn't it?"

Mike laughed and said, "yes, I guess you were up later than you wanted."

I told him about the guy wanting to add wood to the fire and a worker stopped him. Robin, Mike and I sat around talking for a good bit. It was no secret between us anymore that I was there for Robin. I just didn't know why. Most of the people had left the chow hall, and a smaller group came in together. I noticed right away they didn't have the uniform of the hippy crowd. These seemed to be more street appearance and they looked scared. Mike seemed serious for a moment and asked if I would come by the office later. He wanted to discuss something with me. I told him I'd come by in a bit.

Mike asked Robin if she wanted to do the trail angel this week.

Robin seemed excited and said "yes, who else is going?"

Mike told her to pick two more people and see if they want to do it.

Robin answered, "Sam and Marshall."

I'm like, now what?

Robin seemed excited and said, "it will be different, we get to go hiking overnight."

She looked to Mike and asked, "do we get to go to town for supplies?"

I think Mike started to say we were well stocked, but the intense stare from Robin changed his mind and said, "sure, why not? You can go tomorrow, I've some business in town anyway."

Mike said, "have a great day and drop in any time, I'm not going anywhere today."

Then he left. Robin and I finished up and went out to sit in the rocking chairs on the chow hall porch.

Robin was excited and said, "this will be fun!"

"Which?" I asked.

Robin gave me a sideways look like I should know what she meant.

"Both. I've been stuck up here for weeks, I'm ready to go get some real food, go shopping, see something different. And I want to hike up the mountain and camp out."

"Camp out?" I must have said that a little harsh. "So, what do you call this?"

Robin leaned over, laid her head on my arm and looked up and said, "please, I want to do something different."

"Okay, what do we have to do?"

Robin slid her chair over, so we were face to face, "all we have to do is carry supplies up to the shelter, hang out and hike back down. We don't have to stay overnight, but I want to."

I couldn't help but think about my trip to get up here. Truth is, it would have been nice if I hadn't been in a hurry and my mind wasn't pre-occupied with the case. If you can call this a case. I sat back and closed my eyes. You know that might be fun after all. Robin pulled her rocker next to mine, and we rocked in silence for a few minutes. I was almost asleep when I felt someone take my hand.

Andrea took my hand and placed it on Robin's hand and said, "that's better."

And she walked away. Robin moved her thumb over the top of my hand to show she was okay with this. I didn't question it and closed my eyes again.

I woke to the sound of kids laughing. I guess my snoring was funny. Robin was gone. I guess it is funny to the kids. I know I sometimes snore like a cartoon bear. I had no idea what time it was or how long I'd been asleep. I got up and walked around The Commons track toward Mike's. I saw what Robin was talking about. There were groups around the huts, and they seemed more relaxed than the organized groups. I could hear a lot of laughter and music, and some were dancing. I only saw small portions of the scheduled groups before, but they seemed serious. The topics seemed to surround people in crisis situations and decision making. I guess that's why I didn't hang around and listen.

I reached Mike's cabin and a young man about college age was leaving. He seemed in a hurry and left the door standing open. Mike appeared in the front hallway adjusting his clothes. I guess he wasn't expecting me at that particular time. I went and sat down on one of the rockers. Mike came out and sat down.

I looked at Mike and said, "you know, I've been doing a lot of rocking and taking naps, since I got here. I wouldn't mind having one of these at my cabin."

Mike laughed and said, "I'll have one delivered."

I wasn't sure if he was serious or not. I wasn't blackmailing him; it was just conversation to ease an uneasy moment.

Mike got right to the point. He said he knew I was coming to look after Robin. He was thrown off when I didn't admit to why I was there. He explained he had met Christy by accident. He had gone to a store close to the school to do a rescue. One of the girls from the school had called the hot line and wanted to be picked up.

Mike paused and said, "I guess you've figured out this isn't your typical Summer camp?"

I just shook my head and motioned for him to continue.

Mike said he was unsure about Christy for a good while, but several girls recognized each other when they arrived in Haven. They got to talking and compared their stories. The girls came to me and told me about the school and how the preacher was allowing prostitution and drugs to be sold there. The regular school kids and Christy didn't seem to be involved.

Mike said he went back several times and talked to Christy about their Summer Camp Programs for Teens and Adults. All the advertisement shows all the arts and stuff like that. There is no mention of the rescue missions. One day I get a call from Christy telling me not to come back and see her. At first, I was afraid she had discovered what we were doing and was about to expose Haven. I have to admit I was scared. I found the girls that had been to the school, and they convinced me Christy did not approve of her husband's dealing and Christy was as much a prisoner as the kids there.

I'm not sure how much Christy knows about Haven. About a month after the phone call. I get a letter from her saying her daughter was coming to Haven. A man was coming to keep her safe, and they were both to stay until she comes to get them. There was a money order for $5,000 in the envelope to cover the fees. I tried to call and only got voice mail. I sent a letter to the post office box, but Robin showed up at the landing the next Friday. Robin was here about three weeks before you arrived. "I know you're a licensed private investigator, so now, do you want to tell me what's going on?"

I had to think about this for a moment. Mike showed me the letter and a copy of the money order. Normally, I was bound to privacy issues in an investigation, but I had no instructions other than to stay close to Robin. If I declined to talk, Robin and I could be escorted off the property.

I decided I'd admit to the obvious, that I was sent there to look after Robin, and I agreed there is something serious going on at the school. I told Mike I was in the dark about the details involving the school and explained the mysterious text messages and my efforts to communicate with Christy. This seemed to ease Mike's mood, I told him I was unsure what to do at this point. It's pretty obvious Christy has figured out the connection and sent Robin and me here.

I told Mike, "I swear, I'm not here to spy on Haven, I have no idea of what I'm supposed to be doing other than to watch over Robin."

"Mike, I promise I can keep secrets and I'm not here to expose Haven."

Mike got up, looked directly at me, and said, "I'll just have to trust you at this point." He then got up and went inside his cabin.

I was about to leave when he stuck his head out the door and added, "be at the lift at 9:00 with an empty backpack." He paused and muttered, "yea, you can have a rocker too."

I left Mike's, and I just wanted to walk around by myself and think about this. Part of me wants to go find Robin and do as instructed, but she has expressed her desire not to be hounded. I have to respect that since she is of age to make her own decisions. I guess we can discuss this since we're going to be stuck together the next couple of days. Then I actually stopped in my tracks and said out loud, "you're such a dumb ass."

I walked around the track and went out to The Point. I crawled up on the rock and looked over the edge. It was more of a drop than I'd want to do, but Sam is in really good shape, so I guess jumping off was no big deal for her. I hate that I reacted so badly. I was thinking about my trip up top and the narrow ledge Merlin led me across. I hadn't thought about Merlin until that moment. I wondered where he had gotten off to.

I walked around the gravel path near The Commons. I waved to the groups of people but didn't want to stop. I went to the workshop, but it was locked. I was glad I took the sax to my cabin. I considered going to get it and go play at the fire pit. To be on the safe side I walked over to the path and looked down. Unfortunately, there were people sitting on the stage area, so I continued on. I found the library and went inside. The selections were limited. It looked like the rejects from a thrift store. The trip to town was starting to sound much better to me.

Once again, I forgot to bring my Haven book along, so I decided to just go and explore. I went to the canteen to get a drink since I would be out walking. I encountered a group of kids out front eating ice cream. It didn't take much to change my mind. I went inside and bought a large cup of soft serve. I went outside and walked to the front of the chow hall and sat at the picnic tables closest to the shop side. It is quiet here and just out of sight of The Commons.

A young girl came along and sat on top of a picnic table across from me. She sat on the top and her feet rested on the seat. I didn't look at her at first, hoping she would get the hint and move along. That didn't work. I asked her if she wanted an ice cream, I'd pay for it. She just sort of shrugged her shoulders as if she didn't care one way or the other. I pulled out a dollar and laid it on the table closest to her. She got off the table and picked up the money. Instead of going to the canteen she got back on the table across from me.

She was wearing a loose-fitting t-shirt type of dress. She pulled her arm out of the sleeve and pulled it down to expose one breast. Then she raised one foot up on the tabletop and began playing with herself. She asked if I was staying in a cabin or a dorm? I didn't answer. I asked her age. She looked to be about the same age as the kids on the other side of the building. She told she was old enough to rock my world and offered to give me a blow job for $20 or fuck for $40.

Luckily for me, the kids from the other side came around the building. The girl dropped her leg and put her arm back in to cover herself. The other kids came toward the tables.

Before they got any closer, she whispered conspiratorially, "I'm Amy. I'm staying in dorm B bunk 12 if you want me. Just put a note on the message board, time and place."

She got off the table and walked toward The Commons before the other kids arrived. The kids caught up with her just before they reached The Commons, and they all walked out of sight as a noisy little group.

Holy cow, I've been approached by a lot of prostitutes while working undercover and surveillance jobs, but this was way different. This was scary. My mind was racing at all the things that could have gone wrong during that encounter. I was so glad the other kids came along.

Feeling pretty shaken, I walked to the other side of the building in front of the canteen. *Yes, I was shaken, but I'm going to sit at a different table and finish my ice cream.*

Finishing up, I saw Sam walking up from the cabins. I waved for her to come over.

She looked into my empty cup and laughed, "looks like I'm too late."

Sam leaned over and whispered in my ear, "buy me an ice cream and you can have me."

I actually laughed out loud and spewed my last bite of ice cream on the table.

Sam was mad and tried to walk away.

I told her, "No, you've got to hear this, but first you need an ice cream."

We got her an ice cream and a couple of bottles of water, and I led her back to the other side of the building where we could be alone. I told her about the encounter and why the timing so funny. I pulled Sam close to me and looked her deep in the eyes and said, "I intend to collect on your offer." It was Sam's turn to laugh, and I think I have been forgiven.

Sam kissed me deeply. Although we slept in the same bed last night, this was the moment we connected. We sat and talked about Haven and the people that come there. She was aware of the rescue missions performed by some of the workers. There are not many, but they do exist. Mostly it is as it appears. Right now, there seems to be more than usual. Sam suggested it would be a good idea to avoid the B dorm area since that is the area where they stay.

Sam continued, "Robin is staying in the A dorm area which is on the opposite side of The Commons, but she doesn't like to be there with so many people. A dorm has divided rooms just big enough for a bed and locker. It's loud at night. That's why Robin stays at my cabin a lot."

She was quiet for a moment and said, "I'm sure you've heard I have a friend, Gladys? It's true I'm bi, but trust me I'm not trying to get in Robin's pants. We just sort of became friends and talked a lot. I was aware of her situation when she got here. Like you, I was the first person she met, so we sort of bonded."

I tried to find out more about Sam, and her connection to Haven and her background. She seemed distant and reluctant to talk about herself.

Sam explained to me that she lives in the moment, she doesn't think about the future and anything in her past is just that, the past. She held my hands, "when we're together I just want to enjoy the moment."

Sam was trying to come across as the hippy, soulful, live in the moment kind of girl. I see this as something to hide, but what the heck. *It's Haven, she's hot*, and I seem to be the only person on this hill that seems to care about a person's history.

Sam broke the moment when she exclaimed, 'Oh, How the hell did you get a rocker delivered to our cabin?"

I noticed she said, "our cabin."

I made sure I repeated it back to her. "Our cabin?"

Sam seemed to change into the shy little girl and asked, "can I stay in your cabin?"

Since our conversation was shifting from in the moment, to asking if she could move in, I gave the only answer I could think of that suited the moment. I said, "sure, but don't move any of your stuff in, just in case the moment doesn't suit you." I made sure it had the sarcastic sound it deserved.

I sort of felt bad about it; I really wanted to know more about her, but she made it pretty clear she wasn't going to enlighten me about herself.

It was at that moment I decided I'd do just that, live in the moment during my time in Haven. I'd have a short heart-to-heart talk with Robin and explain how I ended up in Haven and let her know I'd be there if she needed me for anything. She was welcome to spend as much, or little time with me as she wanted.

I took Sam by the hand and led her away.

Sam asked, "where are we going?"

I said, "I'm collecting on your ice cream."

Sam picked up her pace and was almost leading at this point.

When we arrived, I was pleased to see the rocker on the front porch. It pretty much took up the entire space, but that's okay.

As soon as we entered, Sam pulled off her dress. As suspected, and in normal Haven fashion, that was all she was wearing other than her sandals. She pushed me down on the bed and she crawled on top of me. There was very little foreplay as she pulled off my shirt and unbuttoned my pants. She slid them down enough to mount me and began to hump me hard and fast. Sam played with herself as she leaned back and she was loud when she yelled, "I'm cumming."

That was all it took for me as I shot off inside her.

Sam rolled over out of breath.

I said dryly, "that's not quite how I had fantasized about it."

Sam said, "me too, but I wanted it bad. You're the first man I've been with in four years."

That was a shock.

Then Sam explained, "I've been doing girls for the past four years. Lately, I've been thinking about sex with men a lot. I just wanted to get fucked."

Holy cow, I think I just got used for sex. Truth is, I didn't feel bad about it. It was a moment, and it was damn good. I was feeling like I could go again, but Sam said she had to get some things done before we leave in the morning.

Sam got up and pulled on her dress and said, "make sure you have your wish bag ready."

Perplexed, I asked, "What's a wish bag?"

"Your backpack, so you can bring back all the shit you wish you'd have brought up the first time." She laughed at my expression and then pointed to the sax and said, "bring that too, we're going to have some down time."

Sam and her dress flounced cheerfully out of the cabin, and I got myself dressed still feeling a bit of the sexual rush. I open the case and put the sax together. I stuck a reed in my mouth to wet it and went out to the porch. I sat in the rocker with the horn in my lap. I wanted to play but the sounds of nature were so peaceful I didn't want to disrupt the moment. Sometimes you need a sign. I heard a distant drum and that was it. Those assholes bang those things day and night. I was pleased with the way the horn responded. All the keys worked, and the intonation was good from top to bottom. I squeaked several times because the reed was way too hard, and I had to use a lot of pressure to make it play. It was obvious I was out of practice, and I quickly got out of breath. I hope there is a music store so I could get some reeds. That was a high priority on my wish list. Well, that and a lot of alcohol and books.

It was still early; I wasn't sure what to do next. I walked back to the chow hall and saw it was open for the floating lunch. I wasn't really hungry but went in anyway. There was a serving line, but I opted for the salad and sandwich bar located out in the dining area. I sat by myself and ate in silence. I watched as the people came and went. I was thankful no one came to my table. I had no idea how long I had been there. When I stepped out of the dining hall, I looked at the rockers and sort of laughed, I had no idea how much I liked them. But, not now my friend, I had one of my own. I needed to walk.

I was curious about the trail below The Point. It wasn't marked. I walked to The Point and looked over the edge. I heard voices and then a group of kids came walking by. None of them looked up at me as they passed by. I was pretty sure this led to B dorm. I walked back toward The Commons and found the message board between the last hut and the maintenance shop. There was a map of Haven. I noticed the B dorm and the trail was not on the map. So, I figured this was to keep outsiders from finding it easily. There was a cork board where people left messages. I noticed names or numbers and letters on the outside of the folded papers. I guess no one is concerned about privacy since none were sealed. I was tempted to peek to see if these were like the messages Amy told me to leave for her, but I didn't.

I studied the map a little longer. I saw the trail I came up, and the trail toward the swimming hole, and the area Robin and I had walked. The trail beyond my cabin ended shortly thereafter.

The only road to Haven was behind the shop and there was a note handwritten in that said "Bridge Out" next to what appeared to be a river. Maybe they are going to fix the bridge, since Randy was working on the Jeep. I'll have to remember and ask him about that. I looked over toward the shop and the doors were closed.

The rest of trails were located on the North side of Haven, and they appear to split is several directions beyond the trail heads. The South end looks to be steep declines beyond the B dorm area. There were post notes attached to some of the trails, like "Boys Night Out" and "The Shadow Coven" with times on them. I guess you have to be one of the insiders to know what this means. Somehow, I don't see myself getting an invite. I don't think I fit in their social circles, and I'm not going to try.

The first of the trails seem to start near the back of the maintenance shop. The trails go beyond the boundary of Haven, so I have no idea if they go somewhere or what. I had time to kill so I started with the first trail I came to which was between the fire pit and the shop. I figured I would check the trails one at a time by doing an out and back just to get a feel for the place.

I walked about a half mile when I reached an area near a small stream surrounded by large boulders. There were several men siting the rocks talking. I stopped to speak and be sociable. I saw one guy standing with his back to the group next to a tree. The way he was standing I first thought he was taking a leak. He turned slightly, and I could see another man giving him a blow job. One of the men from the rocks asked if I was there to join in on "Boys Night Out?" I told him "No," just passing through. I didn't continue any further and returned to the shop area.

I sat down on a bench and looked out toward The Commons. I've always considered myself to be an open-minded person. I've been surrounded by all types of people and dealt with just about every situation I could think of. In the past week, I've been challenged head on. I realized through my law enforcement career and even as a private investigator, I deal with people in the aftermath of their situations. Now, here I am surrounded by the people I have always avoided.

I may not be any better since I screwed a lesbian a couple of hours ago. I held on to that thought and realized I fully intend to screw her again if she'll let me. I hope that wasn't just to satisfy her curiosity. I guess only time will tell.

I see a group of people headed toward my direction. Then they spread out a mat and blanket on a nearby picnic table. I had the only table in the shade, so I called out and asked if they wanted that table, I was about to leave. There was an older woman along with two women in their twenties and a guy with purple spiked hair.

The older woman approached first as the other followed. She asked if I was sure I didn't mind sharing the table.

I gestured, "No, I have no plans and was just killing time before going on a walk.

She asked if I wanted to join in, they were about to do a Reiki share.

I had to ask, "what is that?"

The older woman started explaining it as an energy healing technique working with the Chakra systems.

One of the younger women spoke up and said, "you'll have us touching you all over."

The older woman said, "yes, that's true too, but it's not the focus of the share."

I objected at first, but the other younger woman said, "I think he's scared. Or maybe he doesn't like women touching him."

She looked to the purple haired guy and asked him, "what do you think?"

The guy looked at me, and I gave him a hard stare. He sat down at the end of the table and didn't speak.

I looked to the older woman again and asked, "What is this?"

She explained this is a healing method that realigns the energy field surrounding the body. Reiki means Universal Life force. The body had a field of energy that can felt and arranged to put yourself in balance.

"These are my students; I was going to instruct them on clearing methods today. Having an outsider and someone with no preconceived knowledge of how this works would be of great help in teaching them to trust the energy and feel the changes as they work."

The older woman introduced herself as Linda, she is a Reiki Master teacher, and her students are Lisa, Jane and Seth. "This is their second level of training, and what they are about to experience is totally new to them. If you agree to be our subject?"

"It sounds strange, what do I do?"

Linda indicated, "nothing at all. Just lay back and follow my instructions."

I agreed, and Linda set out a cushioned mat and covered it with a colorful blanket. Linda explained the colors represent the chakra regions of the body. Linda asked me to lie on the table and relax. As soon as I did, I felt someone removing my shoes. I looked up to see Lisa at my feet. I looked at her, and she froze and locked eyes with me. She said, "oops, I forgot to ask permission."

I smiled at her, "go ahead, seems like no one wants me to wear shoes around here."

Linda told me that each student would scan my body and determine which parts of my chakra need to be adjusted. She said I would feel them as they moved to different parts of my body.

Linda said she was going to do a meditation and a clearing. During this process she would guide me into deep relaxation and remove negative energy. During the process, I would meet someone that had a message for me. I was to accept the message as truth. After that she would instruct me during the clearing phase to speak if I wished to do so. I wasn't required to speak, that part is optional.

Linda spoke words I didn't understand and repeated them three times. The others were moving their hands on various parts of my body and putting light pressure and just remaining in position. Linda instructed me to ignore the others and listen to her voice.

She placed her hands on my forehead and on the top of my head. She directed me to allow myself to imagine I'm sitting high on a mountain looking out over the hills and valleys off in the distance. I'm alone and there are only the sounds of nature all around me. I'm comfortable being here and content to just be here and relax.

You watch as the sun moves closer to the horizon. As the sun touches the distant mountain you become very sleepy. You feel your body relax beginning at the top of your head. All the muscles let loose, and you feel your forehead relax. Your eyes are heavy, your cheeks droop with relaxation. Your jaw hangs loose. You allow this feeling to continue down your neck, chest, arms. The fingertips relax and all your energy flows out of your body. Allow this to continue down your legs. You will feel a tingling sensation which is a sign you are beginning to relax. Allow this to continue and go one hundred times deeper into relaxation.

I could feel Linda move her hands, but my body was so heavy I felt like I had been drugged. I felt wonderful and relaxed as deeply as I could.

Linda said the sun was sinking deeper beyond the horizon and as it faded away, I was to relax to my deepest level. The sun is gone now and the sky is turning dark. Stars are beginning to appear in the distant sky. Little by little the sky became darker, and the stars were brighter.

Allow your body to drift up toward the sky. Soon you will find yourself drifting weightless among the stars out in space. I had the sensation of floating, and I was surrounded by stars off in the distance. Linda said to find the brightest star and go toward it.

I rolled around and found the star way off in the distance. It seemed the furthest away, but it was the brightest. Suddenly, there was a bright flash of light which startled me, but I remained there in space. I regained my focus and there was an old man standing in front of me.

He was wearing a black robe trimmed in gold. And he had a tall hat similar to what the Pope wears. He appeared to be Asian, with long gray hair, and a long facial hair. He was laughing and seemed happy to see me. He didn't speak but pointed back toward Earth. He placed his hands on my shoulder, gave me a hug, and smiled. He shook his head yes, smiled as he turned me toward Earth and gave me a gentle push. I was back on the table.

I could feel my body returning to normal. I could feel the hands on my body. Linda was still at my head; I could feel her hands close to my throat. I could feel her move around as if she was scooping her hands. She said I could talk if I wanted to. I didn't speak. I wanted to go back to the deep relaxation, but my mind wanted answers to what I had experienced.

After several minutes, Linda instructed me to open my eyes and begin to feel the presence of my surroundings. I felt as if I had just awakened from a long nap. My body was so heavy I could hardly move. Lisa and Jane helped me sit up on the edge of the table and Seth handed me a bottle of cold water.

Linda must have known I had questions, but I didn't want to speak to the group. I answered their questions about being able to relax and get the feeling I was drifting into space. I described everything except the old man. Linda excused the group, and she came and sat down on the table. She asked if I had a visitor? I told her about the man and described him.

She seemed very pleased by this and asked if he had a name. I explained that he never spoke a word, and I described his actions. Linda seemed surprised that the vision was of an older Asian man. She explained the technique was discovered by an Asian man and invited me to join in their sessions to learn Reiki.

She then asked, "what do you think the message was?"

I pondered this a moment and then replied, "the man seemed pleased and wanted me to continue what I was doing. Problem is, I'm not sure what I'm doing here."

Linda smiled, sat back and said, "interesting he didn't speak, and he was pleased in what you are doing. In that case, I guess you need to keep doing what you are doing."

I must have made a sound of displeasure in her statement.

Linda asked, "do you watch television?"

I said, "yes, why?"

Linda said, "life is an illusion, and all the people are actors just like television. It's not necessary for you to react to the things they do or have an opinion about them just because you don't understand them. Just for today, I want you to not anger or judge anyone. Just observe and make this the best day possible."

Linda got up and again invited me to join the classes, as she walked toward the dining hall. What I have observed is everyone telling me to just observe. I wonder *if my secret is known to everyone here?* At this point it really doesn't matter.

Reaching down to put my boots back on, I hesitated and thought, *what the heck?* I took off my socks and walked out to the middle of The Commons. The grass was cool and soft. I'm amazed on how well groomed the area is. I guess this is why they clean it every day and don't allow shoes on the grass.

When I reached the center, I laid down looking up at the white fluffy clouds. I remember doing this as a kid and trying to imagine all the shapes. Mostly, I would see animals. I loved being outdoors when I was a kid. I still do, but somewhere along the way I seemed to only be outside when work called for it.

How is it I can be here and feel rushed, like I need to be somewhere else or doing something. I forced myself to stay despite the urge to go to my cabin, or just be somewhere else.

I closed my eyes, and the bright sun penetrated by eye lids causing me to see red. It felt good and relaxing. I'm not sure if I dosed off or just really relaxed.

When I opened my eyes, there was a pair of big brown eyes looking into my eyes. Andrea was seated cross legged at my head looking down on me. I rolled over, so I wouldn't be seeing her upside down. Andrea laid down too so we were facing each other.

Before I could ask, Andrea pointed toward the chow hall, and said she was over there. I could barely see her, but Cassie waved, and I waved back. Andrea asked if I wanted to go swimming with them. Will everyone be naked? Andrea laughed, "well yes. Mom says boys don't like the cold water because it makes their Winky shrink."

I rolled over and motioned for Cassie to come over. I don't think I want to have this conversation without a witness. I distracted Andrea by talking about the cloud shapes while I waited for Cassie. As soon as Cassie was within shouting distance, Andrea yells out, "he's afraid his Winky will shrink up and fall off!"

Cassie stopped in her tracks and covered her face. I couldn't tell if she was horrified or laughing. When she fell to the ground rolling around, it became obvious she was laughing. I just went back to cloud gazing.

A moment or two later Cassie lay down on one side and Andrea was on my other side. Cassie points up and says "rabbit."

I guess Andrea has never done this. She sat up looking for the rabbit. Cassie then explained the game.

Andrea calls out, "Winky!"

Cassie started to scold Andrea, but she pointed upwards to our left, and sure enough I could see what she was pointing at.

I'm not saying it was obvious, but it was easier than finding Cassie's rabbit. I'm not sure how long we were there, gazing at the clouds and pointing out the shapes. I think the is the most relaxed I've been in a long time.

Cassie kind of whispered, "I better keep my promise. You want to go?"

I declined, by folding my hands and bowing toward Cassie and said, "Namaste."

Cassie responded, "thank you and namaste to you, as well."

I laughed, "Na, I'm a stay right here."

I wasn't sure she liked my joke, but she kissed me on the cheek and said, "we'll see you later." They got up and headed toward the swimming trail.

I watched as they walked away and turned around to wave before disappearing out into the woods. As much as I'd love to spend more time with them, especially Cassie, I'm too modest and not comfortable being around the kids. *This is such a strange place.* I'm laying out in the middle of The Commons. Off to my right is the meeting place for everyone. Then out into the woods, the people that gather there are something like a time warp of hippy free-spirited people. Then off to my left are the drug rehab, prostitutes and rescues.

I'm not sure how this place works. I got up, walked out to The Point, and looked out toward the rolling hills and waited to see if any of the people from the B dorm area would come by. I was curious about them. I figured there was no point sitting here thinking about it. I walked back toward the picnic tables and found the unmarked trail head.

The B dorm was only about a half mile from The Point area. It was a two-story wood building. It was the largest building on the property as far as I could tell. It was surrounded by a grassy area. There were tables on both sides of the building. A lot of people were sitting around talking. I could smell a mixture of food cooking and marijuana in the air.

There were kids playing basketball on a half court area in the rear. From the reaction of people stopping their conversation to check me out, it was obvious I was from the other side of the tracks, so to speak. A woman came up and asked if she could help me. I informed her that I was new to Haven and was just out exploring. I told her I was out looking for the waterfalls, but my encounter on the trail behind the shop led me to believe I was on the wrong trail and this one was not marked.

She laughed loud and hard since she knew what I was talking about. She introduced herself as Tina. I told her I was Marshall, and I was sort of on a working vacation. She looked puzzled, and I told her I'm a private investigator.

Tina first looked surprised, then said "so, you're the one we heard about?"

I took a big chance in doing that, but since this case was a bust, I didn't see the need in hiding it any longer. It actually paid off. If I'd have lied, she would not have trusted me.

Tina asked, "I guess you want to go to the big fall?"

I had no idea what she was talking about but agreed. Tina sort of sized me up and gestured, "follow me."

We entered the door at the end of the building closest to the trail. We walked through a large open bunk area. There were a lot of teen-age kids sitting around. The next room was a dining area, and at the end was a kitchen. We walked up to the counter and Tina called to one of the workers, "two cans, please?"

A man stepped into a walk-in cooler and came out with two canteens, which he placed in insulated holders and handed them to Tina and me. He walked away without saying a word. Tina led me out the side door and walked toward a wooden staircase. We stopped at the bottom and looked up.

Tina must have thought my reaction was funny. She slapped me on the back and said, "it's a nice view if the climb doesn't kill you. And if it does, you'll be that much closer to heaven or further from hell."

Tina was a good ten steps ahead of me before I took my first step. *Holy cow, I can't even see the top!* The steps just keep going up the side of the mountain. I climbed until my legs were on fire. The wood railing ended and a large cable began. I held on to the cable and kept stepping one after another. I still could not see the top as the stairs turned out of sight.

Tina was out of sight too. I sat down to rest and get a drink. A few minutes passed and a couple passed me on their way down. The man stopped, looked at me, and indicated about "one third" and walked away. *Crap, was I only one third of the trip or one third left to the top?*

I started climbing again and about fifteen minutes later a few more people passed. I guess I looked like I was about to die. Without asking, a young girl said, "not much more."

Well, about twenty minutes later I still couldn't see the top. I sat down for another drink. My heart was pounding so hard, I felt it in my ears. I was also a little dizzy from the elevation. When I was able to catch my breath. I could hear voices, and I could smell the water.

I got up and started climbing again and when I rounded the next set of large boulders, I could see what I was hoping was the end of the stairs. I could hear the water fall now. It sounded huge. I was feeling energized now and pulled myself up the steps tugging on the cable.

When I arrived at the top Tina was sitting on the other side of a waterfall with a group of people. The water seemed to be coming right out of the ground and shooting a tremendous amount of water out into the air before falling out of sight somewhere below. The water was coming out with such force it didn't even touch the face of the mountain it was coming from. It wasn't much farther to the other side, and while I sure that was an amazing view, my legs were weak, and I didn't see a cable to hang on to. I sat down and marveled at the sight. Tina and the others cheered as I waved to them. Of course, they all motioned for me to come over. I pointed to the ground to signal back. I was staying here. I wish someone was close by to use my namaste joke again.

I would love to see more, but I used my better judgment and didn't chance the trip across to the other side. I crawled up onto a large boulder and tried to get a better look. I could see further down between the mountain peaks but could not see the bottom. The spray felt good, so I laid there relaxing and trying to regain the feeling in my legs.

I stayed on the rock for about a half hour before the group on the other side started back across to my side. The others spoke as they passed but didn't stop as they descended the steps out of sight.

Tina stopped, shook my canteen to see how much was left, then handed me hers. She said, "it's easier if you go down backwards." Then she headed down herself.

I figured I better get started since it looked like I was the only one still up here. *Oh crap, my legs hurt.* I took a few steps and realized every step hurt. I held on to the cable and eased myself down one step at a time. This was going to take twice as long as getting up here. I then realized what Tina meant. I turned around and started walking backwards, holding on to the cable. She was right. This was a lot easier. In fact, I was making pretty good time.

Before I knew it, I had passed the place I had stopped to rest on the way up. I didn't stop this time. As pretty as it was up here. I really wanted to get to the bottom. I took step after step until I reached the grassy area. Again, my cheering squad cheered when I laid down in the grass.

They all came over and poured the remaining canteen water all over me. There was a time when this would have totally pissed me off. Right now, I just said, "thanks."

All the others went inside, but Tina came over and sat down on the grass beside me. We didn't speak for a good while. She finally asked if I was hungry. I had no idea what time it was, but I was pretty sure I couldn't make back to the chow hall on the other side of Haven.

I rolled over to speak and noticed people sitting at the tables eating. The guy that gave up the canteens came out with a tray and put items out on a table. He pointed toward us and then at the table. Tina helped me up. And I needed the help. We went to the table and there was a bowl of spaghetti, bread and water.

Tina explained, "we do simple meals on this side, everyone can go to the regular chow hall when they want to. But a lot of us would rather just hang out here. It's not as nice, but it will keep you alive."

I dug into my food, and said, "it's pretty dang good."

One of the guys I recognized from my cheering squad came and sat down next to me. He asked if I was the spy he had heard about?

I wryly said, "yes, but I must not be very good since everyone knows who I am. Unless that's part of my cover, to tell everyone who I am and make everyone trust me and tell all their secrets?" I don't think he followed what I was saying, and he didn't speak to me again.

Tina got the joke and just smiled. We ate in silence at that end of the table for a while. Tina broke the silence when she asked about the saxophone.

That brought a happy smile to my face, and I said, "yes and I got my own rocking chair too. I might not ever leave this place."

Tina asked if wanted to come over later and join in the drum circle. I must have made a funny face and didn't answer right away.

Tina asked, "what's wrong?"

"I hear drums all the time on the other side. I don't know where they are coming from. Not sure if I'm missing a party or the natives are about to attack?"

Tina wasn't amused, but one guy almost choked. Tina punched him and said, "not funny."

The guy said, "That was my first thought when I got here. I mean we're all sitting around a campfire, torches burning and all of sudden drums were banging all over the place. Like some kind of jungle telegraph."

"I'm Kevin, by the way."

"Good to meet you, Kevin. It's nice I'm not the only one thinks it a little much."

Tina interjected, "if it brings people together, how can it be wrong? It gives people a reason to get together and just let loose."

"Tina, I agree, but there should be a limit. By the way, how did you know about the sax?"

Tina told me she was looking for Sam and heard me playing on my front porch.

I became interested in finding out more about Sam. I asked Tina what she knew about her.

I probably should have eased into that topic. Tina seemed a bit guarded on the topic of Sam. She explained that Sam is more of a mystery than you. "Well, sort of."

Her big grin led me to think Tina and I had something in common. I think I'll just avoid the topic for a while. I apologized to Tina if I seemed cold to her invitation.

"I love a chance to play with other people. I'm not very good, so don't expect much.

Tina asked," So, does that mean you'll go get it?"

I asked Kevin if he knew where he could get a wheelbarrow.

Giving me a puzzled look, he answered, "there should be one over at the shop, why?"

I groaned, "because there was no way in hell I can walk to my cabin and back, can you go get it and give me a ride?"

For a minute I think Kevin thought I was serious.

It was Tina's turn to make fun of me. "Kicked your ass today big boy."

"Yes. Yes, you did. My legs are still burning. I dread walking back to my cabin." My cheering section was laughing at me now. I really don't mind, it's all in good fun. The B side is nothing like I had expected, as if I had any idea of what to expect in the first place. Several people came over to join our little group, No one introduced themselves. That's fine, I wouldn't remember their names anyway. *Heck, I'm not sure anyone uses their real names here anyway.*

A few people asked again about me being a private investigator and why I was here. I told the story a few more times, that the case I came up for did not pan out, so I just decided to take a vacation. I think my story was believable, mostly because it was pretty much the truth, and I had been seen just roaming around the camp and being seen with the people that are in charge of the place. It would seem I've been under surveillance since I arrived.

I enjoyed being on the B side. lots of people to talk to. People off in the distance playing guitars and singing. I can see drums, but thankfully they hadn't started banging yet. It didn't appear anyone was drinking, but I could smell marijuana pretty strongly. I still wonder what Orangejello did to get kicked out. I mean this place is pretty wide open.

As I look around, I'm trying to figure out what is the difference in hippy and homeless, or if there is one. Not everyone is having fun. I notice a lot of the teenagers, male and female seem to keep to themselves, and they are not interacting with each other. I'm not going to ask and sound like a detective. But I'd bet these are the rescues I've heard about.

I needed to get back to my cabin and get ready for my trip into town. I've been gone most of the day and no one knew where I was at. I wonder if anyone cared. I guess I'll find out when I get back and see if anyone missed me. I thanked everyone for letting me hang out and with an obvious groan I got up, stretched, and it took me a bit to stand upright.

Tina took me by the arm and asked if she could walk with me. It had the tone of a scout helping an elderly person cross the street. I agreed, she was obviously just being nice since I saw her kiss a young pretty girl when we arrived back at the B dorm. So, I'm obviously not her type. I welcomed the escort and that gave us a chance to talk without the others listening in.

When we were out of range of the others, Tina asked if I was part of the team. I told her, "no, I was actually telling the truth about how I arrived in Haven, but have since become aware Haven was not all as it appeared to be. I think Mike and Sam are still trying to figure me out."

Tina sort of snorted when she laughed. "Sam told me you two had sex."

I had to ask, "did she provide a positive review?"

Tina laughed and said, "I'm pretty sure she'll be back for more."

We walked in silence the rest of the way to The Commons. Tina seemed like she wanted to talk more about the Haven operation but didn't. I decided not to ask her anything.

When we reached The Commons, I could see people lying on the grass. It was starting to get dark. Tina let go of my arm and went to a table and came back with a canvas tarp. She took off her boots and started out on the grass. She looked back and motioned for me to follow her.

Bending down to remove my boots was quite painful but I managed. I walked out near the center of the field and collapsed on the tarp face down. Tina poked me and said, "you have to roll over if you want to see the stars."

I grunted loudly as I rolled over.

We laid there for some time without speaking. Nothing about this seemed romantic between us at all. I'm pretty sure Tina is all the way lesbian, but I'd just hang out and see what this was all about. I noticed Kevin and some other guys close by, but not close enough to overhear their conversation. It was pretty quiet out on The Commons. There was an occasional gasp as a shooting star sped across the sky.

Tina finally broke the silence and asked what I really knew about Haven.

I reassured her I was telling the truth about how I came to Haven but realize there is a lot more than it is made out to be. I told her I don't think anyone believes me, so I haven't really tried to convince anyone otherwise.

I asked Tina what she thought, and why she was here with me now.

Tina was silent for a bit, then said, "I noticed you with Sam, and Mike. I figured you were part of the team. I don't know anything about the new girl, Robin, I've seen you with. I've heard she's a runaway, but she never was part of the B dorm, so that means she, or someone pays for her to be here."

I sort of chuckled and said, "for a bunch of free love hippy types, there sure is a lot of paranoia going on."

I was getting annoyed at the game and started to get up to leave. About that time, Andrea dove onto the tarp between Tina and me. She pulled on the back of my shirt, and told me to lay down, the show was about to start. I didn't want to explain my sudden departure, so I laid back down.

A moment later, Cassie arrived as if on cue. This seems to be a common thing with these two. Cassie, said to Andrea, "you shouldn't interfere, they might want to be alone."

Andrea let out a squeal of laughter and said, "Mom, you know Tina likes girls. They need to be here."

Cassie didn't question the situation and spread out a blanket next to us and watched the stars. As the sky grew darker, the Milky way became clearer and there were more shooting stars than I'd ever seen in my life.

After a while I could feel the dampness, and I thought about the trip to town in the morning. I didn't get all the details, so I hope Sam and Robin will fill me in when I get back to the cabin.

I told everyone good night and stood up to leave.

Andrea stood up and gave me a hug. Then she said, "Tina will tell you everything when you get to town."

Tina looked as if she'd seen a ghost. Then her expression softened when she and Andrea locked eyes.

Andrea and Cassie said their good nights as Andrea sort of pushed me in the direction of my cabin. Once again, I realized I didn't have a flashlight, and I had to fumble my way back in the dark. Luckily, I could see the battery lantern on my front porch, so I at least had something to aim for. I was determined to make it on my own and not call out for help.

I was hoping Sam would be there waiting for me, but it was Robin. I wasn't expecting her to be there. Robin had already consumed a bit too much wine and offered me the bag which looked to have been a couple of gallons at some point. There was still plenty left, so, we sat on the porch and drank together. *I'm perplexed in my role here.* It's obvious I was sent here on a false pretense, but now I have a drunk eighteen-year-old on my hands.

We sat in silence. Robin had fortunately stopped drinking and was nodding off to sleep with her head against the porch rail. I looked out toward the path as long as I could stand it, hoping to see a Sam coming down the trail. Robin got up without asking and went inside the cabin and fell onto the lower bunk bed and fell asleep.

I sat in the rocker a while longer sipping warm red wine. I have no idea what kind it was, but it was pretty good. All along I was hoping Sam would show up. I stayed long enough that I was getting sleepy, so I headed inside. Robin was curled up in a ball on the bunkbed. I took the sleeping bag off my bed and laid it on her. I figured I'd be sleeping in my clothes tonight anyway.

Sunday

I woke the next morning as the sun was shining through my window. Robin was gone, and she had returned my sleeping bag at some point. No one has filled me in on the game plan for the day. I figured I better empty my pack, or my wish bag as it would be called today, and make my way to breakfast, if it wasn't too late. As I was unpacking, I decided I'd grab a quick shower first. I could always eat in town.

I was in a hurry since I didn't know what my time frame was. I glanced at the mirror as I was passing, and an old scruffy guy was looking back at me. I thought it was kind of funny I was beginning to look the part, but I didn't have to smell the part. I took a quick shower and changed into fresh clothes before headed to the chow hall.

I arrived in time to eat, but most of the crowd had come and gone. I was surprised to see Robin and Tina at the same table. I went through the line and was able to gather enough of the remaining portions to sustain me until we reached town. The coffee in the insulated container had pretty much gone cold, but at this point I wasn't complaining.

Robin looked really tired. It was obvious she wasn't going to enjoy her trip to town. Her first words were, "I'll never drink again."

I sort of chuckled at that, which I received a hard look from Robin. I told her I was sorry, it's just because we've probably all said that at some point. I put my arm around her and pulled her close. Robin laid her head on my shoulder and seemed to go limp. I told her I wanted to respect her privacy, but I was also concerned about her safety and overall well-being. I didn't want to come across like I was about to start keeping a closer eye on her, but the truth is, I think I should.

Robin didn't pull away as I expected, she just sat there with her head on my shoulder, as I ate my breakfast.

Tina said she would be going to town with us and Sam would meet us there. I didn't ask about Sam, I wanted to but didn't. I asked if there was anything I needed to know before we went.

Tina answered "no, we should just go and enjoy our day, get whatever we need and meet up later to return to Haven."

I guess I had a puzzled look.

Tina explained they have a standing order for the trail angel supplies, but they had other business in town. We were just going along for the ride. I was looking forward to getting a few items for my wish bag, but I was concerned Robin wasn't going to have much fun on the trip.

Mike came into the chow hall and motioned for us to follow him. I roused Robin, and we made our way to the door. Robin retrieved her bag sitting at the door, and we made our way toward the lift area. Randy was running the lift controls. We waved across the room, but didn't stop to speak. Madison and Tony were in the lift. This was the first time I'd seen them since our meeting in town. They seemed friendly enough, so I guess I'm not being escorted out of Haven for misbehaving.

The lift ride takes about fifteen minutes. Robin slept the entire way down. When we reached the landing, we made our way to a white passenger van with dark tinted windows. Madison got in the drivers' seat and Tony sat up front as well. Robin disappeared into the back seat and went to sleep again.

Tina, looked back toward Robin, then looked to me and said, "poor baby, I hope she gets to feeling better."

I said, "me too, what's the plan?"

Tina said, "you guys are going to be dropped off downtown to do whatever you want to do. Just enjoy the day."

She looked back at Robin, and added, "or do the best you can. We'll meet with our team and get a time and place to meet this evening for out return trip."

I didn't bother to ask any questions. I've been on enough undercover operations to know I was not part of the plan and no need to know what was going on at the moment. I was armed and had money and my cell phone if we needed to get away.

The ride into town was silent except for the snoring from the back seat. About thirty minutes later we arrived in Asheville, North Carolina. We drove around for a bit going up and down some of the same streets and seemed to be looking for something or someone. Finally, we pulled over at the curb of a small park area. I should have known this was the place. Right away I hear drums and see a bunch of people with hula hoops dancing around. Our crew, less Robin, departed from the van. Everyone sits down on a brick wall.

Tina said, "we'll get her up before we go."

Tina points to the sax case and says, "you might as well start blending in."

Playing by ear cold is not one of my strong suits. I tend to read music, but I don't have any with me. I noticed this area has a lot of buskers, so, for now I just want to watch and see what's going on around me.

I moved over to a bench closer to the center of the park, but close enough that I still have a direct view of the van. The people around here are much like the folks back in Haven. It's kind of hard to tell the hippies from the homeless. If there is a difference. I guess the biggest difference is watching to see which ones display signs of mental illness or serious drug burnout.

As I'm looking around, a woman in bright red sweatpants, a tie-dyed shirt cat eye sequin glasses and a multicolored tam sat down beside me. I tried to ignore her in case she was one of the nuts that seem to dominate the place. She leans in close and whispers in my ear, "I hear you're a good fuck."

I had a moment of confusion and reconnection at the same time. I'd have never recognized Sam in this get up.

Sam apologized for the disappearing act, but said something came up, and promised to make it up to me when we get back to Haven. Our conversation was cut short as Robin emerged from the van and walked over to the bench. She laughed when she saw Sam and gave her a hug. Robin was still unsteady on her feet and told Sam she owed her a box of wine. Sam assured her she was well supplied and not to worry about it, "we'll indulge again tonight."

Robin seemed a little green at the thought of that and said, "no, I think I'll pass."

Robin sat down next to Sam and leaned against her shoulder. Sam stroked Robin's hair and said, "as nice as this is, I've got stuff to attend to. I'll meet you guys back here between 6 and 7, if all goes well."

Sam handed me an envelope and said," if I'm not back, call the number on the form and someone will came get you and take you back to the landing."

Sam kissed me on the cheek and jumped up. Robin pretty much fell over and her head landed in my lap. Sam and the others drove away in the van. So, here we are. A hung-over teenager surrounded by a bunch of…well, whatever. I opened the envelope hoping to find some sort of explanation of what was going on. It only contained a list of places and directions to get the things we might want for our wish bags. At the bottom as a number to call if we needed a ride to get a ride back to the landing. Other than that, it appeared we had a whole day to do whatever.

Robin finally sat up and said, "I'm hungry."

I'm kind of familiar with the area, so I'll let Robin decide on what kind of food she wants. It was too early for the normal lunch menu items to be ready but hopefully some breakfast types of places would be open. I'm normally in a motel so I don't think about those things, or I could just drive where I want to go. This was strange to me. I feel stuck and totally out of my element.

Robin took charge and said, "lets walk, we'll find something."

We didn't have to walk too far before we saw a restaurant on the corner with outdoor seating. We approached the hostess booth and asked for a table. Right away the patrons seemed to eye us as less than desirable. I guess when you show up looking as scruffy as we were with your backpacks and saxophone case, you automatically fit the profile of street buskers or even less desirable street people.

The hostess showed us to a table in a corner away from the others. Truth was, I really liked our location. Robin and I had not really had a chance to talk. Our waitress was obviously new and seemed very uncomfortable trying to take our order. She was unfamiliar with the menu and could not make recommendations or provide advice on the timing of the items that might be available at this time of day. We decided the breakfast items would be the best bet and be less of an issue for our waitress if we just ordered the standard combinations they offered.

Our waitress was very friendly and seemed to have a cute personality. She apologized often for not knowing what she was doing. We noticed the hostess and some of the other waitresses seemed to find it amusing in her fumbling and didn't help her when she dropped a plate of food at another table.

We assured our waitress that we were in no hurry and not to worry. She had nothing to apologize for. It did take a long time for our order to arrive, but everything was fine. This gave Robin and I time to talk a little. We stayed a lot longer than normal customers would normally stay. Our waitress was accommodating the entire time. I think the manager and hostess was concerned we were just looking for an opportunity to jump the fence and skip out on the bill.

Robin and I discussed the church school. She told me it had not always been a bad place. The Reverend got caught having sex with an underage girl, and instead of being arrested, he became friends with the detective and before you know it, lots of strange girls started showing up at the school. They did not attend classes and stayed in trailers out back. Robin was sure they were selling drugs too.

Our hostess and other employees seemed to be hovering closer to our table so we decided we should just leave so we could discuss this further later on. I motioned for our waitress to bring the check. A few minutes later she arrived and apologized for the service.

Robin took the check and looked at the amount. She took out a twenty for the bill. The waitress said, "I'll be back with your change."

Robin held out her hand, "wait, I forgot your tip." She took out a one-hundred-dollar bill and handed it to her and said, "keep the change."

Our waitress was stunned and could barely speak as she thanked us. Robin was sure to depart with a "Fuck you" comment to our hostess as she passed by.

We walked about a block before Robin spoke, "that really felt good."

Curious, I asked her. "Which part?"

"All of it. I've never bought anyone a meal in a restaurant, I've never left a tip, and I've never said Fuck You to someone that looked down on me before."

I chuckled and told Robin I was glad she had the opportunity for a bunch of firsts but reminded her that was kind of an expensive first.

Robin looked at me and said, "I understand. but it's something I'll always remember, and I'm sure our waitress will too."

I had to agree to that. I was curious about the money since I got a glimpse of the wad in her bag. Robin told me her mother gave her plenty to escape with and gave her a credit card and a cell phone. I stopped dead in my tracks.

"You can call your mother?"

Robin said, "sort of. I can text. And set up a time to call her. She can only use her phone when no one is around."

I guess I already knew this, but was hoping Robin had a better arrangement.

Since we had all day to walk around, I figured we should have a plan. I didn't want to walk around all day with a heavy backpack. Robin agreed, so we elected to do the tourist thing and hit all the museums and what else we might be able to find. What we found right away was people not wanting us to bring our packs inside. We tried looking up storage lockers and asking the locals, but I wasn't pleased with the results. I wasn't about to repeat this process several times a day, we started talking about our options. I was about to pull out the sax when I realized we were sitting in front of a parking garage. They had bike storage but denied us the use of our bags. The attendant suggested we rent a car or a hostel room. I liked the idea of a car better, since we needed to do some shopping.

I guess we were not the first to have this issue and the attendant suggested we can take the Trolley and gave us directions to the rental agency. The process was quick and before you knew it, we were in our rental and driving around Asheville. Robin had never been there, so we headed up to the Blueridge Parkway first since we were close to the entrance. We didn't want to get too far away, and our cell signals went away pretty fast.

I noticed Robin was talkative when we were sitting or riding in the car. She was easily distracted by the sights or tourist attractions. Robin was mostly a home body and not by choice. Her first adventure on her own was to be shipped to a remote mountain camp, with very little to do.

We stopped at a couple of overlooks along the way. Robin was quick to point out the distant city and other structures more than admire the view of nature.

On the way back down, we stopped at the Art Center. Here was another place Robin where she got quiet and spent a lot of time reading about the exhibits and admiring the difference in techniques.

I wanted to get to know Robin without the usual questions and answer sessions. My limited experience with teenagers is they clam up if you ask them personal questions.

We left the Art Center and headed back toward town. Since I knew we'd be stuck downtown later I decided we should go somewhere else. I headed to West Asheville. From what I remembered, it was more of the hippy scene without the obvious homeless population. I hoped it would still be the same.

This side of town is much smaller with not as much to take in. There were restaurants and bars. Not much to hold Robin's attention. She seemed more interested in the people. She stopped to watch the artist and buskers, then I noticed she took extended glances at well-dressed women.

This concerned me since she and Sam had spent so much time together before I arrived. I guess I'm no better since I'd been with her myself. Maybe I'm reading too much into this. I'm just trying to observe her likes and dislikes.

There was one restaurant that looked interesting, so we ventured inside. At least this time we were welcomed like royalty. Robin wanted to sit outside again. She said she likes to watch the people and traffic. I had to get my big hamburger fix, but Robin chose a sampler appetizer plate. She said she couldn't make up her mind. Our conversation while waiting to order had been about her being confined to the school and the repetitive cafeteria food and then she gets shipped off to Haven where she again had to stand in line to eat.

It amazes me the things I take for granted such as the ability to travel and experience so many things. Robin lived such a sheltered life, then she is thrust into the middle of forced sex and drugs, then she ends up in Haven where it much the same, except the sex is pretty much open and plenty of it.

I don't know how much time we'll have together, but I want to try and bridge our gap and help her have better experiences. I can't imagine being eighteen years old and having never seen the ocean, or have the freedom to choose anything for myself.

Learning this about Robin made me look at her in a different way now. I watched her as she ate and tried new things. I barely know her and all of a sudden, I want to give her the world and protect her from it at the same time.

After we ate, Robin wanted to go back to the downtown area. Now that we were able to secure our packs, she wanted to check out the stores and just walk around. We drove back toward the downtown area by way of the Biltmore Village area. Robin saw the sign for the River Arts District. I had never been there myself, so we went to check it out.

Again, this seemed like something that interested her. Robin mentioned that she liked to draw, but she had to keep it hidden since the school was strict and any form of expression was forbidden. If it wasn't all about God, you were the Devil.

"That's kind of fucked up, since you can buy a teenage girl on the other side of the fence."

Robin got upset talking about the school. She walked out of the building and headed to the car. We drove downtown and had to circle around looking for a parking space. Robin seemed excited looking at all the stores she wanted to check out.

There were buskers on just about every corner, and she asked if I had ever done that. I had to tell her about how I taught myself to play the sax and only had a few lessons. I wasn't very good, but yes, I have played on the streets three times. Once here in Asheville and twice in Wilmington.

Robin asked me, "do you want to play today?"

I suggested that I might if we have time later. Right now, this is her day. I can play pretty much anytime I want, but today I'll do whatever she wanted to do.

We finally found a place to park and went out walking. I loved watching her as she looked in store windows and lingered at the restaurants as we passed by the people dining outside.

I hope we weren't making them uncomfortable, but I enjoyed seeing the excitement in her eyes.

We stopped to watch some buskers on the corner. We sat on a bench close by. Robin was looking around and asked if I would wait there while she went into the store next to where we were sitting. She promised she wouldn't go anywhere else and would come back there as soon as she finished.

As much as I didn't want to let her out of my sight. I agreed. After all she is eighteen years old.

I was tempted to look into the window to watch her, but I resisted and just watched the people busking and take in the sights and sounds downtown.

I had been there long enough that I was getting uncomfortable with her being gone so long. When she finally returned, it was well worth the wait. Robin had bought new clothes. She was wearing a red and white sun dress, white sandals, and a white hat. She had a large canvas bag over her shoulder.

She looked like a dream and was laughing as she spun around to show me her new outfit.

"What do you think?"

"I think you look amazing." That was putting it mildly. I knew Robin was pretty, but she suddenly transformed into someone else right before my eyes.

Robin wanted to walk some more. This time it was different. She was still excited as she looked around to see all the new things, but now she seemed like she was part of it. I loved to see her light up when she saw her reflection in the windows as we passed by.

I was lucky enough to find a music store and a used bookstore on the same block. I made short work getting my reeds and cleaning supplies, and then hit the bookstore. I pretty much knew what I wanted and located the a few mystery paperbacks and a couple of sailing novels.

Robin wandered throughout but lingered a few times around the romance section. It hit me I should give her some space. I told her to take her time and be out front of the café next door.

I really want to order a beer, but I'm armed and not sure how this day may play out. I hadn't thought about Sam and the others until now. I had been left out of the loop on what they were doing, but it seemed dangerous, so I better play it safe rather than sorry.

Robin had spent about thirty minutes in the bookstore. When she came out, she wanted something to drink.

It only took a few more moments to find an inviting little café. We went inside and found an open booth near the back. Today had been so full of new sights and sounds, we talked, but it was mostly about the things around us.

Robin had opened up a bit earlier when we were eating lunch. She talked about the school and her limited freedom. I know it bothered her a lot. I wondered if she would bring it up again. I sat back in the booth with my back against the wall. I took out a book with a sailboat on the cover.

I opened the book and attempted to get an idea on what it was about. Truth is my mind was more focused on Robin.

She seemed uneasy and shifted around in her seat. I pretended not to notice. Finally, she turned sideways in the booth with her back against the wall facing out like the way I was sitting.

Robin fumbled with a book, looked up at me and asked, "are you religious? Do you believe in God?"

It took me by surprise, and I wasn't sure how to answer her. I was silent for what seemed like a long time.

I sighed, "I have given it a lot of thought over the years. It took a while, but I finally came to the conclusion that it didn't matter what I believed, at least as far as a religion was concerned. It feels more like politics and another excuse to judge and separate people. So, I guess I can say I really just don't know."

Robin showed me a book on witchcraft. She said there are a lot of witches in Haven.

I took the book and sort of leafed through a few pages, trying to get a feel for what I was seeing.

Robin said, "they've really been nice to me."

I looked up as she said, "the witches."

They meet up near the swimming area. I realized that was the note I saw on the message board about the Shadow Coven. I asked if that was the same group.

Robin said, "yes, but there are a lot more."

I can still hear Mike's voice telling me to observe. So far that seems to be working out, since there is nothing I can do about it anyway.

"Hmmm, okay, tell me more."

Robin seemed excited telling me about all the people she met in Haven and how different they were from people she knew back home. At first no one told her they were witches. It's just not something they talk about. They just seemed like nice people. They seem like they care about people, animals and taking care of the Earth.

I guess I looked concerned, and Robin responded by saying, "I'm not looking to join the club, I'm just curious. I mean these are witches. They're supposed to be evil, devil worshiping mean ugly people. At least that's what I've been told all my life."

"I met a group of girls close to my age while we were working with the younger kids cleaning The Commons. I heard them talking about where they were from and their home life. These girls were happy and so sweet. None of them knew each other before coming to Haven. They connected somehow. I wanted to know more about them since they were so different. On the surface they were poor, hippy types, but happy. It was the happy that drew me to them."

"None of the kids back home were happy, not like this anyway. Unfortunately, they were all near the end of their stay, so I didn't get to learn all I wanted from them. We only had a couple of days working together before they left. Sheri was the last to go. She was the youngest of our work crew and was more open than the other about her home life."

"Sheri told me the other girls' parents were witches, and they travel to places like this to meet others like them. Sheri and I went up the trail to see what the witches were doing."

Robin stopped talking, I half expected her to tell me something shocking, but she said, "they were sitting around naked in the woods talking. We got bored and left after a while."

I sort of chuckled about that and asked, "if that was all they were doing, why are you interested?"

Robin said, "oh, it's not so much about witchcraft but why the kids were so happy. These kids had nothing. They were poor and didn't care. The kids I knew from the school came from nice homes, or what I perceived to be nice homes."

"How is it I've been told my whole life these people are evil, and Christians are so superior to them. None of the kids back home were like this. I mean I live in a church that sells drugs and girls. I just need to know."

As much as I wanted to hang out and talk, I figured it was time to finish our shopping and return the car. We made our way back to the rental and headed for the nearest big box store to stock up on the rest of our wish list. Then I had to calculate how much room and weight I could stand in my pack for the most important items. Since a couple of cases of cold beer was out of the question, I opted for a run to the ABC store.

I wish I'd asked Sam about her supply before we left but I forgot. I guess she'll have to deal with what I bring back. Wine and beer take up too much space. I never dreamed I'd someday have to calculate how much buzz per pound or volume I'd need for a backpack. Now I have to decide on what to get. I would have bet the better stuff doesn't come in plastic bottles. Turns out I was wrong, well sort of. I'm sure the really high end doesn't, but as it turns out, there was a good selection since a lot of campers come to the area and request plastic bottles. I probably bought a lot more than I needed, but I'm one of those better safe than sorry types. That's my story anyway.

I filled my wish pack and wondered if I'd have to haul all this stuff down the mountain. I'd be in trouble, so, I hope I get to stay in Haven for a while. I should be set for a while. Now, I have a few more changes of clothes, plenty of reading material, and alcohol. I'm sure I'll think of something I forgot when we get back up top.

We returned the rental car and made our way to the trolley stop. The pack was heavy enough, and I was questioning why I brought the horn along. I was in pain by the time we reached the stop. It would be another thirty minutes before the next trolley came along. We were too tired to talk at this point, Robin laid her head on my shoulder and went to sleep.

I started thinking about the different perspectives people must have. Robin grew up in what was supposed to be a place of high moral standards and, yet it was pretty bad.

My time with the B dorm crew has been limited, but they seem okay. I thought about Amy. I've had plenty of contact with strippers and prostitutes throughout my career. They've all been older. I'd never given it much thought about when they get started, or why.

When the trolley arrived, I woke Robin up just long enough to find a seat. As soon as we sat down, she was out again. It was a short ride back to the downtown area. We got out close to the park area where we last saw Sam and Tina. I was still full but wanted something. Robin suggested ice cream, and that sounded like a good idea.

We found a place about a block away and went in to place our order. It was small and hard to move around with our packs. We managed and made our way back out onto the streets. As we sat on a brick wall eating our ice cream, I noticed all the people around us. Everything from the well to do, to the down and out zombie types. People amaze me. How do you arrive at such a place in life where you can barely function? I see two teenaged boys digging through the trash looking for food. I watched them as they unwrapped something and consumed it as they scurried away.

There are beggars and hookers of all ages. I work here a lot, and pretty much just do what I have to do. Rush around working and when I'm walking downtown, I see the people, but just in passing. Now I'm forced to just sit be among them, almost as if I'm one of them at the moment.

After we finished, we made our way back to the park and wait some more. We grabbed some bottled water from a street vendor and found an empty bench near the street.

Robin was quiet for a bit, then said, "I hope I didn't freak you out with my book."

"No, not really, Haven is a different kind of place. It kind of makes you look at things differently. I even had a Reiki session."

Robin busted out laughing and almost choked on her water.

She managed to say, "I can't imagine you doing any kind of woo woo stuff."

"And, why not, may I ask?"

Robin was still trying to regain her ability to speak and managed to get out, "because you just don't seem the type. You look like one of those guys that throw you out of bars when you get out of hand."

I wasn't sure if I should be flattered or offended. I wished I was young and in shape to still be that guy. That's actually how I got my start before becoming a police officer. I think I'll just keep all that to myself for now.

"Well, I did it, and it was pretty interesting."

Robin just looked off in the distance like she was in deep thought.

Then she blurted out, "I want to go see the witches." Then she waited for my response.

"Okay, do you want me to go with you?"

"You'd do that?"

"Sure, unless you'd rather someone else go."

Robin seemed excited and said, "no, I want you to go."

I wanted to discuss it further, but Sam showed up. When Sam saw Robins' outfit, she squealed like a teenager as Robin got up and spun around showing her the new outfit. Then Robin pulled out two more from the large canvas bag to show off.

Sam asked if I wanted to do anything because it may be a little longer. I really didn't want to walk anymore, and I wasn't hungry, so I indicated we would just wait. Sam kind of nudged the sax case toward me and gave me a flirty smile.

I was tired and wanted to resist, but I reached for the case. I felt very uncomfortable about playing in public. I had to do some self-talk to get motivated. Off and on today I watched other performers and noted some were pretty good and some were really bad, so hopefully I can land somewhere in the middle.

I put a new reed in my mouth and made a production of getting it ready to play. I was sort of stalling too.

Sam asked, "why do you have to put the reed in your mouth first?"

I took the reed from my mouth and looked at it as if I was giving it a close inspection.

I told Sam that a reed was like a woman, soft, delicate, sensitive, fragile. After a short pause, I then said also like a woman, it is much more cooperative when it's hot and wet.

Sam kicked me in the shin as if she was offended but laughed anyway. I was terrified since I hadn't played in a long time. I hadn't had a chance to become accustomed to this horn. My nerves were obvious by the squeaks as I was biting too hard on the mouthpiece. I took a long deep beath and decided I'd just play like I don't care, or I'd suck. I blew a few scales and arpeggios to test the horn, and she was acting pretty good.

I know about ten songs I can play from memory. *Misty* has always been my favorite since it was the first piece I learned to play by ear. At first, I was playing too fast just wanting to get it over with. Then I realized the acoustics were actually pretty good here despite the sounds of the city blending in. I slowed down considerably and listened to the sounds almost as if I were hearing someone else playing. I was starting to enjoy this. Maybe I've found a new hobby? Maybe this would give me a reason to start practicing again?

I hadn't paid much attention to the people passing by. After about five songs I realized I'd collected a pretty decent amount of money. I was about to play some more, but the van pulled up at the intersection. Tony called out for us to meet them in the parking lot down the street. I collected the cash from my case and stuffed it in my pocket. I didn't have time to count it. I was curious on how I did. I'll figure it out later.

I got in the van and saw a teenage boy and two girls in the far back seat. They were all crouched down like they were hiding. When we were all in, Tina slid the side door shut.

There was a commotion on the sidewalk and one of the girls screamed. My attention was drawn toward the scream, but then saw Tony as he spun around and kicked a guy in the face. There was a lot of blood, and I'm pretty sure a few teeth went flying too.

This all happened so fast I didn't realize there had been two of them. I saw the second guy laying on the sidewalk with his arm bent in an unnatural angle. Tony jumped in the van and gave Madison a high five as we drove away.

I remember my law enforcement days and that rush when we'd get into a hot situation. I looked back toward the kids in the back of the van. The girls were still hiding, but the boy was peeking over the seat looking back toward the guys on the ground.

Madison took out a cell phone and called someone. All I heard him say was, "we need a blocker." Then he hung up. Everyone was silent. We drove out of the downtown area and it seemed like we were just going in circles, and ran a few red lights. I've done a lot of surveillance work and could see that Tony is doing maneuvers to spot a tail.

Madison's phone rang and all he said was, "okay, we'll head there now."

I had been watching traffic looking for a tail. Unfortunately, these windows were so dark all I'm seeing is headlights and dark outlines of cars. We pulled onto the Parkway and two cars were sitting on the side of the road. I felt my heart skip a beat as they both moved when we passed by. Both vehicles pulled onto the parkway and turned sideways blocking both lanes. I saw several people getting out as we drove out of sight.

I'm accustomed to dangerous situations, but I'm really pissed that Robin was put in danger, and I had not been informed on what was going on. I'm not going to make a scene in front of the kids. They are obviously the targets, rescues, or whatever they are called, but there will be hell to pay when we get back.

Sam acted like she wanted to speak, but Tina stopped her. It's obvious Tina is higher on the pecking order of this mission.

The route was obviously longer, and we all remained silent during the trip. When we reached the landing there were others present which appeared to be on guard. I'm not sure if this is normal since I didn't come up this way. The new kids went up first even though there was plenty of room in the lift. About ten cable cars passed before Robin and I were allowed to enter our car. Again, no one else got in despite the fact there was plenty of room.

When we reached the top the new kids were no where in sight. I didn't recognize the guy running the lift. And I didn't want to wait for Sam. I figured she knew where to find me.

Robin started to walk toward the A dorm area, but I stopped her. I told her I wanted her close by because I really don't trust these people.

Robin asked, "what about Sam?"

I told Robin that I wasn't quite ready to kick her aside, but I won't be sharing any secrets with her. Robin seemed to accept that answer. Although she didn't say any thing, I think she felt the same way.

Robin and I walked toward my cabin but detoured slightly at the dining hall to rest before making the final leg to the cabin. We each took a rocking chair and sat in silence for several minutes. I guess we were both waiting on the other to break the silence and discuss the events if the evening. I looked over and saw Robin was crying. I took her hand and the silent tears turned into sobs and shaking. I stood up and held her as she clutched me as hard as she could.

Robin cried out, "I'm so scared."

I told her everything was okay, we were safe now.

She protested, "no, I mean all of it. Why am I here? I thought I was here to get away from this shit. Why would my mother send me here? And why isn't she telling us what's going on?"

"I don't know if she's safe or anything." All I could do was hold her because I had no idea what I could do to help sooth the situation. I don't like being kept in the dark about everything.

"This is going to stop right now. I'm either getting some answers, or we're leaving."

I didn't want to go straight back to the cabin. I wanted to talk to Robin and not run the risk of Sam showing up. This is not how I normally work. I don't like others making plans for me. I decided to change this situation. I asked Robin how she felt about Sam and if she trusted her.

Robin hesitated before answering, "I really don't know. She has been a big help to me up until this point. I have to admit, I'd have been lost the past couple of weeks. She seemed to know I didn't fit in with any of the groups here. The B dorm people were not nice to me and the people in the woods were just plain weird."

I had to laugh at the way she said it more than the fact she found them weird. I'd have to agree with her about the woods people. I've done a lot of traveling and met a lot of people, but this place is so strange. There are people from all walks of life here, like some kind of dream or a nightmare depending on your way of looking at it. I've mostly kept to myself other than the few people I interact with out of necessity.

Sam, I couldn't figure her out at all. She's hot, and I love being with her, but I know nothing about her and tonight made me wonder if it was worth the effort.

Robin seemed to be able to read my thoughts and said, "you know, it's not like you're going to take her home with you."

"Well, I'll be damned, you're right." *Why do I care?* It seems like people around here keep telling me how life is an illusion, I just need to observe and be in the moment. You know all that hippy shit.

I guess I could have sat around and had some kind of great awakening that would have transformed my whole way of thinking, but just then I detected movement off to my right. Something big and black was approaching us in the dark. Thank God, it was upon us before I could react.

Robin was still holding me, and Merlin decided a group hug was needed at the moment. He pounced up, licked me on the face and nearly knocked us down. I was really glad to see the old boy, but his timing could have been better. I wanted to have a deep conversation with Robin. There is so much I want to know about her and this whole situation. She started playing with Merlin, and I wasn't going to bother trying to reengage her in the conversation. Tomorrow is another day, and if I understand our task, we'll be on the trail all day and overnight if we want to. Right now, that sounds like a plan.

We headed off toward my cabin. I told Robin I wanted her to stay with me tonight.

Robin took my arm and in a flirty voice, said, "I thought you'd never ask."

For a moment I thought I had screwed up, but she laughed, and it was obvious she knew what I meant.

When we got back to the cabin, we dropped off our wish bags, and I got my stuff together for the bath house. Robin asked me to walk with her to Sam's to get her things together too. I did, and noticed this was the first time she wanted me to stay with her. Up to this point, she had been independent and didn't want anyone to hover over her.

I stayed on the porch as Robin got her things together, and we walked to the bathhouse. Before we separated to our own shower areas, she asked if I got out first to wait for her. I told her I would. It was still very quiet and no one else was out walking around tonight.

I was feeling pretty grungy, so I shaved, showered and put on fresh clothes. There's something about a camp shower that feels so good. I wanted to just stand under the hot water and relax, but I didn't want Robin to have to wait on me.

I walked out and Robin was not in sight. She came out a moment later. I'm pretty sure she was waiting for me to come out first.

I said, "that was good timing."

I didn't want her to know I noticed the difference in her. She was walking closer than normal and looked around as if she was scanning the woods as much as she was looking down the dark trail.

As we approached Sam's cabin Robin asked me to come with her while she got something else she had forgotten. I did as before and waited on the porch. A moment later she came out with a large, insulated water bottle. I didn't bother to ask what she had.

We proceeded over to my cabin, and I went in to drop my stuff and grab a bottle of Scotch. I remembered I still had Merlin's bag that Ms. Mattie gave me. Merlin perked up as I walked out on the porch. I poured him some water and food. He was obviously in need of both.

I took to my rocking chair, and Robin and Merlin sat on the porch. Merlin laid his head on Robin leg, and she stroked him until he went to sleep. Robin asked how long I'd had him. I had to tell the story about meeting Ms. Mattie and the trip up the mountain. As I was telling the story somehow, I remembered it as being a great adventure and not the hell I remembered before. I wish I could re-tune my thinking and learn to enjoy things as they are happening and not just think about the end goal.

We didn't talk a lot tonight. I sipped Scotch, and she was obviously getting tipsy on whatever she had.

In her slurred speech she asked, "do you think Merlin would be a good guard dog?"

"He obviously likes you; I'd say so. Why do you ask?"

Robin asked if he could stay in the cabin with us.

"Yea, I'd love for the old boy to hang around."

Robin got up and took Merlin inside the cabin.

I wanted to sit up a bit longer and listen to the night sounds. It was nice tonight. Just nature sounds and no drums or hoop and hollers from the woods people. It didn't take long before the scotch and soothing sounds made me fade off into a deep relaxation. For a moment I wondered where Sam was at, but quickly decided I didn't care. I went to the cabin to find Robin in my bed.... right next to Merlin. They were both sound asleep, so I crawled into the single bunk and went to sleep.

Monday---Trail Angel

I was awakened to the sound of someone banging on the side of my cabin. Robin and Merlin were gone. I'm not sure who was banging, and I didn't try to find out. The sun was up, and I knew I had something to do today.

I wasn't sure what I was supposed to do or what I would need. I figured someone would tell me. I got my day pack together and headed to the bathhouse. I guess breakfast was in session since I was the only one there. I knew I'd be hiking all day, but I didn't want to start out all stinky. Since I had shaved last night, I indulged in a wonderfully long, hot shower. I dressed and made my way to the chow hall. Luckily, the line was still open and there was plenty of food out. I guess being late is not always a bad thing, I was loaded up with a large portion of everything.

As I entered the dining area, Robin, Sam and Mike were all seated out toward the middle. Robin went and got me a coffee and pointed toward the table for me to come sit. Robin didn't speak and neither did I. The tension was obvious, and Mike asked if we were ready for the assignment.

Robin was looking forward to this and there was no way I'd disappoint her no matter what the tension between Sam and I.

Robin was excited and asked Mike what we needed to do. Mike motioned to one of the chow hall staff, and he brought over a large paper grocery bag.

Mike said, "it's pretty simple. Just hike up to the shelter and put this stuff in the cabinet. Just be sure to engage the bear lock."

Robin looked concerned, "bear lock?"

We all laughed. I guess she had never considered the wildlife around here. Sometimes I forget she not only lived a sheltered life, but this was her first time being in a remote area.

Mike assured her she would be okay, and not to be surprised if she came across one. "They are plentiful, but rarely cause a problem."

Robin, again, made us laugh at her reaction, "What do you mean by rarely?"

Mike had to explain how they would break into things if they smell food. Just be sure to lock up the supplies and do not store any left-over food in or near your sleeping area if you decide to stay overnight.

I asked, "do you still want to go?"

"Yeeeesss, I just didn't think about bears."

Sam had not said anything during the entire conversation.

I asked her, "are you going too?"

Her eyes were misty, and she had a slight sniffle as she said, "I'll go if you want me to. I'll understand if you don't."

Mike excused himself to avoid the situation. I wanted Robin to have the hiking experience and camping overnight. If I knew the way there, I think I'd have asked Sam to stay behind. At the time I still didn't know what her involvement was with this organization, so I decided it may be best to have her along.

I made a bit of a production with a heavy sigh before saying it would be okay for her to go along. Truth is, even though Mike said that was all there was to it, things never go as easy as planned. Having someone else going along that has done it before would take the guess work out of it.

Sam seemed relieved and her mood lightened up a bit.

"Is there anything we need to know? It seems too easy."

Sam smiled for the first time. "Yea, it's pretty easy, just put the food in the box and lock it up."

Robin picked up the bag and shook it before looking inside. "What is this, it's so light?"

Sam explained, "those are dehydrated meals for backpacking. We leave a few days' worth of meals up there in case there is an emergency, or someone runs out on the trail. We do this pretty regularly. Sometimes the cabinet is empty, and sometimes it's not."

Robin asked, "do the bears steal the food?"

Sam reassuringly hugged Robin, "no, I've never seen them take the food."

Sam instructed us to go get our backpacks and everything we needed for an overnight campout. Robin headed off to her dorm, since that is where the majority of her things were stored. Sam and I walked toward the cabins.

Sam looked to be sure Robin was far away before she spoke. She was tearing up again and said, "I'm really sorry for last night."

I stopped her and said, "either tell me everything or don't bother to tell me anything. This game you're playing stops right now."

Sam was crying and pleading ignorance about the pick-up and why things got out of hand. I'm not sure I believed her, and we didn't have time to get the full story before getting to the cabins and then back to meet Robin. We were about to spend two days in the woods. I figured I'd get my chance to pin her down on some details. If not, Robin and I would hike down the mountain and not look back.

When we got to the cabins, I went to mine, and she went to hers. I wasn't sure what I'd need. So, I just packed like I was going on an overnight backpacking trip. I forgot to tell Robin what she might need, so I packed a little extra. I looked in my wish bag goodies and stuffed a bottle of scotch in with my food and water. I made sure I had my gun, and, of course, a flashlight. I brought two just in case.

Sam was waiting out by the trail, when she saw my pack, she asked how long I had planned on being away.

"Better safe than sorry."

There was no further discussion. We stopped by the Quartermaster shed, and he gave Sam and Robin packs with everything they needed. It was obvious I had all I needed…and then some.

Sam led the way. It's a good thing since I didn't know how to get there or how long it would take. Robin was in a more forgiving mood I guess and excited to be doing something different. She and Sam walked ahead, and I held back a bit. I overheard the discussion. Sam was telling her the trip really wasn't that long, we could easily make it up and back before supper if we wanted to, but half the fun was staying overnight in the shelter and seeing the stars from the mountain top. I didn't get in the conversation, but wondered how much better it could be than the view from The Commons.

Robin told Sam about her witchcraft book and told her about some of the people she had met.

Sam looked back to me and asked if I minded a little detour along the way. It wouldn't take long. There was something she wanted to show Robin.

I called back, "I've got all day and night, whatever you want."

I let them get a bit further ahead because I didn't want to get in the conversation.

The route took us past the swimming hole and near the area where Robin and I had walked before, except this time we turned off to the right where the trail went downhill toward another stream. I'm amazed at how many streams there are up here and how they branch off in so many directions.

When we got closer, I could see people sitting by the water. They were sitting in a circle of white rocks. And, as in Haven fashion, they were all nude.

Sam turned toward me and said, "sky clad, I'll explain later."

Actually, I already knew what it meant but, no reason to explain. I'll butt out and let Robin get a lesson in Witchcraft.

When we arrived at the circle, Sam asked the older woman if she could and her friend could enter.

The woman responded with a wave of her hand, "yes, all are welcome who wish to embrace the magic."

Sam dropped her pack and her clothes and entered the circle. She looked at Robin and motioned for her to come too. Likewise, Robin undressed and entered the circle.

I stayed up the trail and waited. I could see Sam and Robin sitting on the ground next to the older woman talking. The older woman motioned for the others to come closer to her. The others moved in and it looked like they were answering Robin's questions. I guess we were there for about thirty minutes. It gave me time to think. I'm sitting here alone in the woods. Well, sort of alone. Just alone for the moment. But that's the point. I work alone, I sail alone, pretty much everything alone. *Do I like it? Or is it just a hazard I've created?* I think about the people I avoid, the religious freaks and the people I've met here, the people back home. I don't get it.

I didn't get a chance to dig deep into the subject before I saw Robin and Sam dressing and gathering their packs. When they arrived, I asked Robin if she had found the answers she was looking for. She grinned, "yes, but you have to be naked if you want to find out."

That was actually pretty funny. I guess I won't be finding out what they told her.

Robin and Sam seem to have rekindled their friendship, and I wasn't sure I'd be able to get them apart long enough to have a come to Jesus meeting as they call it with Sam. Maybe the key to finding the answers is getting naked. Which got me to thinking about our time together. The more I thought about it the more I wanted to forgive her too. At least for a little while.

Right now, I don't want to think about this case, Sam, or last night. I just want to be here. I feel like I missed the hike up to Haven. I was so focused on getting to the top, I barely remember the scenery along the way. This is nice, but nothing compared to the hike up. I'm hoping to get a little more like that on this trip.

When we reached the intersecting paths near the swimming hole, Merlin came running up the hill. He was wet, and, of course, he shook and rubbed against me. I'm not sure if this dog likes me or hates me. I started up the trail behind Sam and Robin. I was glad to see him, but I didn't have his bag.

I called out to Sam, "it would appear we added a new member to our excursion. Should I go back and get his supplies?"

She shook her head, "no, he can eat what we eat."

I don't know why I bother to ask. Merlin is on his own and seems to be doing fine. We walked on, and Merlin stayed right beside me.

As far as supplies go, I know we have plenty of food, and I brought enough water and a filter if we needed it. I looked at the girls' backpacks, and I was not sure either of them had ever slept outside before. I guess one night of roughing it wouldn't kill them.

Sam and Robin walked ahead. I could hear them talking, but I have no idea about what. Little by little they were moving further away. I'm older, out of shape, and carrying a heavy pack. I had Merlin for company, so I guess I'm okay. This place is so beautiful with the dark forest and views of the distant hills and valleys. I don't think I've ever been to a place with so many streams and waterfalls. I kind of feel ridiculous that I brought so much water to carry, but I didn't know what to expect.

I didn't have to worry about Merlin getting thirsty, he spent a lot of time wading in the stream and drinking. And, I got to wear some of the water when he'd come running back. After about the third time, I didn't yell at him. I have accepted it for what it is. I have a change of clothes, but I figured it would be in case of bad weather.

I kind of liked that they walked ahead. I thought about the hike coming up to Haven and how I'd like to do it again, but not in a hurry next time. Even this feels a little rushed to me. I have such a hard time just being in the moment. It's a shame, too, since I'm in resort areas all the time. Just rush in, work and rush to the next case. I really need to stop that.

I tried to talk to Merlin about it, but he didn't offer any advice. I thought about how he doesn't truly belong to anybody, but he seems to be happy and healthy. Just come and go as you please and jump in the water any time you feel like it. Just do whatever I please and not worry about it.

As I hiked around a heavily treed bend in the trail, Robin and Sam came in to view. They were sitting on a rock resting. As I approached them, Sam raised her shirt to wipe the sweat from her face exposing her breast as she did. When she saw me looking, she smiled and lingered a bit longer. Sam is a knockout, it's a shame she's so elusive. Merlin brushed up against me and looked up at me. Maybe Merlin can talk. I'll take this as a hint to go with the flow and see how things work out.

I sat down for a quick rest too. I needed it more than I realized. I guess the look on my face must have showed it.

Sam said, "about an hour and a half."

Which means we're about halfway there. Sam leaned against me and apologized for last night and assured me she didn't know anything about it. Sam told me that she has been coming to Haven for a few years on vacation. So, while she helps with office stuff and is aware of the rescue missions, this was the first time anything like this had happened.

I tried to ask her more, but she stopped me, said we'd talk later, and cut her eyes toward Robin. I took the hint and didn't ask anything else. At least the conversation had started, and I had no intention of just dropping it. I fully intend to get some answers later on tonight.

Merlin's ears perked up and he looked back down the trail and barked. We all kept quiet and looked to see what he was barking at. I was able to calm him down with a piece of jerky. Then we were able to hear the faint sound of the siren from The Commons. My first reaction was for us to return to camp. Sam informed me that it could be anything, and since we were accounted for as being off site, there was no reason for us to return. We were a long way from camp and whatever was going on may be over before we could get back. I asked if it had ever gone off before while she was here?

"Yes, once a couple of kids came up missing overnight. Turns out they found a bottle of booze, got drunk and passed out behind the woodshed. They showed up at The Commons and tried to act like nothing was wrong. I wasn't happy about the situation, but I'm not in charge here, so I'll take her advice and finish what we started."

Since we were all on our feet by now, I picked up my pack and started walking again. Merlin was frozen in place looking back toward camp. I half expected him to break out running back. Merlin is a smart dog; I wasn't going to influence him one way or the other. I walked on for about ten minutes before Merlin came running up the trail.

I patted him on the head and said, "I hope we're not making a mistake here." Merlin didn't answer so we kept walking.

I noticed I was walking much slower now. I wasn't in a hurry, and I'm still feeling a little uneasy about not returning to camp. Here I am in the same situation. In a great place and can't relax.

Merlin brushed against my leg as we were walking. Our eyes met as I gave him a pat on his head. He looked happy. I think I'll take his advice and try to do the same.

Every now and then the trail zig zags between the edge of the mountain overlooking rolling hills and valleys, then turns back to view the distant stream flowing between us and the next ridge. The scenery is amazing, part of it looks like something from a fairytale. The view from the side of the mountain is spectacular, but I seem to be drawn more toward the lush dark forest. Something about being in the thick trees feels peaceful and relaxing.

The girls were out of sight again, which was fine with me. I just want to take my time and enjoy the hike. Merlin hung close by as we walked along. This section was rocky and a little hard with the uneven stones. I had to be careful not to turn an ankle. My mind drifted back to the other trails I'd been on since I've been here. I already dreaded the trip back down on these loose rocks.

Unfortunately, thinking about a hard-descending trail also reminded me about Tina, which almost put me in a bad mood. That whole situation in Asheville really pissed me off.

I stopped for a moment, and Merlin stopped too. He looked up at me and as our eyes locked, I said, "I know, I've got to quit thinking." Merlin seemed to agree, he didn't say anything, but he started walking and looked back to see if I was coming.

Thank goodness, the rocky section only lasted about twenty minutes of slow walking. I just hope I don't have another section like that. The next thirty minutes were rather uneventful as far as views go, but the trail was hard packed and not much of an incline. I'm getting pretty tired by this point, so I'll trade views for easy walking.

I could hear the girls up ahead, but I couldn't see them. A few minutes later I could smell the water. Merlin must have smelled it too and ran off and left me. I came to a small clearing where I could see the shelter off to my left, and all I could see beyond that was sky. As I got closer, I could see the large gray rocks protruding out over a huge gorge. Sam was standing near the edge and dancing around. I swear if she jumps off, I'll never speak to her again.

I got close enough to see that jumping off of this ledge was not an option unless you want that to be the last thing you ever do in this life. I walked out just a few feet on the largest rock, and I didn't feel the need to get any closer. Sam tried to get me out to the edge. I told her it looked about a mile to the bottom, a few feet closer wasn't going to change the view that much, so I'll stay where I am. Just as I said it, I thought that would have been a good time for my Namaste joke. Too late now.

Now that my heart is no longer pounding in my ears, I could hear the water. I walked out in front of the shelter, and I could see a small waterfall. I walked closer and Robin and Merlin were in the water just below the fall. Merlin was jumping in and out of the pool, and Robin was bathing. I hope I didn't unpack my soap in all the packing and unpacking I've done lately. I'll wait until Robin is finished, and if Merlin is still down there, he's getting a bath too.

The shelter was divided into two sections, each having four sleeping bunks, a table and a stool to sit on. I found the supply room located on the back side. There was plenty of food still in the lock box, so we could eat anything we wanted and have more than enough to leave behind.

I found a broom and a dustpan; that was all the cleaning supplies I could find. I took the broom into the shelter and began knocking down spider webs and making sure the bunks were void of any critters. I picked out a bunk that I hoped would not be in the direct sunlight in the morning.

I blew up my mattress and laid my sleeping bag on it. After that, I checked my pack, and my toilet kit and a change of clothes were all there, so I'm feeling good about this trip. I heard something behind me, and I turned to see Robin standing there totally naked.

A bit shocked, I grinned and said, "I purposely didn't go down to the water so I wouldn't embarrass you. It appears that wouldn't have been an issue."

Robin just laughed and said, "you need to lighten up. I have shampoo if you need some?"

I rolled my eyes up as if I was looking at my bald head.

Now Robin was embarrassed, realizing what she had said. She laughed awkwardly as she went into the other section of the shelter. I figured this was as good a time as any to go get cleaned up. I got my stuff together and went down to the water. I was feeling self-conscious about bathing out in the open, but I just have to get over it.

Damn, the water is cold, but it felt good to get clean again. I tried to make quick work of it…get in and get out. No, that just wasn't going to happen. Robin and Sam came down to the pool.

Both of them laughed at me conspiratorially knowing how uncomfortable I would be. It didn't surprise me when Sam took off her clothes and got in, but it did surprise me when Robin undressed again and joined us. Sam came over, wrapped her legs around me and started kissing me. I looked over at Robin.

She put her hands over her eyes and peeked between her fingers, saying, "don't mind me, I promise not to peek.

Right now, I'm having one of those angels on one shoulder and the devil on the other telling me what to do. Sam and I kiss for a while. Robin must have sensed I was uncomfortable with her watching. I actually think she wanted to watch, but she left and walked back toward the shelter. Sam is a kinky girl; she seemed a bit disappointed and watched as Robin walked out of sight.

Sam stood up, turned around and said, "fuck me."

Even with the cold water, I was hard and entered Sam from behind. The cold water made her skin cold in contrast to her warm soft inside. She felt amazing. I went slow, because I didn't want this to end too soon. But Sam makes that hard. She is loud and plays with herself with enthusiasm. She cums easy, and there's something about a woman having an orgasm that sends me over the top. I pushed in her as deeply as possible to let loose inside her.

As soon as we finished, she turned around and wrapped her lips around me. *Oh my god, I can't take it.* I had to make her stop. I mean I love it, but I'm way too sensitive right now. I think Sam knows this; she just likes to be in charge. Which is fine with me. *Why are the crazy girls so good at this?*

We both bathed for a while without talking. I was getting used to the water, and now I was in no hurry to get out. Sam started the conversation by asking how much I knew about the school where Robin came from. I told her how the situation unfolded that led me here. We had talked about this before, but this conversation was different. Sam told me the reason she approached Robin in the first place was because she knew about the school and her parents running the school. Many of the rescues were runaways and kids from the school, which was one of the recruiting places for the rescues. Since Robin was coming here, she wanted to keep a close eye on her.

I still wasn't sure which side she was on.

"So, you do work here?" I inquired.

Sam shrugged noncommittally, "no, not really, I've been here several times, and I got involved in the office stuff. That's how I found out what was going on. I don't know everything. Just that there is a connection."

I didn't like what I was hearing.

"Do you think Robin is involved or what?"

"No, I don't. All she talked about was going to get her sister and coming here to hide out. I don't think she'd bring her here if she knew some of the girls had been at the school."

I thought about the things I saw at the school, which makes sense, *Robin might not know what was going on, but what didn't make sense was her mother sending her here if she knew the other girls were here.* I guess I was thinking out loud.

Sam said, "her mother might not know."

My look may have been enough, but I asked anyway. "How could she have not known?"

Sam's face reddened, and she teared up. "This was the part I helped with; Haven is billed as a hippy commune resort. It is, but we don't talk about the other stuff. We target places where troubled kids are. If they are identified, we secretly make them an offer to escape. Even the rescues don't know where they are going until they get here."

I really don't know how or who contacted her mother. Maybe the recruiter got caught and used the backup plan. They all carry Haven sales packages."

"So, how long have you been doing this," I demanded?"

Sam was visibly upset and pleaded that she was telling the truth, she only comes a few weeks a year, she just happened to know how to do the brochures and set up the website stuff. Sam went on to explain she found out this year about the B dorm kids and thought it would be exciting to go on a mission.

I'm not sure if I believe her or not. I got up and walked out to the rock ledge and sat down. Here I am again in a place that should be a paradise, and I'm having to deal with shit. *It's no wonder I like to spend so much time alone.*

I sat down on the ledge looking out over the distant hills as far as I could see. A part of me wanted to get my stuff and walk back to camp, but I don't think I could make it before dark. I wasn't out there long before Robin came out and joined me. Neither of us said anything for a long time.

Robin spoke first and simply said, "I believe her."

"Why," I asked?

Robin remained quiet for a bit. "I don't know, I just do, and it really doesn't matter anyway. From what I see everything around here is just make believe. People come here to get away from something, be free, do what you want, then walk away when your time is up. We're going to do the same aren't we?"

"I guess we are."

I laid down looking up at the sky, thinking about all the people I've met on this adventure, and I have to admit I think she is right. No one has made me any promises, or commitments. Sam may be fun, but she's full of crap as far as I can tell. She's here to play her game and go back to whatever life she has elsewhere.

Cassie made it clear she was unavailable. *So, why should I care?* I seem to be the only one looking for answers.

Robin laid down and put her head on my shoulder and said, "Rabbit."

"What?"

Robin pointed up to a cloud and giggled, "it looks like a rabbit."

I lightened up and laughed a little and agreed that it did look like a rabbit.

I don't think I've done this since I was a kid. I wanted to see things in the clouds after the rabbit shifted into a fluffy undescriptive cloud again. Maybe my imagination was lost. All I can see is blue sky and large white plumes.

Robin pointed over to the western sky and says, "Teddy bear."

"I don't see a teddy bear," I said disagreeably.

She tried to point out the features, but I didn't see what she meant. We laid there a bit longer, and she said, "helicopter."

I scanned the clouds and didn't see it. Then I heard it. I was a real helicopter flying low coming up from the gorge and disappeared between two mountain peaks.

Sam came out to the ledge and asked if we saw the helicopter and wanted to know where it was going.

We both pointed toward the last place we saw it, and Sam said, "that's toward Haven. There's nothing else in that direction for a long way. What kind of helicopter was it?

Neither one of us knew since it came and went so fast and was a long way out. Sam seemed concerned, but there was nothing we could do about it. By this time, I knew we couldn't make it back before dark. After a brief discussion we agreed there were a million possibilities and, in every scenario we discussed, the answer was the same. There was nothing we could do about it, if there was a problem in Haven. They've gotten along without us long before we got here.

I'm not saying I don't care about a possible situation in Haven, but I'm not going to worry about it either. Maybe I'm starting to get it. *I don't have to have the answers.* Right now, the only things I'm concerned with is gathering firewood and cooking something. I'm getting hungry.

We walked back to the shelter, and I found Merlin asleep on my bunk on top of my sleeping bag. *That damn dog better be dry.* Either way I made him get off. Sam and Robin seemed to think that was funny. Just to be sure he didn't sneak back in, I moved everything to a top bunk. I'll move it back when I'm ready for bed.

We went out and gathered firewood for the night and got it going. I got out my backpacking chair and assembled it to sit by the fire. It was obvious neither of them had done any real camping since they had never seen a backpack chair before. I finally asked what they carried up for their overnighter. Both looked surprised and neither answered. Robin brought a sleeping bag and a change of clothes, and no food. Sam pretty much the same except she also had a box of wine.

I guess I should have asked before we left, but since we were hauling food up to stock the shelter, I can't be mad. I was well stocked, and the quality of food in my pack was better than what we hauled up. I dug out my gear and boiled water for our dehydrated meals. One of my favorites is teriyaki chicken, rice and vegetables. I bought two of the big packs since that was the only size that had at the store. I had plenty of other meals, but this is what I'm fixing.

I hope we can find utensils in the storage area, or we'll be taking turns eating. I sent the girls out to look. I checked my stuff as well, but didn't come up with any extras. I figured I could always whittle a spoon from a wide stick if I needed to. I started looking among our firewood for a possible spoon, but they showed up with plastic utensils before I got started.

The water was starting to boil, so I poured the hot water into the pouches and checked the time. I took my chair and sat by the fire waiting for our food to be ready. I like Sam and Robin, but I'm not giving up my chair. They rolled a couple of cut logs closer to the fire and plopped down after their struggle with the logs.

We all pulled out our drink of choice and melted ourselves into a relaxing campfire mode. Sam had a collapsible cup she used with her boxed wine, and Robin was drinking from a leather bota bag. I didn't bother to ask. I didn't know if she brought it up with her or if Sam supplied her. I really don't like it. My gaze must have lingered longer than I thought, and she was reading my thoughts. Robin sternly informed me I was not in charge of her anymore. I guess she's right. I'm not sure what I was hired to do, and since I was provided false information in the beginning, so any contract was voided. *Or, at least that's my story.* I guess I could fuss about it, but what good would it do.

It looked like enough time had passed for our dehydrated meals to be ready. I divided it all out between us from the two bags. There was plenty to go around, even Merlin got a good portion.

I wasn't sure how he would react. I love the stuff. Merlin dug in and finished it off pretty quick and took turns begging from all of us until we gave in and shared more with him.

Darkness had settled in upon us, I was beginning to feel the warming effects of the scotch, and the girls seemed to be having a good time laughing and whispering back and forth. I'm sure they were talking about me part of the time from the glances as they went back and forth. I'm feeling pretty good, so I really don't care.

I needed to pee, so I walked away from the fire to the edge of the woods and was amazed at how cold it was away from the fire. My equipment is good stuff, I hope their sleeping bags will be enough to keep them warm tonight. I got back to the fire as quickly as I could and got close to warm up. Sam and Robin weren't dressed for cold weather. I hoped they had something warm to put on.

They were both sitting close to the fire, getting cold a little at a time when you don't realize it until it's too late. I suggested they put on warmer clothes, and it was obvious they didn't have what they needed. We all went into the shelter to see what they had. Neither of them had a jacket, so they put on layers of what they had. While we were there, I checked their sleeping bags which were also not up to keeping them warm.

I checked the supplies and there were no other blankets or sleeping bags, but there was an extra ground pad. I took it and my pad and put them on the floor. They were narrow, but if we just use them to support our upper body, then we can use one bag under us and the other two along with my bag liner to cover us.

I boiled some water and filled a water bottle to put between us. I was getting tired by this point, so I laid down in the middle of the pad and covered up. Sam and Robin both got under the covers too. We hadn't discussed an arrangement, but I ended up in the middle, which was fine with me. Merlin came in and laid at the end of the sleeping bags on top of my feet.

At first this seemed cozy between two women and a dog to keep my feet warm, but it didn't take long before I was feeling cramped and it since it never fails, I had to go pee again. I slid out doing my best not to fan the covers and stumbled outside. The fire had burned down to just embers at this point, and I think it had gotten colder. I took care of business as quickly as possible and went back inside.

Sam and Robin had huddled up together. I slid in beside Sam this time. I wanted to be on the outside in case I needed to get up again.

Merlin moved between mine and Sam's legs, which kind of pushed me to the edge of the pad and nearly uncovered. I scooted over and covered myself as much as I could without uncovering Robin.

Tuesday

I must have been more tired than I realized. The next thing I knew, it was morning. Sam and Robin were still asleep. The sun was coming up. I was glad to see the deepest portion of the gorge was East, so we got light early, and it didn't feel half bad when standing in the direct sunlight.

We hadn't discussed our plans for the day. I didn't know if we were hanging out or headed back as soon as we got up. I decided I wasn't in a hurry to get back, so I put some wood in the pit and got the fire going again. We had plenty of water, so I put on a pot to boil. I could get used to this. I hate feeling rushed, and right now I have no place to be. I made coffee and oatmeal, then sat by the fire to eat.

It's quiet here. I can hear the waterfall and birds chirping in the distance. My body was feeling heavy, like I could go to sleep again. I could feel a presence…I was no longer alone. I didn't want to open my eyes. I lingered as long as I could.

When I opened my eyes, Robin came over, kissed me on the cheek and said, "thank you."

She sat down on the log near the fire. I took off my jacket and put it over her shoulders.

"You hungry?"

Robin asked, "what do you have?"

I pointed to the bag where I had gathered all mine and some of the storage food together, just in case we stayed for a while.

Robin wanted oatmeal as well, so I fixed all I had which should be enough for her and Sam.

I fixed Merlin chicken and rice. His took a little longer, and he begged for a bite of oatmeal while his was getting ready. I took a bowl into Sam while it was still hot along with a cup of coffee.

I hated to wake her up, but this was the last of the oatmeal that I had brought up.

Sam rolled over and took the coffee. After a few sips she said, "I'm worried about you."

"Why," I asked?

Sam laughed, "you had two women in bed with you, and you fell asleep!"

"That worries me too, but in my defense, I have to behave around Robin. She's the daughter of a client so she is 100% off limits."

Sam just shook her head as if she understood.

This seemed like a good time to put a suggestion out there to see what kind of response I'd get.

I told Sam, "I'd love to come back up to Haven for a vacation. It's an interesting and beautiful place, unfortunately, I haven't been able to actually get involved and enjoy it."

She replied, "yea, I like it here."

It looks like I'm not going to get an invitation to make future plans so I let it go and went back out by the fire. Merlin's food should be ready by now. I poured it in a bowl. It was hot but he did his best to eat it anyway. Sam finally emerged, and I fixed another round of coffee for all of us.

It was still cold but sitting in the direct sun and close to the fire felt nice. I was relaxed and enjoying myself for a change. I don't know why I don't hike and camp more. I like it a lot. I don't know why I feel guilty when I get away and try to relax. I hate being rushed, and I'm the one doing most of the pushing.

Robin was waving her hand trying to get my attention. I must have been in deep thought. Sam and Robin seemed to think it was funny that I was so zoned out.

I wryly growled, "I'm glad I can entertain you."

I don't know why I thought about this just now, but I flashed back to a scout camping trip. *Everyone thought I was asleep, if fact I'm not sure I wasn't. but I joined in on their conversation for a few lines, then started snoring again. The guys talked about this a bunch the next morning.*

Sam moved her log next to me, sat down, and leaned against me. "So, what's on your mind?"

"Just trying to figure myself out, I guess?"

Sam looked like she was about to slip off in thought as well as she shrugged, "me too."

We must have been thinking the same thing as we asked Robin, "How about you?"

Robin responded after a big sigh. "I'm beginning to think I'm the only sane person on the planet. I just want to be safe, happy and healthy without all the games and make-believe crap." Then she got up and walked down toward the waterfall.

Sam and I sat there in silence. I'm not sure if that was aimed toward us or not and right now may not be a good time to go ask her. I'm trying to think back and remember if I'd done anything that would have caused that reaction. As far as Sam goes, she is a game. I know nothing about her other than she likes sex. I remember in my younger days that would have been my preferred relationship. I prefer something deeper these days, and I know that's not going to happen.

I thought about Cassie and how much I really liked her, but it was obvious that wasn't going to happen either. I need to get my head in the game and realize I'm just a passing observer. No matter what takes place up here, I'll be leaving it all behind soon. Having that revelation, I felt much better and sort of had a don't give a damn moment. I got up, took Sam by the hand, and we went in the shelter and had sex. Nothing mind blowing, but one of those things where it might be our last time, and I'd regret it if we didn't. The strange thing is I felt like we connected that time. Not like we were going somewhere, but more like an understanding, we just needed to use each other.

It was beginning to warm up, and I decided to go down by the fall. I didn't invite Sam and didn't go looking for Robin. I just wanted to get in the water by myself. I undressed and eased into the cold water. It took several minutes to overcome the shock before I was able to swim around. I rolled over to swim on my back and saw Robin up at the top of the fall. We waved to each other but didn't speak. It was too late to be embarrassed about being naked in front of her, and I figured I might as well not fight it anymore.

When I looked up again, she was gone. I could hear other voices so I got out of the water, got dressed to go see if others had arrived. When I got back to the shelter, there was an older couple I didn't recognize from Haven. I learned this was a loop off of one of the larger hiking destinations. The main attraction was the gorge and the waterfall being so close to the shelter. It was a good place for a quick overnight hike. This is definitely something I'd like to do again, but under different circumstances.

While we were talking a helicopter flew up through the gorge again toward Haven.

The man said, "it's a good thing you were up here, you missed all the excitement last night."

Our surprised reaction was obvious, and the man wasn't expecting that. He seemed afraid for a moment.

Sam asked, "what excitement?"

He hesitated before speaking again. He'd heard there was a big fight and two of the campers were missing. He went on to explain they weren't there but heard some other hikers talking about it back on the main trail.

I had wanted to stay longer, but it looked like our plans had changed. Sam went into the shelter and packed her bag. I asked Robin what she wanted to do. Personally, I have no obligation to the people in Haven. In fact, I was there under vague pretenses, and my ultimate mission was to locate Robin and keep her safe. With that, it might be better if we stayed away. We talked about our options, and Robin felt like we should at least accompany Sam back to Haven then decide on what we were going to do.

Sam was stressed when we got back to the shelter to pack. She was upset that we had not already packed up and ready to go back. It only took a few minutes to get my stuff together. Sam's behavior was not that of a person distant from the working of Haven. Robin and I looked at each other as if we were reading our thoughts.

I asked her again, "what do you want to do?"

Robin wanted to make sure Sam got back to Haven. We got our gear together and left the couple sitting by the fire.

We were walking at a quick pace and not talking for a long while. We reached the section with the large loose rocks. I fell and cut both knees. Sam seemed agitated with the delay. I got out my first-aid kit to clean and bandage my knees. It wasn't too bad, but blood had covered the top of my socks. Sam was growing impatient. I told her to go ahead, I'd catch up in a bit. In most situations, a team wouldn't separate, but Sam walked on agitated.

Robin sat down on a rock beside me, and we watched Sam walk out of sight. I tried to get Merlin to go with her, but he sat down beside me.

I could have gotten up, but I wanted her to get a good distance ahead. I needed to have a conversation with Robin about this entire chain of events. I was getting my thoughts together and thinking of a way to convince her we may need to leave Haven.

Robin spoke first, "I want to leave."

Well, that went better than expected, I thought to myself.

"That sounds like a good idea to me. Any place in mind you want to go?"

Robin was crying. "Let's go get my sister and run away."

This was the first time she mentioned her sister to me. Sam had said Robin talked about her in their conversations. My mind went straight to all the legal reasons I couldn't do this. I'd have to convince Robin I wanted to help her, but I couldn't go to jail for kidnapping her sister.

The only option I can think of at the moment would be getting her mother involved. When I mentioned this to Robin, her gentle tears turned to sobs. I hated that I caused such a bad reaction, but I didn't see another option at the moment. I held her close and let the situation play itself out. I opened my pack and found my only clean shirt and handed it to her as I helped dry her face.

She pulled it away and looked at it.

I said, "it's clean, go ahead."

As if on cue, she blew her nose on my shirt. After giving herself a final wipe of her face, she offered the shirt back. I grimaced and told her to hang on to it, just in case.

Robin stood up and put on her pack.

We better get going. I got my stuff together, and we started down the trail. It didn't take long and she began to talk. Robin began by telling me about her mother, who was really her aunt. This I knew, but I remained quiet and let her vent whatever was on her mind. Her parents were killed in a car crash, and her aunt took her in to raise. She later met the Reverend, they got married and had her sister.

Things were not always bad. The school was much smaller, and, of course, the others were not there. The Reverend had a big ego for as long as she could remember, but he wasn't mean back then. It all changed when he molested an underaged girl, and she reported it.

Mom cried a lot during that time. She talked about her plans to leave, but didn't know how. I was only six at the time, but I remember it well enough. My sister was around one, so she doesn't remember the times before. Mom expected her husband to be arrested and the school to close.

But that didn't happen. What was to follow became much worse.

She continued, "instead of him going off to jail we all were imprisoned at the school. It took me a long time to figure it out. A lot of new kids showed up at the school. Boys and girls at first, they would come and go. Then, later on, the property was divided, and we were not allowed to go near the fence. By this time, it was all girls staying there."

We still have boys and girls in the school, but it was all girls on the other side of the fence. Every Friday afternoon all the school kids would go to the gym and later on you wouldn't hear the girls on the other side of the fence until late Sunday night."

One Friday, I snuck out and saw the girls getting into van and leave. I got caught, and the Reverend beat me and my mom when she tried to stop him. I remember him saying he'd go to jail if we talked about it."

I got grounded and was locked in a dark room and didn't get fed for a long time. I'm not sure how long I was there, but I was starving by the time I got out. As long as I stayed away from the fence and didn't talk about it, I was left alone. I didn't talk about it, but it was obvious these girls were prostitutes living on the other side."

Little by little things changed. People would come and go, and I suspected drugs were being used and sold. The police came and went regularly. At first, I thought the Reverend was being investigated, but it became obvious he was part of the scheme. Mom moved into our bedroom. She said it was because he snored, but I knew better."

Mom and I talked, but we had to whisper, and she always turned on music when we did. She talked about a plan where we would run away to this magical place where we would all be happy, and we could do anything and eat anything we wanted. She would describe this place, and it was always in the mountains. It looked a lot like the mountains around Haven, but she never mentioned other people being there. I loved hearing the stories, and she described all the adventures we would have. I loved her stories, and she said she would tell me the greatest secret of all when we got there."

I wished those nights would never end, but they did. Mom moved into her own room. Some nights she would stay there, and some nights she would stay with the Reverend. I could hear them having sex."

Robin sort of chuckled as she said her mom made a lot of noise when she was in her room alone too. Her tone then changed at that point as she described how her mother started staying in her own room most of the time and stopped taking care of herself. She didn't wash her clothes and rarely brushed her hair. Robin stopped talking for a while.

Then she said, "I really miss when we used to take turns brushing each other's hair."

Robin sat down on a rock and took off her pack. She wiped off her face with my shirt and took out a water bottle.

I was getting hungry, so I dug into my stash and held up several options. "You want cold trail food or hot trail food?"

"Cold would be fine."

I laid out all the stuff for her to choose from. I started with a protein bar and some dried fruit. Merlin was giving me a hard stare. I didn't have much in the line of cold trail food I thought a dog would eat. I handed Robin a pack of salmon, and I opened the other pack and spooned it out on a rock for Merlin. He lapped it in about a second and asked for more. I didn't have any more.

I opened a small pack of peanut butter, and Merlin began to whine eagerly and wiggle around. I removed the top of the pack and let Merlin lick the container. He didn't stop until all of it was gone. I think he would have continued until the taste was gone from the container.

I was still hungry, but didn't want to take the time to fix hot trail food. I packed up our trash and got ready to leave. Merlin took off down the trail before I could get my pack on. We caught up with him about a mile down the trail as he was lying in a creek. I told Robin to keep walking as I stopped to see if my suspicion was about to be confirmed. Robin passed by and spoke to Merlin. At first, I thought she would get the greeting, but no, he came running over and gave me a doggie shake and covered me with doggie water.

I grinned and couldn't get mad.

Robin laughed so hard, she had to sit down and said, "I'm going to pee on myself."

Speaking of which, this seemed like a good time for a pee. I turned away and had to keep moving so Merlin would stay out of the stream. *You'd think a dog would know better, but I guess not.*

Robin called out, "guys are so lucky," as she stepped off the trail dropping her pants as she did.

I held on to Merlin. I didn't think she needed his assistance at the moment.

Once again, I smelled like wet dog as we continued on our way. Funny thing about hiking, the trail looks different when going in the opposite direction. I wish I'd have picked out some landmarks coming up so I'd know how far away we were. Robin had never been here either, so that didn't help.

We walked for about an hour without talking. We both heard the scream at the same time. "Stop it! Stop it!"

We were frozen in place, then we heard the sound of splashing and laughter. Merlin knew where we were as he ran down to the swimming hole. The next sound was a big splash. I didn't have to be there to know Merlin had jumped from the ledge out into the water.

I could use a rest, so we walked down to the swimming area. As usual, it was full of naked people. I was tempted to jump in clothes and all. Not from modesty but to get rid of the doggie smell. I was too tired at this point, so I put my pack on the ground and laid down using the pack as a pillow. Robin came over and laid her head on my shoulder. That lasted for about a second as she sat up waving her hand in front of her face to move the smell away.

It was my turn to laugh hard enough I was about to pee in my pants. I was content to just lay there to rest looking up at the clouds trying to find shapes. Robin undressed and jumped in. The water must have been pretty cold from the sound she made as she came up for air.

For a church girl, she holds her own at cussing.

I must have dozed off for a few minutes, when I felt myself being sprayed with water. I was about to blame Merlin, but it was Cassie and Andrea doing their imitation of a doggie shake with their hair. I didn't mind them doing it. Cassie put a towel down on the ground next to me, and Andrea went back in the water.

Cassie asked if I heard the details from last night.

"No, we just got back, and this is as far as we made it."

Cassie said, "two of the kids are missing from the B dorm. I heard they were taken after a fight with some of the staff. We were called to The Commons, but they didn't give us any details. They just did a roll call and let us go."

Cassie asked about Sam.

I told her Sam was in a hurry to get back, so she left us and rushed back.

Cassie noticed my knees, "ouch, that looks like it hurt, how'd you do that?"

I didn't want to go into to details about how Sam had left us when I got hurt. Her tone seemed a little off when asking about Sam, and I didn't want to give her more reason to have hard feelings toward her. *Not that I care at this point.*

Cassie was being more friendly than normal, almost flirty. I wanted to tell her that we were leaving, but I didn't. There are several things I'm going to miss about this place, and she is one of them. Cassie called out to Andrea that it was time to get ready for dinner. I didn't realize it was so late. Robin, Andrea, and a bunch of other girls were playing together on the other side. When Cassie called out, all of them came over to our side and got out.

I was ready for food too. My trail lunch had long since run out. I was feeling overly protective of Robin since we didn't know what had happened yesterday. I asked her if she needed to go back to her dorm to get ready for chow. I was glad to hear she had everything she needed at Sam's cabin.

We got our packs together and headed to the cabins. We parted ways to go shower and get ready for chow. I didn't want her to know I was concerned for her safety because of the incident. So much of this felt connected, and I don't like it. I showered as fast as I could and waited outside the bathhouse for her to come out.

I am feeling so much better now. Robin leaned close to me and made a display of sniffing me.

"Funny," I said sarcastically.

Smiling, Robin took my hand, and we walked to the chow hall.

There was talking going on, but it wasn't loud like normal. Kids were sitting with their parents and not up running around playing with the other kids the way they usually did. I never thought I'd miss seeing that and hearing all the rowdy voices, but I did. I don't like to see people scared. The staff may not be talking, but it would appear the guests are.

Mike, Randy, and most of the usual staff were not in their normal places in the chow hall. Little things like that are noticeable and cause problems. Robin and I made it through the line, and we sat at Mike's usual table. I was hoping some of the crew would come in, but they didn't. Sam didn't show up either.

Cassie and Andrea joined us. Andrea didn't seem phased by the events, which is strange, since she is so in tune with things. I didn't get a chance to ask before she moved in close to my face and said," some things I know and some things I don't."

Cassie gave Andrea a stern look and said, "don't be rude."

Andrea looked hurt and apologized. Then added, "I just want to be a kid; I don't want everyone thinking I know everything about everybody. I don't!"

I was surprised by her outburst; she is normally so quiet and ladylike. I guess you can only hold back for so long. I also have to admire her for standing up for herself.

She was still steaming mad. I leaned closer, almost nose to nose.

"You may not know everything, but there is something I really need to know right now."

She put her hand on her hips and huffed, "what?"

"Do you know if the frozen ice cream machine is working tonight?"

Her mood lightened, but she didn't answer my question.

And I had to go check for myself. It wasn't. That's okay, the canteen will be open later, and they will have it.

Robin went to a table where some of the other kids were sitting. I went out to sit on the porch and rock. Cassie and Andrea came out a few minutes later. I love having them around, but right now I have a lot of thinking to do. I closed my eyes to relax. It didn't take long before my body felt heavy and relaxed. I guess they got the hint and didn't hang around.

Robin and I didn't discuss an exit plan. It's Tuesday and the lift wouldn't be running today. The thought of hiking down didn't sound like much fun at the moment, and we had acquired more stuff since I got here. I really don't want to pack it down. That heavy feeling gave way to sleep.

I woke up to the sound of a whistle off in the distance. I could see to volleyball court from when I was sitting. This was the first time I had seen anyone using it. The kid standing near the sideline must have been the scorekeeper, ref, or something like that. One thing for sure, he liked the whistle a lot. It was as good a time as any to go looking for Mike or someone that would operate the lift so Robin and I could leave.

I checked Mike's cabin first, and no one was there. Gladys was in the laundry, but she didn't know where he was at. I checked the garage, the door was unlocked, but Randy was not there. I checked the lift and the guy there said he just got there and didn't know if anyone had come or gone, he was just there to give a break to the regular guy. I didn't know where else to look other than the B dorm people and right now, I don't know if I trust anything they might say, and I didn't want them to know we were thinking about leaving.

I heard a banging noise, at least it wasn't drumming this time. It gave me an idea to go see the people in the woods. I hadn't actually made an attempt to have a conversation with any of them. So, now is as good a time as any to give it a shot. I was hoping to find Robin first so she could go with me, but I couldn't find her. I walked out behind the chow hall and Merlin was laying on the deck next to the back door. It looked like he had just finished a bowl of food. When he saw me, he came over and went with me out into the woods.

The camp areas started about a half mile behind the chow hall. I'm not sure how far the trail goes. I just wanted to find a group and see if they knew anything about the missing kids.

I could smell smoke, and I'm sure there should be people close by. We walked on for about fifteen more minutes before we came across a group of six people camped at a lean-to.

They seemed friendly enough, so Merlin and I asked permission to enter their camp. They greeted Merlin like an old friend which didn't surprise me. They didn't pet me on the head but welcomed me in also. It was no secret, everyone seemed to know I was an investigator. They just didn't know why I was there. In this case it worked to my advantage, since they assumed I had information about the missing kids. Their questions pretty much filled in the blanks. They thought it was funny they tried to keep the rescues a secret, but everyone there knows. The kids sneak out to the woods to hang with the hippies and smoke pot. I didn't have to convince them I didn't know anything, since it was common knowledge we had been doing the trail angel the previous night.

It concerns me a bit that so many people know who I am and keeping tabs on my location. I didn't question any of this, I just listened to see how much they would tell me. I became concerned when I found out one of the kids was Amy, the young prostitute that propositioned me and another was one of the kids that rode up with us. They had no way of knowing, but they mentioned the kids knew each other from some kind of religious school.

That scared me. I wouldn't be surprised if there were others in similar situations, but it is just too convenient. Robin was sent here to a place where some of those particular students show up. I don't trust anyone at this point, so I'm going to find Robin and get out of here even if we have to walk down.

I again checked Mike's, the garage and the activity building to see if Robin or any of the workers were around. I went back to my cabin, and Robin was there. She had heard the same information and was suspicious about the connection too. Robin had decided to move out of A dorm and brought everything to my cabin. She said no one acted suspicious about her move since most of her stuff was at Sam's cabin anyway.

We discussed walking down, but we were tired and it would be dark before we could get to town. The best option was to find Mike or Randy and get permission to get a lift down. I told Robin about the woods people. She was interested and said she hated that she didn't get to go.

I told her if we don't get a ride down, maybe we can move out into the woods also.

I said that as a joke, but she sounded like she'd like to go stay in the woods for a while and live like hippies. It's been nice being with her on the trail and the thought of going on a hippy retreat with her sounded like fun. I'm ready to be finished with whatever this is and just maybe we can be friends after.

Robin and I hung out at the cabin reading and talking. I even got the sax out a played for a few minutes. I couldn't get into it, so I put it away. I went in the cabin and got out a bottle of scotch and took it out to my rocker. When Robin saw what I was doing she excused herself and walked over to Sam's cabin; a few minutes later she returned with a bota bottle which I'm sure she filled with wine. I think I'll ignore it and claim plausible deniability. This place is crazy anyway. In fact, this girl has no idea what makes for a normal life. Robin asked me about the woods people, and in exchange, I asked about the school and the B dorm people.

Robin met some of the people that had been at the school. She had not met them before arriving here. It was pretty much by accident that she met them. She attended one of the sessions around The Commons, and they mentioned some of the businesses and local attractions which led her to believe they had been at the school. She never tried to have a conversation with them in fear she would be accused of being a part of the scheme.

I had to laugh at that part, since I had gotten the same reaction from some of the people here.

I told her about the woods people and how they reminded me of the people I met when I was doing security services for rock groups way back in my pre-law enforcement days. I look back on those days and I'm somewhat envious I can't just live day by day and not give a shit about anything. I'm feeling the scotch kicking in, and I wondered out loud about just playing my sax on the streets and living a simple life.

I held up my bottle to see if was close to the bottom, close enough I went ahead and finished it off. I had a good supply from my wish bag run, so I went in to get another one. I was a little unsteady on my feet, and I was okay with that. I got a feeling before this night was over, I'd be a lot unsteady on my feet. I picked up Robin's bota bag...it was about half full.

I told her to go reload, we were going on an adventure.

Robin came back with a filled bota bag and wearing a day pack. It looked like she was well supplied.

I said, "wait a second." I went and got another bottle, one of the bigger ones. I might find some drinking buddies along the way.

We set off holding hands and walking like we were on a mission. By the time we reached the bathhouse area, I was about out of breath, "we need to slow down, this might be a long night."

I was thinking I may have made a mistake, but it was too late now. I started this, and I'm going to see where it leads. We walked on, not really talking much.

Thank goodness, I remembered my flashlight this time. It was getting dark when we reached the first camp. I recognized one couple from my previous trip. There were about a dozen more around the campfire. This looked like a mellow bunch and there were no drums in sight. *I hope it stays that way.* The smell of marijuana was heavy in the air and everyone looked high and just having a good time doing nothing.

We were welcomed into the group and without so much as an introduction, we were offered a hit on a large bong. I waved it away and hoped Robin would too.

I held up the big bottle, "this is more my thing."

They looked happy enough about that and seemed eager to join in. I broke the seal and took the first of many pulls before passing it to the woman next to me.

It was strange no one cared who anyone was in the real world. Someone had seen me with the sax and the next few minutes I was the center of attention. I talked about buying my first sax in a pawn shop and had to bend the keys with pliers to make the pads seat. I taught myself how to play and read music. I played in two big bands, and I was the weak link, so I quit. I loved busking and this was something this crowd could relate to.

I only busked a few times...in Wilmington and Asheville. I was nervous as hell, but I liked it. Someone asked how much money I made, and I can't remember if I counted the last time, so I didn't mention that one. I told them I didn't know because I gave the money away to some homeless kids. Which is the truth, I might add. I got a lot of, "that's so cool."

After that, the conversation moved around the group and people talked about traveling around, staying at various shelters and sharing tips of the areas they go to. To hear them tell it, it sounded like a great adventure. I guess it is all in perspective. I go to resort areas several times a month, work and run to the next assignment. Sometimes I take a moment to go look at the ocean or gaze at a mountain view before I rush off again.

Work and travel alone just plain sucks. The more I'm away from it I become more aware of it. This place is kind of like a break in reality for normal people. *If normal is a real thing*. There are no expectations and there seems to be very few rules. This is different than any place I'd ever been to. I'm wondering what Robin thinks. I hope we get away from here tomorrow and get some answers. I hate the fact she went from one nut house to another. As far as I can see, the only thing they both have in common is lots of sex.

The free and willing kind sounds like a lot more fun than the forced and abusive sex from the school. I thought about Amy and how she didn't escape prostitution even when she didn't have to.

I guess my buzz and being in deep thought made me zone out. I felt the woman next to me give me a nudge. The bottle had made its round and was back to me again. I took a smaller hit and passed it on. I knew I was getting drunk, and I wondered how Robin was holding up. I made sure she was close by the entire time we were there. I didn't want anyone to take advantage of her. I also wanted to be sure she would be able to walk back to the cabin on her own. She's small, but I don't want to carry her.

I heard drums off in the distance and someone yelled, "enough already!" I thought that was funny as hell coming from one of the hippies. I actually fell off my log laughing.

Robin came over to help me up and said, "I think I need to take you to bed."

I know she didn't mean that in a sexual way, but everyone applauded and congratulated me for the score.

When we got away from the fire, the night air was cold, Robin wrapped her arms in mine, and we walked the best we could under the circumstances.

Robin said, "I hope you know what I meant back there?"

I sighed, "yes, but my ego needed the boost, and no reason to explain."

The rest of the walk back was quiet, other than to state to obvious that it was cold. We made a quick stop at the bathhouse which was nice because it was warm, then a quick dash to the cabin.

I was worn out. I got in my bunk and was out in a flash. I must have been sleeping pretty deep. I woke up in the middle of the night to go pee, and Robin had moved over to my bed and put her sleeping bag over us. I was able to slide out without waking her. I was still unsteady on my feet as I took care of business behind the cabin in the woods. It was too far and too cold to make it to the bathhouse. I tried to be careful and slid back into my side of the bed.

I brushed up against Robins legs and she yelled out, "damn you're cold."

I replied, "damn you're warm," as I wrapped my arms and legs around her.

It was then I realized she was naked, and I have to remind myself she is the daughter of a client. I moved away and apologized for freezing her. She got out of bed. I thought she was mad when she said payback is hell. Then she went out of the cabin naked. I knew she was going to freeze me when she got back. I had another one of those angel and devil on my shoulder moments.

I got my sleeping bag and got in the other bed. I really think she was honestly trying to get warm, but you never know.

When she came back, she searched the bed and asked, "what are you doing?"

I let out an obviously fake snore.

"Fine, but I'll get you back." Robin got in bed and covered her head.

A few minutes later she whispered, "are you awake?"

"Yes."

"Where's the light?"

I reached over and turned on the battery lantern.

Robin got up and opened her bag. She took out sweatpants and a shirt, got dressed, and crawled back into the bed.

"Now, get back over here with the good sleeping bag, I'm cold."

So, I did. Truth is, I was cold too, and I really wanted to go to sleep. I was tired and sore from the trip. It took me a while to get warm, but I must have fallen asleep as soon as I did.

Wednesday

The sun was shining and lit up the cabin. Robin was still asleep. I got my stuff together and made my way to the bathhouse. I took a long hot shower and thought about all that had happened. I can't quite wrap my head around the whole situation.

Why would Christy send Robin here if she knew the other kids would be here? Maybe Sam was right that Christy may not know the whole situation. I heard others come into the bathhouse, so I got my stuff together and got out. When I got back to the cabin Robin was gone. I figured I'd catch up with her later on.

Right now, my biggest concern was seeing if we could get a lift down to the landing. It was early and the chow hall wouldn't be open yet. I went anyway. I would love to see Cassie, and I still needed to see Mike. It was a quiet morning as I made my way up the path. Not many people are out yet. When I reached the chow hall porch, I did see a familiar face waiting next to my favorite rocking chair. Merlin was there and had his hiking bag lying next to him.

I sat down and gave him a pat on the head and asked if he brought the bag there, or someone else? Merlin didn't answer. I didn't think he would, but it was good to see him anyway. I closed my eyes and listened to the faint sounds of distant voices and nature as it was waking up. I don't know what it is about the rocking chairs, but I think I could go to sleep again.

I heard footsteps approaching, and I guess I got lucky. Mike and Randy were together, and they went into the chow hall. I shook the sleep away, gave Merlin another pat on the head, and went into the chow hall. Mike and Randy were seated near the coffee pot. I got a cup and joined them.

Mike asked if I enjoyed the trip to the shelter. I told him so far that was one of my favorite parts of this mess.

Mike and Randy were stressed, and they asked if I had heard about the kids missing. I told him that I had heard something about it but no details. Then I filled him in on the so-called rescue mission, and I wasn't happy about me and Robin being in the middle of it.

Randy kept quiet during the conversation. Mike seemed genuine when he explained that had never happened before. They've only been taking in the troubled kids for three years now, and it looks like they may have to stop. It sounded like a good idea, but something has changed.

I can't help but think people are still suspicious about me being here. Now is as good a time as any to ask about a special ride down the lift. Randy finally spoke up and said it would be late tonight or tomorrow morning. They were doing maintenance and needed a part to get it running again. I must have sounded concerned when I asked if it was going to fall. They both laughed, but Randy explained we could actually go now, but if the relay failed again, we might get stuck halfway until the part comes.

"I think I'll wait for the part." Again, that got a laugh.

Randy said it would be a quick fix, he just didn't know if the part would be there today or tomorrow. If I was in a hurry, I could walk down or take a chance on the lift. I told him I would wait.

Then the topic turned to the kids. Mike was talking to me and Randy. It sounded like Randy didn't know what had happened either. Which I found comforting.

When Mike told Randy about the problem in town, he looked shocked and said, "I was afraid something like this would happen someday."

Mike went on to explain to both of us how several men hiked up undetected and one of the boys from last night and Amy left with them.

I asked if anyone tried to stop them?

Mike said, "Tina got in a fight with one of the men. She's okay. Her pride was hurt more than injured."

I asked if they had notified the police?

Mike said, "Tina can take care of that."

He didn't come right out and say it, but I just realized that Tina is the police or used to be. Up here no one is who they say they are.

"What about the missing kids?" I asked.

Mike said, "there's nothing we can do about that. It's all volunteer to be here. They can go if they want to. Heck, we don't even know their real names."

I chuckled a bit when I said, "I've noticed that around here."

What was really funny at the moment as I glanced over was that Randy was wearing a work shirt that said "Frank" on it. Randy turned the name tag up to look at it, and he thought it was funny too.

The chow line was about to open, Mike and Randy got in line. I wanted more coffee first. I didn't mind waiting. I wanted to see if Robin and Cassie would come in. I took a seat at a table on the far end away from the serving line to wait. I was watching the line when Merlin came in and went to the serving area. No one seemed to mind him cutting in line. About a minute later a kitchen staff came out with a tray and set it on the floor near the clean-up area. *That dog has it made.* I remembered Mattie saying he wasn't her dog. I then realized this place doesn't operate year-round. I wonder what he does then.

I was busy watching Merlin and didn't see Robin come in. She had her tray and sauntered over to sit down. She was wearing a new outfit and had on perfume.

Surprised, I asked, "do you have a date?"

Robin said, "I was hoping we were leaving?"

I told her about the lift situation.

She was upset but wasn't surprised since nothing has gone as she expected since she arrived in Haven.

We discussed our options and decided we would wait to get the lift down. Neither one of us wanted to leave anything behind and chance it turned up missing, and we weren't sure either of us would be coming back.

We talked about the things we liked and didn't like about Haven. I think we both agreed it was an okay place in itself, but the drama has sucked the fun out of it. We agreed if either one of us comes back, we'd go stay among the woods people and just come out to eat.

The line had thinned-out, so I got in line to get some food. As I entered the serving area I was greeted by Cassie as it was her turn to serve. I saw Andrea sitting in the back near the cleaning area. Cassie asked if Andrea could hang out with me since she would be busy until after lunch.

I knew I wouldn't be leaving anytime soon, and since I had no immediate plans, I agreed as long as I didn't have to get naked. I got a few hard looks from the other servers. I'm not going to explain the inside joke.

Cassie motioned to Andrea and pointed to me. I guess they had already discussed the plan. Andrea perked up and came running. I guess anything would be better than watching the kitchen staff work. I got an extra portion of everything. I guess that's my pay for doing the good deed of the day. Andrea got a tray and got in line. Cassie asked her if she had eaten before.

Andrea replied with, "I'm a growing child."

Cassie loaded her tray.

I've never been a sitter before, but I was actually looking forward to it. Andrea is interesting. I wanted to see if she had any predictions or maybe she could tell me what she meant when she told me it would hurt, but I'd be okay in the end. I'm not going to ask her anything, just observe…as I've been told to do.

When we arrived at the table, Robin and Andrea seemed happy to see each other. Andrea complimented Robin on her outfit and moved closer as she took a deep breath to smell Robin's perfume. Both of them are not dressed in typical camp clothes, so I wondered what this day would be like. Despite the differences in their ages, they chatted like old friends.

They talked about clothes and their homes. Neither revealed anything I found interesting. There was a little whispering and looking around at the boys. I don't think Andrea has an older female friend to share with, and I know Robin misses her little sister. I heard Robin mention her sister, but she didn't go into details. They finished eating before I did. Robin asked if she could take Andrea to the music building. I didn't see why not, and I told them to stay there until I could get there.

I let Cassie know she was with Robin at the music building, and I was going there too. Cassie was due for a break, so she got us coffee and we went back to my table. This was the first time we've been able to talk alone.

She asked how Haven was treating me.

I answered by telling her about the problems we encountered, and I was unhappy about Robin being exposed to the dangers.

Cassie told me she was unaware of the B dorm situation too. So far, she hasn't had any issues, she's only heard about some of the problems.

She explained that she and Andrea spend most of their time out on the trails or visiting the art groups in The Commons. So, she hadn't encountered anything obvious.

Cassie went back to work after her break. She strikes me as someone that wants to see the best in people and wouldn't recognize the troubled kids, even when they were right next to her. I may be wrong; I actually envy people who can go through life and not see the evil and have a good outlook. I wonder if I spent time with her, *would I start to see things in a different way, or would my poor outlook corrupt hers?*

I left the chow hall and headed to the music building. When I got there, I saw Robin showing Andrea how to play the piano.

Feeling surprised, I said," I didn't know you played?"

Robin flatly responded. "I don't like to play; I was forced to."

"Oh, I see." I sat down and listened.

Robin explained the scales to Andrea, and she showed her how to press the keys. Andrea did a decent job for her first time.

She said, "this is fun. Now play something you're not allowed to play in church."

Robin seemed shocked at the request and just looked at Andrea.

Andrea got up and came over and sat next to me. She petulantly crossed her arms, "I'm waiting."

Robin started playing something I didn't recognize, but it was really nice. It was slow and had a bluesy feel. She played and swayed back and forth with her eyes closed. It was obvious she's played this many times before. I don't think she was forced to play like this. I'm not surprised she had been forced to learn how to play. But this couldn't be forced. Robin looked satisfied with herself.

I was about to compliment her, but Andrea said, "I knew you could do it. Now let's go paint."

And she went out the door.

Robin's eyes were tearing up as she rushed out the door behind Andrea.

I'm sure I missed something important, and, in usual Haven fashion, I'm just supposed to observe. Maybe I'll find out later what that was all about. I just figured that was one of those Andrea moments, and I got to see the tail end of it.

Robin and Andrea had a good lead on me, and Andrea was getting her art supplies together. Robin was seated with her back toward me when I walked in. Robin didn't turn around as she spoke, informing me they were fine, and they didn't need a sitter. I'll take that as a que I was not needed nor wanted at the moment. I eased out and closed the door.

I stood on the porch looking around. I swear I've never felt so lost and useless in my life. A part of me just wants to get my pack and walk down the mountain, but I know I have to see this through. Normally, I can function without a gameplan, but this is nuts. I can't wait to get out of here and finish this.

I walked out to the shop hoping to have some news about the lift. No one was there. I went to the lift and no one was there either. I better not find out this is some ploy to keep us here longer. Since I didn't know when we could leave I figured I better pack and be ready in case we can leave this evening.

I went to my cabin and put everything in bags. I left a note for Robin to get her things together and bring everything to the cabin. And to be sure she is never alone. I want someone with her at all times. I wanted to go find Sam in hopes she would provide some information. I don't know why she would talk now but it was a thought. Then I realized that Tina may be a better source.

I had all my stuff ready to go, but I had one piece of business to take care of. I needed to return the sax. I took it out of the case and played it for a bit. I just needed to hear it one last time. It kept me sane a few times over these days when I really wanted to scream. If it weren't for the horn and rocking chairs, I don't think I'd have survived. It had only been in my possession a short time, but I really liked it. I had a much better horn at home, but something about this old beater was kind of cool. It had a dark rich sound and just felt good. I closed the case and said my goodbye.

The shop was still empty, so I left it on the work bench alongside the other horn and left Randy a note of thanks for everything. I took a peek in the art building to see Robin and Andrea still painting. I didn't bother them. I walked the outer trail toward the B dorm. I didn't want to cut across The Commons area. I didn't want to talk to anyone else but Tina. I could still see The Commons from the trail. The Commons were busy today. Kids were playing and it looked like a lot more people were attending the sessions. Since I hadn't checked the schedule, I didn't know if there was something special going on.

When I arrived at the B dorm it was mostly empty. That's what I get for not checking the schedule. Now I had to go looking for Tina, or anyone at this point to get some answers.

On the way back I passed the message board and saw one of the sessions was on sex abuse in the church. It had already started and wasn't too far away. Maybe I could listen in and see if someone there will know something about the connection.

I was in a hurry and about halfway across The Commons before I remembered to take off my shoes. It never fails when you're in a hurry, something goes wrong, as I discovered a knot in my laces. I managed to get my boots off anyway and walked as fast as I could to the other side.

This was one of the bigger sessions today, and I recognized a lot of B dorm kids there. I scanned the group and couldn't locate Tina. I sat down at the back hoping to not be noticed. The moderator was a woman I'd seen around Haven, but I'd never met her. She was around fifty years old and talked about the time she had sex with the preacher when she was fifteen years old. She went on to describe how she had gone to him to talk about problems in her home life and how he was able to groom her to be a secret friend.

She talked about her homelife, and he talked about his wife not being able to understand him and she was cold-hearted. They started meeting after school, and he would buy her things and take her out to eat at nice restaurants. Something her family never did. This went on for about a month before it happened the first time.

She described the time she went to his office after school and no one else was there. They had become friendly and hugged when they would meet. On this occasion the hug was much longer, and he kissed her. That was the start. He pulled down her panties and laid her on the floor and they had sex. She remembered she was scared, and she bled a lot after that. The woman explained she didn't resist, and she had sex with him several more times before they were caught.

At the time she wanted to defend him, because he made her feel special, but later she learned she was not the only one he was having sex with. She attended counseling and this made her realize she was not in a position to make a rational decision to have an affair with this man. She explained that rape was not always forceful, and the victims blame themselves, and they don't talk about.

I was scanning the group and could tell there were several that seemed on the verge of tears. I tried to not make eye contact with anyone. Being the only older male in the group, I felt very conscious. I hope I'm not making anyone uncomfortable, but I really need some answers. I had arrived near the end of the session and there had been a few other speakers before I arrived. She invited anyone that wanted to talk to come by the office and pointed toward Mike's cabin. She said she would be there until late this evening. I had a lot of questions, but the first one was how she was getting out of here this evening.

I'm not sure she will have the information I need but I left the groups and went to Mike's before the session ended. I wanted to be there when she arrived. I knocked on the door, but there was no answer. I sat on the porch and waited. The session lasted about another thirty minutes. I hope I didn't miss anything important, but I was very uncomfortable being there and didn't want anyone to hold back in the group. Too many people seem to know who I am, so no point in making them uncomfortable too.

I watched as the session ended and a few of the kids gathered around several adults that walked up at the end of the session. They all sat on the ground and talked for another fifteen minutes or so.

The speaker walked up and sat down on the porch next to me and said, "hello detective."

I made a pretend frown, "am I that obvious?"

She laughed and said, "you look the part, and I would have suspected, but to tell the truth, word gets around fast up here. You waiting on me or Mike?"

"Both," I replied.

She introduced herself as Marie. She was a licensed counselor and volunteers here one day a month…today was that day. I told her I had a serious question, and I wanted to know the truth. Marie looked concerned and turned toward me and waited for the question.

I asked, "how are you getting out of here today?"

I was relieved to hear she knew about the lift issue and said Mike had promised to do his best to get it fixed ASAP. Luckily, the issue was in the lower unit otherwise they would have to hike the part up.

I was thinking about this conversation and how to proceed since we both have privacy issues at stake.

She broke the ice and offered, "yes, there are kids from the school here. I'm aware Robin was sent here by accident. Mike told me."

I was annoyed at this point, and my tone was obviously pissed off mode. "So, how is it he has all the answers, and I'm left in the dark?"

Marie was calm, "trust issues, we got word you were coming, but didn't know why or who you represented."

"So what changed and why are you talking to me now?" I asked.

Marie responded, "I'm not sure. Mike doesn't tell me everything, and we didn't have much time to talk about it. Besides, I know you want to leave as soon as possible. I guess you got what you were looking for?"

"No, not really. I discovered the connection between here and the school, but that's all. I have no idea why I need to know that. It looks like Robin was sent here by mistake, and we're both ready to go."

Marie said, "I'll see you at supper." She got up and went inside Mike's cabin.

At this point, it seems obvious Robin was sent here by accident. I can only assume, or hope Christy bought the cover story when the scouts were checking out the kids at the school. That's an issue I'll take up with her when or if I ever see her again.

I started back to the chow hall and looked around. I can see most of The Commons and the other buildings. I stopped by the art building and told the girl I'd be on the porch if they needed anything. I was glad to see the porch was empty. I could hear the kitchen staff clashing dishes and running water. I'm hoping Cassie will come out at some point.

I saw Mike and Randy standing at the shop. Randy turned back inside, and Mike came toward the Chow Hall. He waved and called over to me that the lift will be ready in an hour, then he disappeared around the corner of the building. I went inside to look for Cassie, but she was not there. I went to the Art building and Robin was inside putting her supplies away. Somehow, I had missed Cassie leave through the back and get Andrea. I spotted them as they were about halfway across The Commons.

I really wanted to talk with her before I left, but I needed to get my stuff together and help Robin pack too. Robin and I went to the shop and got a wheelbarrow to put her things in.

Luckily, she didn't have as much as I had expected. We took her things to the lift and stored them in a hidden corner. Moving next to my cabin, we loaded up the wheelbarrow again. It was pretty full this time. I forgot Robin had moved some of her stuff there, and I know I had added a full wish bag on top of the stuff I brought up the first time.

When we got back to the lift, I noticed the sax case lying on top of Robin's bags. There was a note from Randy telling me to take it with me, he didn't want to put it back in storage. I was happy to see the old sax but dreading the thought of having to transport everything when we get to the bottom. I hadn't thought about transportation back to my van.

Robin and I sat on the ground talking. She told me again about the changes over the past couple of years at the school and her home life. It was a strict religious upbringing, until the Reverend got caught screwing an under-aged girl. Then little by little new girls were being moved into the trailers behind the school. She noticed the same cops hanging around too.

Robin continued to repeat her earlier stories about her mom and the changes she went through as well. She was distant from her husband, the Reverend, and she started staying in her room at night. She talked about the day we were all going to run away, and that she was going to tell me a secret where we were safe, and then we would all have a great life after that.

I remembered Robin had talked about this before. She seemed to find comfort in talking about the hope of a new life. I just listened. I find it amazing how so many people go on with their everyday life while hiding such pain. I look back on myself and remembered some of the things I endured which I find painful, but they are nothing in comparison to the things I've seen in my career, never mind compared with what I've seen or heard lately.

Robin was silent for a while, then the quiet was disrupted by the sound of the lift as it made a humming sound. Mike and Randy entered the control booth and motioned for us to wait where we were. The lift started moving. We watched as the cars moved past us. It looked like the cars made two cycles before they came to a stop.

Mike and Randy came out of the control booth to help us load the car with our stuff. Randy picked up the sax case first and put it inside. I asked him if he was sure he wanted me to take it. He assured me it would just collect dust if it were left behind. I thanked him and Mike for everything. Mike gave me a note with a phone number on it. He said it's for an answering service. He checks in with them in the evenings.

We didn't have any more time to talk as Marie and a few of the other people arrived and loaded the car.

We were ushered into a different car than our bags. The ride down took about fifteen minutes and there was very little conversation. Just before we reached the bottom, I heard a ding and one of the women pulled out her phone, and I heard her exclaim, "finally back to the real world."

Robin and I looked at each other, and we both seemed pleased too. Our phones were packed away in the other car. I got a feeling we'd be checking them as soon as we could.

The lift stopped, and we could see the workers unloading the car ahead of us and taking our bags to the parking lot. A van was parked at the bottom of the ramp. When we were able to get off, we walked down to the van and learned we could get a ride to town where we would be dropped at Ms. Mattie's driveway. The driver told us to get in last since we would be the first to get dropped off. I did a visual inventory of our bags to be sure we hadn't missed anything.

Just like us, our bags were packed last so they would be easy to get to when we stop. The ride to Mattie's took about a half hour. The van was eerily quiet. I was glad to get down off the mountain and felt apprehensive about our next move.

We unloaded at the end of the driveway and hauled our stuff up to my van. I half expected to see Merlin come running up and was disappointed when he didn't. Mattie came out to greet us. She was in her witch hat, and I think she was disappointed she didn't have a new audience to scare the shit out of. She still seemed happy to see us anyway.

She asked about the excitement up top and asked if we knew what was going on. She told us there had been a lot of traffic in her driveway over the past few days. They didn't hang around and were usually gone before she could get out of here. I told her a couple of kids went missing after a fight with some strange men.

Mattie shrugged, "kids come and go all the time from up there, but I don't like the sound of this."

She looked concerned as she turned and walked back to her house. Robin and I loaded the van and we both got our phones out to check for messages.

We both had a similar message from Christy, saying she has been held up and it may take a little longer to meet with us. Robin and I both called her phone and there was no answer. We both texted to let her know we were no longer in Haven and there is no plan at the moment.

Robin and I agreed to hang out in Asheville in case she calls arrives in the area. We checked into a motel close to the downtown area and freshened up before going out on the town. Robin was obviously upset over the whole situation but didn't want to talk about it.

Right now, all we can do is wait to see what happens. Seems like that's all I've been doing lately is waiting. Being downtown again made me want beer and a burger. Robin liked the idea. However, I made it clear she was no longer in Haven, and I was not going to contribute to her drinking. She looked a little disappointed, but I think that was more show than actual disappointment.

We wandered for a few blocks looking for something that appeared interesting. We lingered at the windows as we passed by checking out the dishes. Neither of us seemed interested in the upscale places. We finally happened upon a dive bar looking place with outdoor seating. I guess we both kind of looked like we were lusting over a big burger a guy was eating. He noticed us, apparently drooling, and I guess he knew what we were doing. He gave us a thumbs up and continued to chow down. We took that as our cue, we went inside to the hostess, and asked to be seated outside.

We both ordered the cheeseburger and the thick-cut fries. I got a large draft beer and Robin looked sad for a moment as she opted for water. You would think I'd get tired of people watching, but that's what we were doing. Downtown was an eclectic gathering. Everything from the well-to-do, to the down and out homeless walking the streets.

Again, I noticed Robin likes to check out the women who dress nice. Several times she made comments on their outfits. That's pretty much all she said up to that point. Then she asked if we could go shopping tomorrow. I told her I didn't see why not. That brightened her mood tremendously, and she pointed out various outfits she liked.

I tried to imagine what it must have been like being a young pretty girl trapped in a place where you were not allowed to express yourself in any way. I was rebellious at the age of eighteen. I was out on my own, working and pretty much doing anything I wanted. Even though she is eighteen, I'm still responsible for her to some degree by the nature of my business agreement to accept this assignment. Robin was happy for the moment, and I wasn't about to spoil the mood by discussing any future plans.

A cheerful waitress brought our food to the table, and we were not disappointed. I introduced Robin to malt vinegar on thick cut fries. One thing we have found in common is our mutual love for common greasy bar food. Robin talked about our plans for tomorrow. She talked about shopping, eating, and sight-seeing. I'm open to all that as well, but in the back of my mind I'm really thinking about Christy and how is all this going to end. I'm a worrier by nature. I over-think and tend to run scenarios through my head with the possible outcomes.

This assignment is too strange, and no conclusions seemed to come to mind. My mind was startled back to the present when Robin asked if I thought she would look better with short hair.

Without thinking, I said, "I love your long, beautiful hair."

She blushed a bit and said, "thank you."

This was the first personal comment I had made to her. She seemed at ease and happy. I may be overthinking as usual; I don't want her to feel uncomfortable. We ate like we were on a mission until we both cleaned our plates.

After I paid the tab, we stepped out to the sidewalk.

Robin grabbed my left hand and pulled me forward, "let's go this way."

We walked without talking until we reached the same store she had shopped at during our wish bag trip. It was closed, but she lingered in silence as she dreamily looked inside.

Robin pointed to a mannequin of a young girl in a short skirt and a white shirt with butterflies on it.

"I want to get that for Sheri tomorrow."

Robin looked at me and said, "my sister."

A tear rolled down her cheek, and she roughly brushed it away as she turned back to the window.

I thought she would be okay, but that only lasted a moment before she turned and buried her head in my shoulder and began to sob; the only words I could make out was she was scared.

Unfortunately, I had no words of wisdom for this situation. Truth is, I'm not only concerned about how this is unfolding, but I'm so in the dark about the whole case, I'm not sure what we will do in the next few minutes. All I can do for the moment is just be there for her.

Robin let go after a few minutes and walked over to a shaded bench and sat down. I joined her on the bench and put my arm around her as she laid her head on my shoulder.

Robin said, "I want to go talk to my mom, but she told me to trust her and stay away until she could come get me. I'm so scared for her and my sister. I wish Sheri could have come with me even though Haven wasn't what I thought it would be. I'd feel better having her here."

I dialed Christy's number and got her voice mail again. I knew I would, but I didn't know what else to do at the moment.

Robin asked, "Can we go home tomorrow?"

Yes, we can.

I actually began to feel better about our situation. This felt like a turning point. I wasn't going to sit around and wait for Christy to send me a half-assed text telling me what to do. It was time to force an answer.

I pulled Robin tight and said, "it's going to be all right, we're going to make things all right together."

Even though we planned to go back to her home tomorrow, I had no idea of what to do right now. In Haven, doing nothing was the norm. Here, everything is moving except some of the street people.

We had time to kill. It was still early enough neither one of us wanted to go back to the room. I was tired, but I feared the silence of the room would force conversations about our situation. Under normal circumstances I wouldn't mind, but I haven't been in charge of this from the beginning and I didn't care to discuss a lot of *what if*, type of questions.

We walked downtown looking in store windows. Robin loves clothes. I can't say I blame her. As far as I know, she had spent her entire life forced to wear the same boring shirt and denim skirt as everyone one else. I didn't want to ask and run the risk of talking about her past. Not that I didn't care. I was still avoiding the risk of upsetting her.

We found ourselves across the street from our motel.

Robin paused, "wait here. I need to go pee."

She dashed across the street and entered the lobby.

I needed to go too, but I wasn't about to chase after her. I just went in the bar across the street and finished well before her and had time to order a beer and sit at one of the outside tables.

When she returned, she was holding the sax case. At first, I wanted to protest, but I wasn't ready to go back to the room, and bar hopping or more window shopping weren't good options either.

Robin didn't want to order anything, so I chugged down my beer and we walked down to the corner.

This area is normally loaded with buskers, but things have changed since the last time I was here. The vibe was off, and the hippy scene seemed more like a homeless camp among the tourists passing by. I figured I might as well give it a shot since we're here.

I cranked a couple of songs, and sure enough a few people dropped in coins and a few bills.

Robin asked how many pieces I could play from memory?

I guess it's pretty obvious I normally play by reading my parts, but I can fake it sometimes. Then she asked if I ever played for someone to sing. I remember one time I gave it a shot at an open mic night. It didn't go well at all.

Robin seemed disappointed, "well do the best you can."

Without warning, she faced me and started singing in a low soft voice. She was well into it before I realized she was singing the intro to "At Last" by Etta James. She stood as she belted out the rest of the piece. I didn't have to do much other than blow some whole notes which seemed to fit. I was amazed at her performance, and the people were no longer passing by. They were stopped and listening. When she finished, she got a round of applause as well as a bunch of bills dropped in the case.

Robin scooped up the bills from the case and nonchalantly said, "pack up, I'm ready to go to the room."

I wondered if I had done something wrong.

She was about a half a block ahead of me and walking fast.

I packed up as fast as I could and caught up to her before she could cross the street.

I could see tears in her eyes. Before I could speak, she shrieked, "that was so much fun!"

"So, why are we leaving then?"

"I was afraid I'd bust out in tears. That's the first time I've ever sang in public. I was scared to death. I wish I could call Andrea and tell her about it."

"Andrea?" I asked, only somewhat puzzled with her comment.

Robin took my hand and led me to a table outside the bar. She said Andrea told me to do it. She told me to sing something I'd never sing in church.

"I'm thinking this should qualify."

A waitress came to the table. Robin pulled out the bills and said, "I'm buying this round. We'll have two beers."

The waitress and I both gave her a lingering stare.

"Okay, make mine a root beer."

The waitress remembered me and asked, "the same as before?"

I nodded my assent, and she went to fill our order.

Robin was almost vibrating with excitement.

I had to ask, "what led to this?"

Robin said, "Andrea asked me a lot of questions about the school and the church when we were together. She also asked about what made me happy, and what I'd do if I could do anything I wanted. I really didn't have an answer because I thought I'd never have a chance to do anything I wanted. Andrea is a special kid. She wants everyone to be happy and somehow knows how to make that happen. I think she can read your mind. Do you remember when she asked me to play something on the piano that I couldn't play in church?"

"Yeah, I remember that."

"Well, when we went to the art room I was humming and sort of singing under my breath. Andrea told me that if I want to be happy I had to sing that song in front of a lot of people. Well, I did it, and I'm happy."

I didn't want to tell Robin what she said to me, but I am curious as to why Andrea seems to be able to read people so well. Interested in her take on Andrea, I asked what she thought about her.

Robin paused before answering. Then she explained she hadn't spent a lot of time with Andrea before I arrived. Andrea and Cassie would come to the music room or the craft room when she was working. They talked, but nothing serious. Mostly, she heard others talking about them. A lot of people made fun of them because they often dressed alike, and usually like they were at some fancy resort, not some place like Haven.

"I kind of wondered if they read the wrong brochure. They seemed to be making the best of their time and were pretty active in the groups. I think that is where people interacted with them the most. I heard people refer to Andrea as an Indigo child. Some of the folks avoided them, but the hippy folks treated them like royalty or some kind of special VIP or something. I thought that was funny since they sure didn't look the part."

After you came, Cassie seemed to pop up wherever you were, but you and Sam had hooked up so she was just sort of there, but not there, if you know what I mean. Andrea and I talked while all of you were hanging out. She asked a lot of questions rather than offer any great words of wisdom as some said she had."

Now, it's my turn to ask something. Don't think about it...just blurt out the answer within one second, otherwise I'll think you're lying."

I wondered where she was going with this, "oh, that sounds scary, but go ahead."

"Who do you miss the most, Sam or Cassie?"

I'm not sure it took a whole second as I blurted out, "Cassie."

Robin sat back and smiled as if she knew something I had not realized.

I knew I was more drawn to Cassie in a lot of ways, but she had made it clear she was unavailable, and I shouldn't pass up and opportunity to be with Sam and enjoy the Haven experience. I shouldn't be disappointed in how it ended if it did end. She just sort of vanished, but that doesn't surprise me either. I was just doing the Haven thing.

I ordered another beer and asked Robin if she wanted anything else?

She yawned and stretched, "no, I'm tired and want to go to the room and watch TV."

She got up and told me to take my time as she wanted some alone time. I watched as she crossed the street and entered the motel.

I can't say I blame her. I bet she was hardly ever alone. All the school and church kids, then shipped off to Haven where she should have had time alone, but got scooped up right away by people wanting to look after her, and then she got me looking over her shoulder.

Not that I needed an excuse to sit and drink beer, but I was following orders to give her some alone time. I guess we could have gotten separate rooms, but I was in protective mode and didn't even ask what she wanted to do. I'll ask when I get back to the room.

Three beers and an hour had passed. I didn't want to just sit here, so I went walking. I wish I'd have had Robin take the sax back to the room. But I hadn't. I walked down toward the more upscale restaurants. There was a guy playing trumpet and singing with background music. I couldn't tell if he was a hired musician or a street busker, since he was standing near the doorway to the restaurant. He was good, so I sat on the brick wall across the street and watched for a while. I have to admit I'm envious of people with talent. But I guess we all look at things and wonder what we are missing.

The beer and my own alone time was making me a bit sappy, thinking about life choices and all that has happened lately. I'm sitting close to where we picked up the kids in the van. So, naturally, that thought came to mind. Screw it, sometimes you have to make a change. I decided to go to a bar I'd never been to and have another beer. That's about all the adventure I can seem handle at the moment.

Most of the bars had outdoor seating, so I chose the one with the least amount of people. I'm not really into the craft beer thing, but after explaining my preferences the bar tender brought me something that should come close. It wasn't bad, I'd order it again if I could remember what it was. I migrated to a table next to an open window for some fresh air.

I guess I just missed the entertainment. The man was breaking down his equipment inside the opening. He asked about the sax, and if I was on a gig or busking. I told him it was just a hobby and didn't go into details. Right now, beer and people watching is all I want to do at the moment. That lasted a good fifteen minutes before the guitar player came out wanting to talk music. I explained I'm just a hobby player and self-taught. As usual, most so-called full-time musicians are self-taught and can't read music. They just play the same stuff over and over. So, I shouldn't feel bad about what I was doing.

I told him my hero was Dexter Gordon, and he was deceased from throat cancer. I guess all the pot smoking got him like so many other players of that period.

The guy piped up, "don't say that, I'm forty-eight years old and been smoking dope and playing full time for most of my life."

I hope the look on my face didn't give away what I was thinking. I'd swear the guy was seventy.

I finished my beer and figured I'd had more than enough. I wanted to give Robin more time alone, so I walked down to the park. It was beginning to get dark. There were plenty of tourists out and about winding down their day. The rag tag homeless are moving in to take their places among the overhangs and doorways of the businesses that have closed for the evening.

I know some don't have a choice, but I'm continually shocked at the numbers that choose to live like this. I see so much pain, no matter the social class, and I try to look at my own life and the choices I've made. *Is anyone truly happy?* Preachers and bad cops selling drug addicts for sex. Sex workers pretending they are just doing it while they are working on the next big thing. The working class digging their selves into debt as they climb the social ladder. And then, here I sit looking like a homeless drunk wishing I could play my sax without making a fool of myself. I know that's not a life ambition, just a thought for the moment.

I'm getting tired, I hope Robin has had enough alone time. I make my way back to the room. I open the door as quietly as possible. Robin is asleep with the TV on. I turned it down a bit and left it on as I slid into my bed. I must have fallen asleep fast.

Thursday

The next thing I know, I open my eyes to see the sun peeking through the curtains. Again, I have a room facing the morning sun. Robin was already up and out for the morning, but she left a note that she had gone shopping.

I knew about where she would be headed since she wanted to get something for her sister. I went down to the motel breakfast nook to make my traditional motel waffle. I was glad to see to room mostly empty and a vacant waffle maker hot and available. I got a cup of coffee and sat down to wait as my waffle maker counted down two and a half minutes.

The TV was on a news station, but the sound was down. I glanced down to see a closed caption about a deputy being arrested on sex crime charges. The story went off as the news continued. I ate breakfast hoping the story would run again, but it didn't. I checked the internet on my phone but didn't see anything related to the school. I didn't panic since that could have been anywhere in the country. I'm not going to mention it to Robin. No need to stir up an issue if there's not one.

I went back to the room and showered and waited for Robin to come back. It's getting close to our check out time, and she hadn't returned. I packed up our various bags and hauled them down to the van. Then I sauntered out to the corner and sat on a bench to wait. The city traffic was loud and crowded.

Robin had been gone several hours now. I hoped she was enjoying her new-found freedom and having a good time.

I spotted her half a block away. She obviously got a new outfit and was loaded down with bags. As she got closer, I could see she was visibly upset.

Robin walked aggressively right on past me. "Let's go, I want to get out of here."

She went to the van and waited for me to unlock it. She loaded her bags and slammed the door when she got it.

I started to speak, and I got "the hand." You know, the universal sign, "don't talk to me." So, I didn't.

We drove about a half hour in silence before Robin spoke up. "Why are people so fucking mean and just plain fucked up?"

I didn't have any words of wisdom, so I answered with a question. "What happened?"

Robin began to cry and speak. Between the gasps I was able to determine she got lost and nearly robbed at a homeless tent camp.

When all else fails, you go get a fast-food fix. I pulled off at the next exit and ordered at the drive thru. I grabbed the food and then parked us in a tree-shaded area.

Robin told me she got turned around and couldn't remember the name of the motel or street we were staying on. She accidentally wandered into a tent city reflecting on our encounters with the woods people as a measure of the types of people that may be staying there. She quickly found these people to be more live vicious animals than people.

Life lessons are hard, sometimes it's better to learn them first hand. Robin is still a trusting person despite all the things she's seen at the school. Maybe she's just been disconnected enough to know about it and not actually aware of what was really going on. I hope she can retain enough of her innocence to keep her a happy trusting soul, but not so much as it puts her in danger.

I let her rant for a while until she finally stopped and looked at me. The only answer I had was, "if people were nice, I'd be out of a job, and we'd have never met."

It wasn't a good answer but there is no good answer. People suck sometimes. I tend to see the suck before the good.

We finished eating and got back on the road. Robin fell asleep a few minutes later. I kept checking my phone hoping to see a text from Christy; I didn't get one. I scanned the radio looking for news stations. Maybe I'd get lucky and see if the news report I'd seen earlier was related to the school. I gave up and concentrated on driving.

We were still about an hour out when Robin woke up. Thankfully, she was in a better mood but concerned about her mother. She called, but there was no answer and then sent a text. I still hadn't mentioned the news report. Robin wanted to ride by the school in hopes of getting a glimpse of her out walking. We had talked about me riding a bike and walking into the woods prior to me going to Haven. Robin asked if we could do that tomorrow.

That thought was dashed when we saw a heavy presence of state and federal law enforcement vehicles in the parking lot. The school vans were missing and there were no students in sight. There were several officers in special ops gear in the parking lot.

I quickly instructed Robin to get in the back of the van and be ready to cover up.

"If we get stopped, just pretend you are asleep."

It was several miles of back country roads to circle back around and take a quick look at the area where I had entered the wooded area behind the school and previously accessed the mobile home and field where Christy walks.

We drove through the area at a normal rate of speed so as not draw attention to ourselves. There were officers parked along the side of the road with two K-9 units out searching. There was one rescue K-9 officer I recognized as a cadaver search specialist. Robin was in a panic and wanted to stop, fearing something had happened to Christy.

I told her we couldn't stop, and I told her about the news report I saw this morning. She was mad and started yelling. I just let her vent, then I told her I only saw the closed caption and had been searching for news stories ever since while she slept without success.

We drove to my office and searched the news web sites and there was nothing listed. It's a good chance I might know some of the officers working in the area, so it wouldn't be unusual for me to drive through this area if I'd been out working toward the coastal area.

I wanted to go alone in hopes of seeing someone I might know but Robin was extremely upset by this time, so I gave in and let her ride along. We circled the area, and all the officers were out of sight. I didn't dare chance pulling into the school to ask. Not with Robin in the van.

As fate would have it, we spotted a news van at the gas station where I had left my van before.

I decided to take a chance: I flashed my PI badge to a guy behind the wheel. I asked if they were covering the school where the officers got arrested.

The driver responded, "yeah, and there are three missing women they're looking for."

I didn't hang around for him to ask any questions from me.

I got out of there as fast as I could without drawing attention. Robin came back up front.

"The good news is there are three missing women."

Robin looked confused, "how is that good news?"

"You, Christy, and your sister," I replied. *I hope I'm right about this.* It's not my norm to give false hope but I can't think straight with a distraught teen on my hands.

We went back to my place and continued to search the Internet for news. There was nothing listed, and we had to wait for the six o: clock news to see if the crew was reporting from the scene. Sure enough it was the lead story.

The news story was vague only announcing a local detective was arrested in connection with human trafficking. A photo of the Reverend appeared on the screen and the reporter asked if anyone knew his whereabouts to please call in...he was a person of interest in a possible connection to the human trafficking as well as information on three missing females.

Next the photos of Christy, Robin, and Sheri were displayed. One of the K-9 officer was interviewed about the missing women. He advised they were searching the area to rule out foul play of the missing subjects and to search for other potential victims.

I looked over to see Robin crying. I wasn't sure how I felt about the story. There was simply not enough information available in the story. I never trust news stories anyway. I've had way too much experience with the media simply filling in the blanks or omitting details to make a story more interesting. Soon as the news reporter ended that piece and moved onto a bit about a car crash. Robin bombarded me with questions hoping to draw on my experience as to what was meant.

Sitting here wasn't going to get us answers, and I didn't want to be shut in with an upset teenager asking an endless string of questions I couldn't answer. I told her to head for the van, we were going to the school. She looked scared.

"We're not stopping...just looking again."

We passed by the front of the school and no vehicles were in sight. I drove around the back route and was surprised to see everyone had vanished. I was tempted to walk in and see if I could find Christy's phone, but further thought, that would be useless other than to see if she had read my text messages.

I saw a sheriff patrol car at the store. I told Robin to get in the back and cover up. I went to find a deputy I didn't know. I got a couple bottles of water and approached the deputy and asked about all the commotion in the area, and asked if there was anything to be concerned about.

Obviously, he didn't want to give a straight answer, just said they were serving a warrant. He didn't mention the missing women. I paid for our drinks and left. As soon as we were out of sight, Robin came back up front. Eyes wide open she started waiting for an answer.

"He just said they were serving a warrant. He's not talking which doesn't surprised me since one of their own got nailed."

There had been a storm while I was away, and I wanted to go check on my boat. Robin and I talked about sailing, and she seemed to be interested in my history. It's kind of funny how that works, people will open up and talk when they are riding. We spent so much time together in Haven, but really didn't connect over to my own personal details. I told her about my time in law enforcement and all the corruption I had witnessed firsthand. I didn't want her to get the idea everyone was like that. I made sure she understood they are mostly very good people, but a few make everyone look bad. Robin looked sad.

I wanted to change the subject and told her about my first assignment as a private investigator. I got a call from a local attorney wanting me to get a video of a renter taking a dog in the rental property. I thought he was kidding at first, but realized he was serious. He said it was okay for the dog to be outside, but it was not allowed in the house.

Not wanting to lose my first client, I agreed to a rate and accepted the assignment. I got to the house just as he described it, and I set up surveillance. After all my years in law enforcement, crime scene investigator, special response team, all I could think about was here I am ending up as a damn pet detective.

Well, I waited and waited and waited some more. I'm well past my retainer and decided I'm not staying any longer.

I got out and went over to take a video of the dog and to show no one had come home. As I was shooting the video a neighbor came over and asked if I was there to take the dog.

I told her, "No, I wasn't there to take the dog."

Then she wanted to know if I was going to feed it.

Irritated, I told her, "No, I wasn't there to feed it either."

Then she mentioned the raid. It was my turn to ask questions. I found out the couple at the house kidnapped someone, locked him in the trunk of their car, took him to his bank and made him withdraw money from his ATM.

Turns out he a was a law enforcement officer, he escaped the trunk and got their tag number. Later that evening they raided the house and arrested the couple. All that excitement, and I'm the pet detective.

Robin laughed and thought I was lying, but it's the truth. I had a bunch of stuff like that written down, and I'd show her when we get back to my place. We checked my boat, and everything looked fine. Robin wanted to look inside. I opened the hatch, and she climbed down into the cabin. It was nice watching her being excited about something new.

She got into the v-berth and laid down, then switched to the stern berth, "can we stay here tonight?"

"I don't see why not. We've still got most of our stuff in the van."

She asked if I would take her out for a sail? There was no wind, but I agreed to motor out and see what it was like out in the main portion of the lake.

Just as I had suspected, the water was like glass and there was no wind. We motored to the marina further down the lake, which took about an hour. We pulled up and docked, then walked up to the marina restaurant. I eat breakfast here often, but rarely in the evening, since I prefer to cook out.

We both got cheeseburgers and fries which were good, but not as good as the ones we got at the bars. I was glad she wasn't talking about her mother and sister missing, even though I knew she was worried.

After we ate, we motored back and stopped near the dam to watch the sun set behind the mountain. A few minutes after we stopped, a bunch of other boats came and sat as well.

I loved showing her new things, she seemed to truly appreciate the things that were common to some but brand new to her.

We sat for about thirty minutes before the sun disappeared behind the mountains far off in the distance. I fired up the outboard and motored back toward the marina. Sailing has always been a great escape for me, since cell phones rarely work out here. As we neared the marina, my voice message tone went off. We were close to docking, so I waited to secure the boat before checking. It was dark, and I needed to concentrate on that.

As soon as I secured the lines, I checked my phone. It was Mike, telling me Christy was in Haven looking for us. I almost dropped my phone in the lake. I called the number I had for Haven, but of course all I got was the answering service. I remembered Mike telling me they have a phone in Haven, but only the service has that number. They do it for security reasons. I left a message for Mike to call me back no matter what time he gets the message.

I called out to Robin as she was getting her bag from the van. She came back loaded down like she was going to stay for a while. I told her about the message, and she wanted to leave right away. She got out her phone and dialed her mother's number and it went directly to voice mail. She also sent her a text. Robin knows the phones don't work up there, but it seemed to make her feel better to try.

We decided to not stay on the boat and go back to my place, do laundry, and repack for the trip back to Haven. I called the answering service again and requested a reservation to be lifted to Haven. I didn't quite know how that was supposed to work. I remembered not seeing the lift operate until after lunch on Friday when the new people arrived. Robin confirmed she arrived at the landing in a van and had to wait for a long time before people were allowed to load their stuff, and then people rode up later after the cars had been unloaded. You don't arrive with your bags. I kind of remember it was later in the day when the people unloaded. The only thing that stood out was a lot of people being upset about the kid that committed suicide before arriving at Haven. That thought made me very sad, since Haven may have been a great place for him.

We got to my place, and I told robin to go ahead with her laundry, I had plenty of stuff to pack.

I unloaded my bags and realized my stuff needed to be cleaned too. It was a little ripe; I don't think I'll wait to get back, but I'll go ahead and repack with fresh items I might need from my drawers.

Robin stuffed her clothes in the washing machine, then went in the bathroom for a shower. It was obvious I'd be getting a cold shower tonight, or I have to wait until later at night for the water heater to catch up. I don't think I can sit up that long, since I'm already tired, and now I have to drive back tomorrow.

As soon as Robin left the bathroom, I jumped in the shower. I'd rather wash clothes in cold water than me be in cold water. No such luck, about thirty seconds and the water was cold. It no colder that the stream in Haven. I thought about the naked girls swimming in the stream, and I did the best I could. The fantasy helped pass the time a little quicker. I found myself already looking forward to going back and how I think I missed out on a lot of the overall experience. I was purpose driven and couldn't let go of that.

I dried off and dressed in sweats as fast as I could. I went to the couch, wrapped up in a blanket trying to get warm. Robin was laughing but apologized for using all the hot water. I accepted her apology even though she was still laughing as she said it. Robin came over and snuggled up next to me to keep me warm.

I am a bit paranoid about our situation. Robin and I have shared the cabin and a bed and been subjected to situations where a man shouldn't be alone with a teenaged girl. Especially one as beautiful as Robin. I'm looking forward to the drama ending, but I'm not looking forward to Robin going away.

Robin asked what I was thinking about since I was so quiet.

I told her, "I really enjoy our time together, but I hate the circumstances behind it." I stopped hugging myself wrapped up in my blanket, pulled her close so I could kiss her on top of her head.

"You're an amazing young lady, and I'm going to miss you a lot."

"Yea, but once I'm out of the way you and go for Cassie."

"Cassie told me she's not available, she made that very clear and pushed me toward Sam."

Robin sat up straight and faced me. "Cassie likes you a lot, but she is overwhelmed in taking care of Andrea. It's not another man, Andrea is sick."

"What do you mean sick?"

"I don't know the details, I just know Andrea told me she would not grow up to be a teenager like me, and I should learn to live everyday as if everything I love could be taken away. Take chances and seek out ways to make myself happy no matter what's going on around me. She said she didn't want to talk about it anymore. So, I never mentioned it again."

"You know how you feel about Cassie, Sam was a distraction, A damn sexy distraction, but a distraction all the same. You gave her what she needed at the time, and she gave you what you needed at the time."

Robin snuggled up close again, "and if you get the chance, you should screw Sam again. I know I would."

I gave her a sideway look.

Robin buried her face in the blanket. "I did think about it. I have a vivid imagination and, dang, I had to shake that one off. I don't want to screw this thing up this late in the game."

I told her to go put her clothes in the dryer. Mostly I'd be embarrassed if she saw the hard on I was having thinking about her and Sam. Sam was a true fantasy girl that I don't think I could have been with under different settings. I don't regret all the amazing sex and, yes, I'd do her again and again if I could.

After I had a chance to relax and Robin went to the kitchen to snack, I went and put my stinky clothes in the washer. I checked my bags, added a few items I thought I might need, and of course I considered the wish bag items. I hadn't planned on staying long, other than to complete my mission, but the thought of staying a couple of days without an agenda didn't hurt my feeling either. I had a couple of bottles of Scotch and Bourbon I didn't get a chance to open, so they went in the bag and well as a few books from my home collection I'd been waiting for the right moment to start. I looked at the sax Randy had given me and wondered what I should do with it. I'll put it in the van and tell Randy I have it available if he wants it back. I have a much nicer horn; this one has a short but meaningful memory attached to it now.

I went back to the couch to find Robin asleep and wrapped up under the blanket I had been using. I went into my office to answer a long list of emails, and to let everyone know I would be back in service in a couple of days. There were a few assignments pending, but nothing was a rush, so I downloaded the information and notified the clients I would get on them soon.

My clothes were finished washing. I put them in the dryer and went to bed.

Friday

It was nice to wake up and not have the sun glaring in my face. I slept a little longer than normal and rolled over to find Robin asleep next to me. For some reason, this is beginning to feel normal to me. I'm comfortable around her. I got up and took another shower, a hot shower this time.

Robin was still asleep when I took my bag down to the van and made a quick inventory. It looked like I had everything I needed. I'm glad I'm not walking up this time. Or, or at least I hope not since I haven't talked with anyone in Haven to confirm we were getting a ride up. I can't imagine otherwise since we got a message that Christy was there.

When I got back inside Robin was still asleep. I woke her up since we still had a three-and-a-half-hour ride ahead of us to get to the landing. I had no idea what we needed to do when we got there, so I wanted as much time as possible in case we had to change plans.

Robin got up and took another shower as well. I went into the den and saw she had packed during the night and was ready to go. She came out of the bathroom dressed and asked if we could eat on the road, since we were leaving later than she wanted to. I agreed we should get moving. We put her bag in the van and headed out. I did a mental run down to be sure I turned everything off before we left. I'm paranoid about that sort of thing.

We drove about a half hour before hitting a drive-thru for breakfast. I swore I was going to quit the fast-food thing, and here I'm doing it every time I go out. Watching Robin eat is entertaining since fast food is another new thing for her, so I'm not going to complain.

"You need a wish bag stop?"

"Only if you're getting me a box of wine, so guess not."

"Lord, I hope Christy doesn't blame me if she ever finds out."

Robin just laughed, "I'm kidding."

"But another drive-thru wouldn't hurt my feeling before we go up-top."

That actually sounds like a good idea, since we may be stuck in the landing for a while.

Robin was reading her witch book during the ride. That's another thing I hope Christy doesn't blame me for. Not that I'm opposed since I found I really liked all the witches I met in Haven.

We rode in silence for most of the trip except Robin would read sections she found interesting. It sounds like this is more of a history of witches that instructions on how to be one.

Robin closed the book and closed her eyes too. Without opening her eyes, she said, "I find it disturbing the witches I've met were more Christ like than the people I meet in church."

I didn't respond, but in my mind, I agreed with her. She looked tired, and I wanted her to rest.

This is another one of those conversations we should have had when we were in Haven.

Our time in Haven was nice, but I realize how little time we spent trying to connect on a deeper level. I know I'm over-thinking this now since we just recently met, and today I will have fulfilled my mission and may never see her again. That's normal for me. I meet a lot of people and face life-changing events with them and then never see them again.

How I wish I could hug her and tell her how much I've enjoyed our brief time together, but I resisted not wanting to come across as a creeper. I changed my thoughts to how I was going to deal with Christy. The easy thing to do was to deliver Robin to her mother, but I really wanted to know what the hell she was thinking and why the hell was she being such a pain in the ass, bitch, running me around in circles.

Robin sighed and readjusted herself to get comfortable and continued to sleep. I figured it best just to keep my mouth shut and let it go.

Not knowing what to expect when we arrive, I decided to make a stop and add to our wish bags. I figured at best I'd be there a couple of days; I'd add a few snacks, and I still had a good stash of alcohol left over. Robin stirred a little as I stopped at the store. She didn't quite wake up, but just enough to say she didn't want anything. I got her a few things just in case.

Since we didn't have a reservation for a lift, I hit a drive through again before we arrived. As I did, I thought, this is something I have to quit doing when this thing is over. My thought shifted to the bar food and the reality is I probably won't be giving that up either. I may slow down, but I'm no quitter. It sounds more reasonable and funnier when I think of it this way.

Robin was still asleep while I ordered, I think I have her figured out as far junk food is concerned. The landing was only a short drive away. As expected, the cars had not started moving yet. The parking lot was mostly empty except for a few workers. I didn't see anyone I recognized, so I guess I'm not getting any favors. I found a woman with a clipboard. Funny how a clipboard makes you look important. Sure enough, she was the one to see for boarding. We were way down the list, but I was thankful we were on the list.

I returned to the van and shut the door a little harder than I intended.

Robin looked up and wiped the drool from her face. "I smell food."

I handed her a bag and a straw.

"How long have we been here?"

"Just got here, and it looks like it will be a while before we board."

Robin looked around, she let out a big sigh and said, "yea, I got here on a bus and waited two hours to board."

"Well crap, I wonder how long it will be before the bus gets here?"

Robin didn't look up, but the sound in her voice was obvious she sounded hurt. "You ready to get rid of me?"

"God, no!" I stumbled over my words trying to find the right thing to say.

I turned to face her and decided to tell her what I was thinking on the ride up.

"Robin, I must admit, I've been very uncomfortable about this whole situation. I'm an older man that's been forced into a situation, where I'm in charge of an unfamiliar teen aged girl. Not only that, but we were stuck in an area where everything is permissible, and I was afraid and unsure of myself most of the time. Everything about this has been way out of my comfort zone."

I'm not going into details but thank God I had Sam to keep me distracted. You made it very difficult sometimes to be the nice guy."

Robin smiled and blushed, "I know, and I'm sorry, I was kind of hoping you'd be my first."

I did not see that coming. My heart was pounding and knew the next thing I said could totally affect everything we had been though.

"Why?" was all I could come up with.

Robin scooted over closer, kissed me on the cheek and said, "because you are a nice guy."

Robin went back to eating as if nothing shocking had just taken place. Maybe it's just me over-reacting and over-thinking again. Robin finished eating and excused herself to go to the bathroom. I watched as she walked out of sight and reappeared later on the other side of the parking lot. She stopped to talk to some young girls sitting on a bench.

I got out to walk around too. I wanted to talk with the workers, but a bus arrived before I could cross over to where they were. This looked to be a new supply of hippies. More of your woods people types. I'm kind of glad we're loading later. I mean they were fun to hang out with in the woods, but didn't look like they'd be much fun in a crowded lift.

They loaded their stuff in a few cars, and it went up without any passengers. I watched as the cars crossed the river and edged up the mountain before they disappeared out of sight as it leveled off at the upper landing. About a half hour later the people started loading the cars and made the trip up top.

Robin came back and said we can go up after the next bus arrives. Before I could ask how long, the next bus pulled into the parking lot. From what I saw from the last bus, it would be at least another hour before we could go.

I reclined my seat and settled in to wait.

Robin started talking as if there had been no break in our previous conversation.

"You are the only person that acted like you cared without a lecture. Even when I did things you didn't approve of you were there to protect me but let me make my own mistakes. Before you arrived, I was playing follow the leader, in which Sam was the leader, and I was doing the Haven thing. In fact, my first sexual encounter would have been with Sam. So, I guess we both have to be thankful for distraction. When you arrived, I was able to break away from Sam and do my own thing. I'm sorry I said and did things to make you uncomfortable. I pushed the limits hoping you would fail and take advantage of me. Why should I be different than all the other girls? All I can say is thank you for being a friend."

Robin was tearing up and said, "I don't want to talk about this anymore."

I scooted over and kissed her on the cheek, then sat back and closed my eyes. There were so many things I wanted to talk about, so many unanswered questions. I keep hearing Mike telling me to just observe.

So far that has worked where Robin is concerned. I'm not going to mess it up now.

I reached over and held her hand. We didn't talk but the energy between us was emotional. In a few minutes we were about to go up top, and we both knew something was about to change and neither of us knew how to feel about it.

A carload of bags arrived from up top and the workers unloaded them from the lift car and put them in an enclosed trailer attached to a small bus. The workers motioned for us to come over.

Robin and I were the last two, so we were able to load our bags and ride up with our property.

That made me happy that I wouldn't have to go looking for my stuff.

Robin and I held hands but didn't talk the entire trip. When we leveled off and approached the landing Robin hugged me and held on until the doors opened. Robin grabbed her bags and got off the lift. She walked out from the station and walked out toward The Commons area.

I can't blame her for being excited. She is about to see her mom and sister. If Christy needs to talk with me, she can come find me later. I wasn't sure what I was supposed to do. I figured I'd find Mike or Randy and find out where I'd be staying or whether I'd be riding back down today.

I dragged my bags to the chow hall. Luckily for me, Mike and Randy were sitting on the porch.

Randy gave me a warm welcome by announcing, "it's about time you showed up, you need to get busy, it's fire night."

I never know if he's kidding or not.

Mike grinned, "same cabin okay with you?"

"Sounds good to me, I don't guess you know if Cassie is around, do you?"

Mike and Randy both had a change in expression from jolly to concerned. Mike spoke up and almost choked on his words.

"We were not allowed to say anything before. Andrea is a very sick little girl. They had to leave yesterday for treatments."

I felt like I was about to pass out.

Mike added, "we don't know what's wrong; we were just given instructions to air lift her out in case something happened to her. And before you ask, I don't know if that's their real names."

Randy got up and motioned for me to come along. We walked around the corner and loaded the Jeep. We drove down to my cabin and unloaded my bags.

Randy said, "I was just kidding, the fire is ready for tonight."

He drove away without another word. I don't think he was being rude. I don't think he wanted me to see him cry.

I sat down on the steps since the rocking chair had been taken away while I was gone. I had nowhere I needed to be, and suddenly felt like I was the last person on Earth. Empty. I can hear people up in The Commons, they sounded happy. That is the last place I wanted to be right now.

I waited at the cabin until the sun was getting close to the horizon. I didn't know if anyone else had been assigned fire duty, and I didn't want Randy to be stuck doing it alone.

I made a stop at the bath house to splash water on my face and try to get a grip on my current situation.

As I crossed The Commons, I saw Robin, Sheri and Christy standing near the dining hall end. Robin saw me and called out for me to come over. Just as I reached them, I saw Madison and Tony running toward us. Robin, Sheri, and Christy had a look of terror in their eyes and was looking past me.

It was one of those slow-motion moments when denial kicks in and everything slows down, nothing seems real.

I saw the Reverend's head explode from the back and small trickle of blood form on his forehead. I saw him fall to the ground just as I realized that I had my 9mm pointed right where his head had been a second earlier.

Time stood still. It seemed like a long time. Then I heard the screams and saw people running away.

Robin was lying on the ground beside me at this point. I looked in Robin's eyes and saw fear. I saw Sam was running toward me when I felt the burning pain in my chest. I saw the blood on my hand as I fell to the ground.

The last thing I remember is seeing Sam's face. I couldn't hear what she was saying. I wasn't afraid at this point. I just thought to myself. This is how it ends.

I felt the pain in my chest. I tried to move but couldn't, I was too weak. I opened my eyes, Sam and Robin were there by my side. Only we were no longer in Haven.

I was in a hospital somewhere. Somehow, I managed to survive being shot in the chest. I had no idea how I got there, or how long I'd been there. I don't remember much about the shooting. I was amazed that I was still alive. I tried to speak, but my mouth and nose had tubes in them. My throat was dry and hurt. The more awake I became the more I realized my whole body hurt.

A group of doctors and nurses came running in and checking me. I couldn't tell if I had just arrived in the emergency room or if I'd been there for a while. I looked around and saw Sam and Robin standing in the corner of the room holding each other. They were both crying. Sam blew me a kiss and the room went dark.

Two days later I became a little more stable. The drugs were wearing off, and I became fully awake. I had lost a lot of blood since it took several hours to get me to the hospital by helicopter. I still had a hard time speaking, and my mind wouldn't focus. I tried to replay the situation over in my mind but couldn't. I was a little scared at this point. I couldn't tell if it was the drugs or the injury causing me to black out my memory. I was in a lot of pain, but at least I was able to move my body, and everything seemed to be working.

I was alone, but I saw Sam's backpack sitting in a chair…seeing that made me feel better. I needed something for the pain, but I wanted to be awake when Sam came back. I had so many questions about what happened, and I really want to see her.

I laid there for about an hour before a nurse came in to check on me. She asked if I needed anything for pain. I wanted it but shook my head no. I still had a hard time speaking.

I pointed toward the backpack in the chair.

The nurse replied, "she's been here ever since you came in. Wouldn't you know the moment she steps out you'd wake up? She just went down to the cafeteria. She'll be back soon."

The nurse left the room after making her notes.

I was expecting to see Sam come back in the room, but it was Robin. She came over and gave me a hug and a kiss on the forehead. She wrapped her arms around me and began to cry.

I wanted to do something to comfort her but didn't know how.

I managed to put one arm around her and stroke her hair. She held me for a long time.

Sam came into the room and stood by the door and looked at Robin and me. I expected her to come over to the bed, but she didn't. I could see her smiling, and she was shedding tears as well.

Seeing this, I knew I was going to recover. I did, however, worry about my future. I am sure I had killed the Reverend, and I'm not sure how or why?

My nurse came back into the room and said my monitor was going crazy. She just wanted to check on me. She asked if I needed anything for pain. I told her I'd take something as long as it didn't put me to sleep. I've been asleep long enough and need to know what happened.

The nurse asked if I felt like talking; there were a couple of people waiting to see me.

I asked, "okay, who?"

Robin and Sam looked at each other and seemed nervous. Sam spoke up reassuringly, "it will be fine" everything is good now.

The nurse left the room for a moment and returned with some pills and some water for me to take. I hardly had time to ask what was going on before a detective from the Sheriff's office came in to see me. I felt panic rising for a moment, but the look Sam gave me made me believe everything was going to be okay.

I didn't even hear the detective's name, he just asked if I was feeling better.

I painfully shrugged, "I don't know. I've never been shot before; I don't have anything to compare it too. Actually, I hurt like hell."

I was expecting him to start asking questions, but he didn't. He said he was in the hospital on another case, he heard that I was awake and wanted to see if I was okay.

I grimaced and said, "I'll make it. So where are we at in the investigation?"

The detective replied, "you're clear."

The detective looked to Sam and Robin, "have you told him?"

In unison they both said, "no."

The detective explained that Reverend McFerrin took the cable car at gun point to gain access to Haven. There was no way to warn anyone that he was coming. Robin was in The Commons, and he spotted her right away, ran up, and shot her.

I thought my heart had just stopped when he said that. For a moment I thought I heard him wrong. I looked at Robin as she was opening her shirt to show me the bandage on her shoulder.

She said, "just a scratch," in her best tough guy voice.

The detective continued, "the witnesses say he shot her first, then you pushed her down, and he shot you before you pulled your gun and fired back. It doesn't get any better than that for a short investigation, not to mention all the other stuff. I'll let them fill you in on the school investigation."

It's like a fuzzy dream in my mind, "I only remember seeing his head explode, and then I saw the gun in my hand. I wasn't sure if it was real or not. What happened after that? How long have I been here?"

The detective said, "you were air-lifted out. You've been here two days. You lost a lot of blood before they could get you here. You stopped breathing, and Doctor Sam here got you going again."

I wanted Sam to come over, but she wouldn't. She stood in the corner with her back to the wall. I could see tears in her eyes.

I reassured her, "I'll be alright."

Sam said, "I know it will now."

The detective said he had to go and headed for the door.

Sam said, "I'll be back in a few," then she went out with the detective.

Robin and I were alone in the room. She laid her head on my arm and held on tight. The drugs were taking effect, I was feeling drowsy and having Robin close was comforting. I soon drifted off to sleep.

Waking up

I woke up alone. The sun was shining through the window, so I assumed it was the following day. Other than being sore as hell I felt surprisingly good. I was able to think and was hungry and extremely thirsty. It took me a few minutes, but I finally found my controller and buzzed for the nurse.

A voice came over the speaker and asked, "can I help you?"

I said, "yes, I'll have the cheeseburger, fries and a beer."

There was a long pause and then the voice responded, "you must be feeling better. I'll have a tray sent to your room as soon as I check your orders."

I looked around the room. No flowers, no cards. Nothing, I was not only alone in my room, I felt completely alone in life as well. I wasn't close to anyone. I work all the time, never getting to really know anybody. Most of the people I know are in the same line of work or something related. I've been out of circulation for no telling how many days now. I wonder if anyone even knew I was missing.

I turned on the TV and scanned the channels. I found a news station and watched it while I waited. I wasn't sure how long it had been on. I didn't see anything about the shooting. I wondered if I missed it. Or maybe it didn't make the news.

My food arrived after thirty minutes or so. Scrambled eggs, something that looked like bacon, toast, apple sauce, and coffee. I ate it all including the bacon-looking stuff.

I really want to leave here now. I realized that I didn't even know where I was at. I never asked anyone what city I was in, or what hospital. The only people I knew in the area were from Haven, and I had no idea how to contact them. I looked at the phone and thought about some of my investigator friends. I didn't know their numbers. They were all stored in my cell phone. I realized that I didn't even know where my phone was. I didn't bother to carry it with me in Haven. I hope the Sheriff's office has my gun. I would really like to get it back when I leave here.

I can't even sit up on my own. I'm fine as long as I'm lying still, but it hurts really badly when I try to sit up.

I buzzed the nurse again. I got the same voice, "how can I help you?"

I said, "never mind…it was an accident."

It was not an accident. I realized that I didn't really need anything. I didn't want drugs that would put me to sleep. I really didn't care what city I was in, or which hospital. I wanted out of here. I felt useless.

I spend most of my time alone, and it never bothered me before. *Why was this so different?* I turned off the TV and thought about my situation. I couldn't concentrate. My thoughts raced back and forth between all the events leading up to my being here. *Where were Sam and Robin? Why did I care?* My assignment was obviously finished when I killed the Reverend.

The orderly came in to retrieve my empty tray. I asked where I was at, but he did not seem to understand English. *Go figure, I finally ask, and I get a mute.* I'd be out of here soon enough and head home.

The nurse came in next and asked if I needed anything for the pain.

I joked, "I'm still waiting for my beer."

She said, "this will have to do for now."

I rolled over on my side and took my shot.

"Better to stop the pain before it starts. I better get out of here soon. I'm starting to like those things."

I started scanning the channels again hoping to find something of interest to occupy my mind before the drugs kicked in. Christy and Robin came into the room. Robin was beaming with a huge smile. I'm sure she was relieved that the Reverend was no longer a threat, but she seemed scary happy at the moment. Robin laid her head on my good side and hugged me as tightly as she could without causing me more pain.

Christy was wearing her traditional blue polo shirt, but now sporting a mid-thigh skirt. Her hair was obviously shorter and fluffy. I made an obvious inspection from toe to head and gave a crooked smile of approval. I didn't say anything to Christy.

I looked to Robin and asked, "Why are you so happy today?"

Robin stood up and looked at Christy and said, "you tell him. I still can't believe it!"

I looked back and forth at Christy and Robin waiting for one of them to say something.

Finally, Christy asked, "how are you feeling today?"

I told her, "As can be expected I guess, what's up?"

Robin was bouncing up and down on her toes, "hurry up!"

Christy looked at Robin sternly and said, "I just want to be sure he's up to getting this kind of news."

I said, "whatever it is I'll probably be asleep again in a few minutes, so better move it along."

Christy pulled up a chair close to the bed opposite from Robin. She took a long look at Robin then back to me.

She took my hand and asked, "do you remember Ashley Simpson?"

I had to search my memory banks and the name is familiar to me. The drugs are kicking in again though, and I'm struggling to stay focused.

I look deeply into Christy's eyes trying to find recognition. I remember bright blue eyes, soft petite hands and really cute legs. I held up her hand and turned it over stroking her palms and the back of her hand as if this would jog my memory.

I looked at her through my increasing fog and said, "Ashley, yes, I remember you."

Christy withdrew her hand; she had not expected that.

Christy said, "No, I'm her little sister."

"We only met once at the camping trip."

I had to think for a moment, but it was coming back to me. I looked back and forth to Robin and Christy thinking the drugs were doing their thing, and I was dreaming. The last thing I remember was the little girl in the hallway at the school. The look she gave me was the same look Christy gave me on the camping trip when I went walking in the woods with her older sister, and we wouldn't let her tag along.

I woke up late in the afternoon. Again, I was alone. I tried to recall the conversation with Christy and tried to figure out what was going on. My mind was still in a fog, and I knew I couldn't distinguish fact from fiction. I laid there for a long time just looking out the window watching the sun fade in the distance. I fell asleep again without the use of drugs. *Hopefully, when I wake up again, I'll be able to think more clearly.*

The next morning a nurse came in to inform me that I had a visitor in the lobby waiting to see me. She left the room and a few minutes later Mike came in. I was happy to see him. I knew I could get the facts about this situation, get my mind on track and get the Hell out of here. I hadn't seen Sam lately and couldn't remember if it was yesterday, or several days since I'd seen her.

I was happy to see him, but I was more interested in answers at this point. I asked Mike if Sam was around.

Mike replied, "Sam is like the wind, she blows in and out. I'm not even sure that's her real name. She came down after they airlifted you out, and she hasn't been seen since."

Mike filled me in, "Sam came to Haven a few years back, and she stays a few weeks at a time and disappears again. This is probably her fifth time in Haven; you never know when she'll show up or how long she'll stay. This was her longest stay of four weeks. The only surprise was you. I really thought she was a lesbian; I never saw her in the company of a man before."

I said, "people say I have an interesting life, but I'm ready to get back to my normal kind of crazy. I have no idea how I got involved in all of this, and not sure it's over."

I asked about Christy and Robin.

Mike said, "Christy and Robin have been staying at a motel close by, at least they were as of last night. Christy had met with me at the landing and gave me this box and asked me to give it to you."

I took the box and thought I better wait to see what's inside after Mike leaves. This is how this whole thing started.

I tried to pick Mike's brain about Christy, Robin and Sam. He didn't seem to know much about their personal lives, and again reminded me that Haven is known as an escape from reality and only knows the least little bit of information people are willing to share. He added that even most of that was pure fiction. I didn't push it further because I believe him. Haven was the most unusual place I had ever been to.

I only know I was sent there to be with Robin. I assumed it was to keep her safe, which I nearly failed at. I don't blame myself for that. Christy was very short on information throughout the whole ordeal. And that thing about being Ashley's sister is very unsettling right now.

Mike only stayed a short while; I knew he had to get back to the landing to shuttle back up. I'm sure they would have made a special trip for him, but knowing Mike, he would not ask for the favor unless it was completely necessary. We said our goodbyes, and he left the room. As soon as he was gone, I realized that we had parted in a way Haven people do. There was no discussion about the future to get together or whether I had plans to visit Haven again.

I can't think of a reason to go back unless it was to find Sam again. That was a shot in the dark according to Mike, and I'm not sure at this point if I should try to find her. I mean here I am laid up in a hospital, and she disappeared as soon as I woke up. The more I think about it the more pissed I am about the situation.

Then there's Christy and Robin. *Where in the Hell did they get off to?* Mike had laid the box Christy gave him on a chair across the room with my bags. I hadn't paid attention until just now that someone had brought all my stuff from the cabin. I've got to call the detective today and see if I can get my gun back when I check out of here. I'm getting pretty annoyed with my present situation, and I'm ready to get out of here. I pressed my call button and waited for the nurse to answer.

A couple of minutes later my nurse came into the room and wanted to know how I was doing and wrote down a bunch of stuff on my chart.

I asked her if she knew when I could get leave.

She told me the doctor would be coming around in an hour or so and I should ask him.

She told me, "Everything is looking good, maybe this afternoon?"

This got me pretty excited, and I asked her to hand me the box on top of my backpack. The nurse handed me the box and left the room.

I opened the box to find another book inside. Again, this one was hollowed out with a lot of money inside an envelope. It looked to be about another ten thousand dollars. My heart starts racing, and I hope this doesn't set off some kind of alarm at the nurse's station. I didn't count the money right away. I opened the envelope to read the letter from Christy. This is what she wrote.

Dear Marshall,

 I'm sorry for the way I've done things. The money is for your services since you've spent so much time away from your other clients. Your hospital bill is paid in full. I came this morning and took care of everything.

 I've not treated you very well through this whole ordeal. I've pretended to be out of reach so I could limit the amount of information you would have access to. I've known for a long time that the Reverend was dealing drugs and was prostituting out some of the girls.

 It wasn't always like this. For years things were going well. Several years ago, the Reverend was caught having sex with one of the students. She was a homeless girl we took in from an abusive drug-dealing mother. One of the detectives started using the Reverend and the school as a front for him to sell drugs and cover for prostitutes. In the beginning, the Reverend was forced to go along or go to jail. After a while he began to use the girls himself, and I'm sure he experimented with the drugs too.

The Reverend lost interest in the school which made it easier for me to hide the money and take control of all the business matters. I'm not going to go into all the details, but I cleaned out the bank accounts and sold the property to a developer.

By now you should have seen the news stories about the school. A bunch of the sheriff's employees have been arrested, and right now I am scared and going to hide until things calm down. I don't know how deep the corruption goes, and I can't trust anyone right now.

The developer was about to announce his intention to build an apartment complex on the property; so, I had to put the plan in action. I had a second recorder on the cameras, and I was able to save all the videos. One of the cameras was in the new dorm building, which was used to catch a lot of the customers with the girls.

I sent the videos to several news stations first, then to the state and federal law enforcement agencies. I wanted the news to break before the law enforcement community had a chance to cover it up.

No one knows that you have been involved in this situation. I didn't need you as an investigator. I needed you out of the way. Again, I apologize for the way I've done this.

Here is the hard part: Robin is your daughter. I wanted to break the news last night, but you went out before I could tell you. That is why Robin was so excited. She cried all night because we didn't get a chance to talk about it. Unfortunately, we had to leave town in fear someone might find out where we were at. I am sorry I can't tell you where we're going right now. We'll be back in touch as soon as we can.

I guess I need to explain how this happened. Ashley told me about you two on the camping trip.

As you know, she and her husband were separated when you two met. The walk in the woods resulted in Robin. About a year later Ashley told me Robin was yours. She said she was going to tell her husband, but I have no idea if she ever did.

Robin and Ashley lived with me off and on. Ashley and her husband were trying to work things out and went away for a weekend trip. They were hit head on by a drunk driver, and they did not survive the accident. Robin was staying with me, so I ended up raising her.

Robin has known for a long time that I am actually her aunt, but she has always called me her mother. I don't think anyone else knows outside of our family. Please don't try to find us. I'm afraid. I have made a lot of enemies, and I do not want to be involved in the trials.

Keeping you in the dark was the only way I could ensure a way for you to spend time with Robin and put the plan in action. This way if anyone finds out you were somehow involved, you can honestly claim you don't know anything or know where we are at.

Again, I am sorry for the way I did things. We will be in touch later.

Christy

I am stunned, my heart is racing, and I am glad I'm in a hospital bed hooked to monitors at the moment. Otherwise, I would swear I was about to die of a heart attack. I searched frantically for the call button to summon my nurse. I closed my eyes and tried to calm myself down so I could think more clearly. I'm listening to the beeps on the monitor and breathe deeply hoping the beeps will slow down.

It seemed like a very long time had passed before my nurse came in.

She looked at the monitor and asked if I was feeling okay. I had no idea what to say. I had no idea what I should be feeling. And could not remember why I had called for the nurse, other than pure panic, and I needed someone else in the room to rescue me.

Normally, I would never include a stranger with my personal dealings, but for some reason I handed her the letter. I closed my eyes again because I was afraid to watch her reaction, for fear I would go into shock. She read the letter in silence. She took my hand and asked if I needed anything, or was there something she could do for me?

I guess to an outsider this didn't seem like a big deal. She handed me back the letter and left the room. About an hour later Detective Morris came into the room. I was in a panic, even though I'd been cleared the thought of something else popping up scared me to death, especially with the news I'd just received. Detective Morris was in a good mood and asked if I needed a ride somewhere, he heard I was getting out soon.

Sure enough, I was discharged and given a ride back to my van. The conversation was light but somehow, I felt like he was prying for information. *Was he being nice or escorting me out of town?* Either way I'm not talking. Detective Morris returned my gun when I got out of his car. I loaded my gear and drove away.

I feel my eyes start to water as I think about Robin. I pull over and look out toward the rolling hills. I never could figure out which mountain top was Haven. I realize I'm too tired and sore to drive home. I watch in the mirror as the sun is beginning to set behind me. I wondered what I'd do if Robin was with me now. Yep, it came to me in a flash. *I'm getting a burger and a beer.*

Epilogue

Well, I got my burger and beer fix, as well as onion rings this time around. I had a different bartender. I asked about Tammy. I also asked about her unusual name and how to pronounce it since I never really heard over the noise in the bar. She said for me to say it slowly after her. So, I followed along as she said, **ON**, then say **J** then **Low**. Like Onjlow, but it is spelled like orange Jello. I asked how she got such a name?

My current bartender smiled and said, "I can't give away all my secrets, but it sure was fun. That was the last time I saw her; it was kind of busy."

I spent the night in Black Mountain since I kind of over did the beer and food. I walked around trying to think about everything I had experienced. Maybe it was all the beer, but it felt surreal, like waking up from a dream. I remember fragmented parts about the people, but not in great detail. I do remember thinking that I would like to go back, but not in any way connected to work. Just be there.

After I got home, it was business as usual. It took a few days to settle in and get back up to speed. Luckily nothing big happened while I was away. No court cases pending, and I was still within the deadlines on the insurance cases. That is what I love about insurance and attorney work. They leave me alone most of the time.

A month passed and still no word from Christy or Robin. The news had died down about the school. I heard most of the girls took off. I figured they were back on the streets working in the sex trade for drugs. I figure it must be too soon for Christy and Robin to come out of hiding. I do remember Ashley, Robin's mother. She and her husband were separated when we met, and we spent time together during a camping trip. We communicated a little afterwards, but Ashley broke it off because she and her husband were getting back together. I never heard from her after that.

I investigated trying to find out more about Haven or Up top. Mostly what I found was sort of the same I had already learned from Mike and Randy. It was a legit, hippy camp after the previous, traditional summer camp programs had failed. The A side was what it appears - just a bunch of people out playing hippie or whatever they want to be at the moment. The B side was something new - Mike and Randy liked to pretend they didn't exist and avoided them.

The rescue program was so new, and the fact I'm an investigator made people un-trusting to talk to me about it. I didn't spend much time on this. I had too much catching up to do on my cases, and I couldn't run the risk of being suspected of knowing more than I do about the rescue program. As far as I know, it all ended because of the publicity associated between the school and Haven. The news never mentioned a link, and the detectives didn't ask me to provide details. I'm letting it all go for now for the safety of all involved.

Mike called from a blocked number. I rarely answer blocked calls, but for some odd reason I did. We had a long talk, but he seemed at a loss too. Sam didn't return to Haven, which was not unusual for her to come and go.

Mike talked for a long time about me coming back sometime and how much fun I'd have just to hang out, hike and escape from reality for a while.

I loved the idea of going back, and we had a good conversation about all the things I missed out on. I enjoyed our conversation, but I knew that was not the real reason for his call. He finally told me that Andrea had passed away about a week after they left Haven. He was aware she was sick but did not know with what. He did not have any details other that a message had come through the answering service.

Mike answered before I was able to ask, that he still doesn't know if that is their real names or where they are from. He offered his apologies for the way they conduct business there, and talked about resigning if they didn't change the policy. Mike claims to be a glorified grounds manager, since he really just does the ordering of supplies and makes out schedules. So much has changed in the past few years. Haven used to be such a fun place and all of a sudden it became dangerous. Thankfully, the cold of winter was just around the corner and the season was ending soon.

After we ended the call, I sat back and thought about the situation and what I had observed. Afterall, that seemed to be my role in the whole thing. I am overjoyed to learn Robin is my daughter and upset that at the same time I found out...I lost her. I would love to go find her, but I have no idea if doing so would put her in danger. I decided to wait a little longer before making that decision.

Overall, the Haven experience was very eye-opening. I hope I can slow down and live more in the moment to take the time to enjoy everything that is available to me. I learned that good intentions and the right attitude can be a powerful thing, but you must be careful. I have spent a lifetime observing people as a law enforcement officer, and now as a private investigator. I had to make a split decision based on short observations. Now, I question all that…because everyone wears a phony face.

Rex Lilly worked 20 years as a sworn law enforcement officer, and 24 years as a licensed private investigator. Rex continues to cover all of North and South Carolina specializing in insurance fraud, criminal defense for murder, and sex crimes.

In a strange twist, Rex is also a Reiki Master teacher, Certified Hypnotherapist, and a self-taught saxophone player.

Such a wide and unusual background has placed Rex in contact with some interesting people.

Made in the USA
Columbia, SC
05 May 2025